BLAZING

CENTAURS

Also by K.L. Mitchell

Kalazad
The Road to Kalazad
Viliians of Kalazad

BLAZING

CENTAURS

(KALAZAD – BOOK 3)

K.L. MITCHELL

Desert Palm Press

Blazing Centaurs
(Kalazad – Book 3)

By K.L. Mitchell

©2023 K.L.Mitchell

ISBN: (book) 9781954213777
ISBN (epub): 9781954213784

Desert Palm Press
1961 Main Street, Suite 220
Watsonville, California 95076
www.desertpalmpress.com

Editor: CK King
Cover Design: Rachel George

Printed in the United States of America
First Edition February 2024

Dedication

Dedicated with gratitude to Mel Brooks.
Please don't sue."

Chapter One

PAINT THE SKY IN purple and gold, streak in red from the setting sun. Mesas burn crimson in the dying light, old and stoic in the desert wastes. Closer now, and see. On the very edge of the largest mesa, there is light. A campfire flickers, a lone trail of smoke winding its way unhurriedly to the stars. Occasionally, the figure tending the fire leans forward and adds more fuel.

Ah, yes. Him.

A long, lean, hairy thing, like a stretched-out coyote, sits cross-legged in front of the fire. He is curiously attired in a rough black vest and tattered dungarees. A beadwork necklace hangs loosely around his neck. A black-felt top hat, now gray with age, allows his ears to extend through two worn slits cut for the purpose. He holds himself with an insouciant air, leaning back against a handy rock when he's not tending to the fire.

Closer, now. His eyes are bright yellow and they shine in the waning light but there's something else, too. Something...not *wrong*, just...off. Something about the way the reflected light of the fire dances in his pupils. Maybe they're off by a second or so; maybe they are showing other fires.

He takes a pipe out of an old leather bag and, with some ceremony, tamps in a little tobacco. A burning twig from the fire, and the pipe is alight. The smoke, when it comes, coils purple and blue into the air. It snakes over to the smoke from the campfire and starts to wind its way around, riding upward.

The creature sits back and watches the smoke drift. From time to time, he takes a long, slow draw on the pipe and blows out another stream of smoke. Sunset fades to twilight then, just as the last sliver of light stands poised to dip below the horizon, there is a change in the air. The smoke bends in a way that has nothing to do with the wind. For a moment, the coyote creature leans forward and studies strange figures that have appeared in the smoke.

After a few moments, he sighs. He douses the pipe and puts it away with care. The fire is put out, the old leather sack slung over his shoulder, and he walks off into the darkness.

Behind him, the last wisp of smoke from the campfire pirouettes, catches the wind, and rides west into the last of the light.

* * * * *

Morning, and the sun is burning away the chill of the desert night as the wagon train snakes its way along the trail. The greenery of the prairie has long since given way to the isolated scrub of the desert. The sun beats down hard on five wagons, all loaded with mail and merchandise, each one pulled by a brace of centaurs. A few hired hands ride alongside, keeping an eye out for danger.

At the head of the train, the trail boss strolls along at an unconcerned pace. Look at him, take him in. If this world ever invented movies, he'd be the undisputed king of westerns. From the waist up, observe a handsome, chisel-jawed cowboy. His red, double-breasted shirt is spotless. A kerchief and a white, ten-gallon hat complete the look. Below, he's a nearly perfect white stallion, lean and graceful and built for speed. And as he strolls along, he strums a guitar and sings:

> *Ever since I was a foal,*
> *knee-high to a gopher hole,*
> *I been plowin' up'n down this dusty trail.*
> *I got no way of knowin'*
> *Just where I think I'm goin'*
> *But as long as I head west, I cannot fail.*

> *I left my darlin' Stacie*
> *way back east in St. Gracie,*
> *and I told her, baby darlin' don't you cry.*
> *I was gone about a week,*
> *when she married my friend Zeke,*
> *and I never got a chance to kiss the bride.*

> *Oh, yo-de-le-hee-hee,*
> *Yo-de-le-hee-hee,*
> *Yo-de-lo-de-lo-de-le-de-lo-de-le.*
> *Yo-de-le-hee-hee,*
> *Yo-de-le-hee-hee,*
> *Yo-de-lo-de-lo-de-le-de-lo-de-le.*

A couple of wagons back, one of the centaurs nudges another. "Uhm, Mr. Sam," she whispers, "pardon me for asking, but does he always go on like this?"

The second centaur takes off his hat and mops his sunbaked brow. "Purty much." Sam is an older fellow, nut brown with a drooping, silver mustache. His mane is braided up tight to keep it out of the way. Besides the wagon harness, he wears a sweat-soaked bandanna and a dingy, old blue shirt.

The first centaur wrinkles her nose in disbelief. She's a Percheron, chestnut brown with long, black hair going down her back. "Really? Because we've only been on the trail since sunrise, and... Well, I'm sure this is probably traditional and everything, and I don't want to step on anybody's hooves, but..."

One of the human escorts sidles up to them. "I think I can speak plainer than Iyarra here. How come nobody's ever yanked that guitar out of his hands and smashed it against the nearest rock?"

"Well, I'll tell ya, Miss Revka. I been ridin' this trail back an' forth for nigh on twenty year, an' under all manner a trail bosses. Ol' Dusty Steele up there is the best boss I ever hauled a wagon under. He's brave. He knows every inch o' trail from here to The Rift, knows ever body, done everything, and ain't never lost a wagon yet."

The woman lets out a low whistle. "That good, huh?"

The old wagoner turns his head maintaining a steady gaze. "Good enough to put up with five solid days worth a yodeling."

The women exchange glances. "Okay," Revka allows. "That's pretty impressive, actually."

The old stallion nods. "Eeyup."

Up ahead, the trail boss keeps strumming and singing:

Well, the desert ain't no fun,
with the sand and heat and sun.
It ain't no place for the delicate or weak.
For the trail is long and wide,
and there's nowhere you can hide.
There's no priv'cy when you gotta take a leak.

Oh, yo-de-le-hee-hee...

And on they went.

* * * * *

It was about the middle of the afternoon, with the sun beginning its long trek down to its home behind the distant mountains. All hell broke loose. They were traveling through a small canyon as they entered the more mountainous territory that led to their destination. Rocky slopes loomed over them on each side, leaving a fairly narrow path for the convoy to work itself through. The old-timers, who had been this way before, seemed keyed up, nerves on edge. The chatter abated, and even the trail boss had knocked off the singing. He slung his guitar over his back and fell silent, only essaying the occasional sotto voce, "Hum."

Revka maneuvered herself next to Sam, who had unslung a rather large crossbow and kept swiveling his head back and forth. "Something up?" she asked.

The old centaur nodded. "McBee's Canyon," he said. His voice was low; something about the place discouraged making too much noise. "Shaves a week off the trip, but it's got its own disadvantages, ya might say."

Revka looked up at the rocky slopes. It didn't take a genius to work out what he meant. "Ambush?" she whispered.

Sam nodded. "Yep. It don't happen too often—maybe one time in ten—but when it does, it can git real bad, real quick." He pointed up ahead. "We've got about half a mile. Ain't no distance at all, really, but if they come down, we're more or less trapped.

"Now, sometimes they don't judge their moment right, or you can see 'em in advance. Which case, you can make a dash for it. The exit's too wide to block, so they gotta catch you in the pinch, if you see what I mean. They can only come down the slopes so fast, y'see. If we get lucky, we can leave 'em behind purty easy, but as I say, it don't happen too often. Probably we'll be all right."

On a mesa, not too far away, the coyote sighed and shook its head sadly. With a long draw of its pipe, it leaned in to watch.

A primal roar echoed across the canyon. The loud nasal bellow sounded like a cross between a charging bull and a wolf, and promised the worst aspects of both. Up ahead, along both ridges of stone, groups of shapes appeared and began to charge their way down the slope.

"Son of a deuce!" Sam groaned.

Revka cursed. "We won't get past 'em from here, I suppose?"

The old centaur shook his head. "Not a chance. They got the jump on us."

"I don't suppose we could turn around?"

"Have a look."

Revka turned. Sure enough, another smaller band was coming down the slopes behind them. "Well, Krep."

Sam nodded. "Purty much." He unbuckled the harness, stepping out of it. "They'll come at us fore an' aft," he said. "Turn the wagons to the side, and we'll have a bit of cover." Around them, the other wagoners were already detaching from their harnesses and moving the wagons into place. Up ahead, Steele carefully unslung his guitar and set it against a nearby rock.

Revka, Iyarra, and Sam managed to get the wagon into position with the others into a rough barricade, three in front and two in back. Revka readied her crossbow, but Sam laid a hand on her shoulder. "Don't waste your time with that," he said. "Those little jobs won't make much more than a scratch on these fellers." He hoisted down another crossbow from the wagon, a big two-hander, complete with a set of big, nasty-looking bolts. "Try this."

Revka, taken somewhat by surprise at the weight of the thing, nevertheless managed to get it braced over the top of the wagon. Sam turned to Iyarra. "Got another one if you want it."

Iyarra shook her head. "I'm more of an up-close fighter," she said.

Sam shrugged. "Suit yourself," he said. The group crouched behind the impromptu barriers, weapons at the ready. Only the trail boss stood out in the open, with no movement except for the slight twitch of his hands hovering over his holsters.

"I suppose," said Iyarra, "that negotiation is out of the question?"

Sam shook his head. "Not a chance. They'll try an' drive us off so they can take what they can. They don't got a lot of nerve. If we can put the fear in 'em, they won't hang around."

"Well," said Revka, "that doesn't sound too difficult."

The old centaur pointed. "Guess again," he said.

Revka peered. The bandits were closer now, almost to the bottom of the slope. They were kicking up a lot of dust as they came, but she could still see their shapes.

"Oh hell," Revka muttered. "Cowboys."

The bandits finished their descent, their cloven hooves hitting the dusty ground and kicking up a wall of cloud. In shape, they were very like centaurs, but stockier, with shorter legs and a lot more muscle. A brutal-looking pair of horns topped each head, and each cowboy carried a pair of handheld crossbows.

The leader, a giant, black Longhorn, charged forward. "Come on, boys," he yelled, "last one in the fray is a steer!" The bandits cheered and mooed, waving their weapons as they came.

Behind the wagons, Revka took careful aim. Next to her, Iyarra laid out several bolts and held one at the ready. Crossbows were effective at short distances but could take several seconds to reload. One tended to be careful about picking their shot. "Wait for it," muttered Sam. "Wait for it...now!"

A volley of crossbow bolts shot out from the wagons. Almost at the same moment, the oncoming bandits let fire. Their bolts flew toward Dusty; he paid them no mind. Somehow, each and every single bolt whizzed past him and wound up lodging itself in the side of a wagon or on the ground.

Dusty just smiled. Then, with speed that would make a rattlesnake swallow its gum, he whipped his twin crossbows out of their holsters and fired. Behind the bandit leader, two of the bandits crashed to the ground, taking down the ones immediately behind them as well. The trail boss dropped his crossbows and put his fists up in the time-honored manner of Gentlemanly Fisticuffs, whereupon the Longhorn knocked him flat as he charged past.

Meanwhile, as soon as she pulled the trigger on her own crossbow, Revka shouted "Bolt!" Iyarra reached down with one hand and yanked back the bow with little apparent effort. As soon as it latched, she dropped a bolt into place and patted Revka's shoulder. "Clear!"

Revka let fly, aiming for the leader. The perfect shot landed dead center of his chest, right where two thick straps of leather crossed over each other. *Amazing. Guy has nothing on but two belts, and I still manage to hit the most protected part.* A moment later, another volley of bolts came sailing out from the other wagoners, who didn't have a rapid-reload centaur. They didn't fare much better.

"Bolt!" One last shot. They were close now, so she just let it fly. It hit the bandit chief in the side, lodging itself a little forward of his left hind leg. He roared, changing his direction so that he was heading right toward them. So that was nice.

The bandits closed with the convoy and the battle began in earnest. The wagons provided a useful barricade, just not a very large one. The attackers split up, charging around the wagons and flanking the defenders.

Fortunately, the group had just enough time to drop their range weapons and brace for close quarters. Revka drew her sword. Iyarra already had her daggers out. As the first few bandits came charging around the wagons, the girls and Sam braced up to face them. In the blink of an eye, four shorthorns, as mean as anyone either woman had ever seen, were on them.

Revka drew back her sword, ready to pick her spot. A big Holstein with muttonchops and black-tipped horns charged toward her. He slowed, a puzzled look on his face. To Revka's surprise, he stopped and pointed an accusing finger at her.

"That's a blade!" he yelled. "That human's got a blade! What gives?"

Sam lay a restraining hand on her arm. "You may wanna put that away," he said. "I know y'all are new out here, but in these parts, we don't take to bladed weapons."

"That's right!" Another bandit nodded. "Just fisticuffs, with allowable use of blunt objects or the occasional piece of furniture."

Revka tilted her head up at Sam. "But...but they're outlaws." She waved a hand at the mob of bulltaurs. "Aren't we supposed to be fighting them off?"

"Well, sure, but there's ways what's acceptable and ways what ain't."

"Exactly!" the bandit nodded. "We may be outlaws, but we got standards! And consarn it, bladed weapons just ain't western."

"That's right." Sam took off his hat. "It's against The Code of the West."

Suddenly everybody, except Iyarra and Revka, bandit and wagoner alike, took off their hats. "The Code of the West," they chorused in perfect unison, eyes reverently shut.

"Now," said Sam. "Go ahead and put them things away and we'll just, ah, pick up where we left off." He looked over to the bandits. "That all right with you gents?"

The bandits looked at each other and nodded. "A'ight."

Revka and Iyarra looked at each other, shared a quick shrug, and put their weapons away.

"Thank you." Sam nodded to the bandits. "Gentlemen, in your own time."

The fight began in earnest. Sam and the Holstein began trading blows, ducking and weaving as each searched for an opening. A big, brown Hereford closed in on Revka and Iyarra, who squared up, side by side.

"No weapons, huh?" Revka muttered to Iyarra. "Not sure how much damage I can do. Guy's a wall of meat."

"Just leave him to me," Iyarra whispered back. "You distract him, and I'll do the rest."

Revka nodded. She licked her lips and moved a little away. "Hey, mister!" she shouted. "Nice ring in your nose. Your mommy pick it out for you?"

"Don't you talk about my momma." He lowered his head and made to ram into Revka. Before he could, Iyarra slammed two massive forehooves into his side. Down he went, howling with the crunch of broken ribs.

A third bandit stepped forward, cracking his knuckles. "Oh, you oughtn't a done that," he growled. "You about to learn you some manners."

A shape loomed up behind the Hereford. As the dust cleared, Revka felt her stomach drop. The Longhorn. He strode forward, coming on with the slow inevitability of an avalanche. He laid a hand on the Hereford's shoulder. "Step aside, Elmer," he growled. "I reckon this one is mine."

Elmer stepped back, giving Revka a knowing smirk. "All yours, Big Jake," he said, moving back to a better vantage point. Revka scrambled backward as the bandit leader moved forward. Without breaking eye contact with her, Big Jake reached back and yanked her crossbow bolt out of his hide.

He held it up for her inspection. "This yours, human?"

Revka bit her lip. "Uhm, possibly?"

The big bulltaur twirled the bolt absently in one huge hand. "Well, now. Seems to me you made a mistake plantin' this in my hide. B'lieve I might just have to give it back to ya." He leaned down, his eyes disappearing in the shade of his brow. "Now, wonder where I'm gonna stick it?"

"I might have a suggestion."

The bandit chief whipped his head around. Behind him stood Dusty Steele himself, swaying a little bit. That shiner over his left eye was going to be there for a while. Nevertheless, there he was, tall and proud. He unbuttoned his cuffs and made a slow, deliberate show of rolling up his sleeves. Clearly, Gentlemanly Fisticuffs was no longer an option.

Big Jake snorted. "Well now, here's a fella who don't have the sense to stay down." He turned, then stopped halfway and pointed to Revka. "Don't you go nowhere." He turned back to Dusty and cracked his knuckles. "Well, now. Mr. Trail Boss thinks he's gonna be a hero. Gotta say, I'm lookin' forward to this. Get you out of the way, my job's gonna be a lot easier."

Dusty just smiled. "Well, now. Maybe it will, and maybe it won't, but I don't think talkin' me to death is gonna work."

The bulltaur charged, his arms out in a grappling position. Steele waited until the last second, then nimbly sidestepped, letting the bandit chief go charging right by. Big Jake bellowed with rage and only just managed to steer himself around before he ran into the rock slope.

By now, Steele was standing a little away from the convoy. He undid his kerchief and waved it mockingly at the bull. "Seein' red, are ya?"

"RED!" Big Jake stomped a hoof. "You know durn well we're color blind, you insensitive clod!" He lowered his head and charged again, barreling toward Steele so fast that he never even had a chance to notice that Steele had once again slipped out of the way.

Some of the wagoners began to cheer. "Olé!" shouted someone.

Steele turned to the appreciative crowd and bowed low. It was just as well he did. The move saved him from getting clipped across the back of the head by Big Jake, who was on the return trip.

The two foes circled each other, each looking for an opening. Steele made a feint, almost catching Big Jake off guard. The bulltaur lurched toward Steele a couple of times, but the trail boss outmaneuvered him each time. Suddenly, they were on each other, grappling and kicking and swinging their fists. They fought like demons, unrelenting in their attacks. All around them, various skirmishes between wagoners and bandits came to a stop as all turned to watch the fight. Clouds of dust swirled around the battle, wagoners and bandits alike watching in rapt silence.

Sam shook his head. "No good," he whispered. "The boss is fightin' like a champ, but there's just too much of that bull and not enough of him. Only a matter of time before he tires out, or that overgrown hat rack gets a lucky shot."

Iyarra fingered her daggers nervously. "Shouldn't we do something, then?"

Sam shook his head. "Can't interrupt a private fight," he said. "That's part of the Code of—"

"Don't say it," Revka growled. "Besides, I'm next, remember? So this is my fight, too." By now, the two combatants had worked their way back toward the wagon train. Big Jake was in front of the nearest wagon, caught in a grappling lock with Dusty, each trying to trip the other up or break out of the hold.

Revka scrambled up onto the wagon and clambered over boxes. Just behind the wrestlers, she watched. Steele landed a punch to the Longhorn's breadbasket. *Now.* Revka jumped onto his back. She scrambled forward and hooked her arms under his horns. She yanked up with all her might. "Now!" she shouted. "Give him one in the—" *Oops.*

Revka heard a soft popping sound. No longer in her grip, the left horn detached itself from the bandit chief's head and tumbled to the ground.

The fighters stumbled to a halt. Dusty stood frozen in place, his fist pulled back to strike. His eyes bulged out, and he slowly began to grin.

"Horn falsies? Are you kidding?" He turned to the onlookers. "Hey everyone! Mr. Longhorn over here's wearin' horn falsies!"

"What? No, I am not!" The brute turned his head away, trying to cover himself. His actual horn, now that Revka could see, was rather short and blunt, no bigger than her hand.

She reached over to the other one and tugged. Sure enough, if you pulled and twisted it just like...ah, there it went. She held it up for the others to see.

"Holy—!" Elmer stepped forward. He picked up the other horn and turned it over a couple of times before looking at the bandit chief. "Boss? Say it ain't so!"

"Shut up!" The not-a-Longhorn snatched the prosthetic away from his accomplice. "Gimme that back!" Jake scrambled to get the horn back on, in his haste pointing it the wrong way around.

A couple of the other bandits stomped over. "All right, all right, just everybody hold everything." A big brown one with a shaved head held his hands out. He turned to Steele. "Look, can you give us just a minute here?"

Steele tipped his hat. "Of course."

"Much obliged." He turned back to his chief. "Jake, you been leadin' this mob for nigh on a year now. You mean to tell me that, all that time, you been fakin' your ann-o-tomical attributes?"

"What? No! It ain't what you think, Roy! Honest!"

Revka peered at the writing inside of the other horn. "ACME Prosthetic and Novelty Goods Company," she read. "Mister Big Horn, Deluxe Model. What the heck is a deluxe model?"

"Oh, that's the one with the all-weather coating," said Elmer, before he could stop himself.

"Oh, fer—"

"Dang it, Elmer."

10

"What? No!" Elmer waved his hands placatingly. "I just happened to see it in their catalog once, that's all! I was just lookin' fellers! Honest!"

The bald one clapped a hand over his eyes and mumbled something under his breath. "All right," he said. "Look folks, I'm sorry, but we're gonna have to cut this short. We gotta go off and sort this out before we can give y'all a proper seein' to. You mind if we just catch you next time?"

Dusty waved a hand dismissively. "Not a problem, I understand perfectly." He turned to Revka. "Go ahead an' give them the horn back, if'n ya would."

"Wait," Iyarra called, "are they really going to stop in the middle of robbing us so they can talk about this guy's horns?"

"Well," said the bald one, "it's like this, ma'am. The horns represent a feller's status within the herd. As he was a Longhorn, we was naturally following his lead, but given current developments," he tapped one end of the horn in his hand, "we're gonna have to have a serious talk about this before we decide who's in charge a this here enterprise."

"That's right," said another. "Ain't no shame in having smaller horns, but bamboozlin' your brother bandits so's you can be in charge, why, that's against The Code of the West."

Again, the hats came off. "The Code of the West!"

"Now, if y'all will excuse us..." The bandits turned and headed back down the canyon the way the convoy had come, their luckless ex-chief in tow.

"Well, I guess that's the end of that." Dusty Steele dusted his hands off and looked around. "How we look, Ted?"

One of the other wagoners saluted. "Well sir, Thompkins got banged up a bit, so I'm having Nathan take his place in harness. Also, one of 'em tried to jump over one of the wagons and landed on a box of surgical instruments, but I reckon they'll be okay once somebody washes the blood off."

Dusty nodded. "All right, sounds good." He cupped his hands around his mouth and shouted. "Get them wagons back in line and harness up folks! I wanna make camp by sundown!" He looked around, smiling. "Now, where's my—"

There was a crunching noise in the key of G. Everybody turned toward the sound, and Revka. A fairly large rock had landed on Dusty's guitar, flattening it.

"Oh dear," she deadpanned. "Looks like this boulder just rolled right on top of the guitar. Must have been knocked loose when they were charging down the hill at us."

Dusty wandered over. He nudged at the boulder with a hoof, then shook his head. "Broke beyond repair," he declared. "Had that made for me in Katt City, the finest instrument I ever known." He sighed, took off his hat, and shed a single manly tear. Then he loaded a bolt into his crossbow and, looking away so as not to see, shot the remains of the guitar right in the sound hole.

Iyarra leaned over to Sam. "Uhm," she whispered, "did he actually just shoot his broken guitar?"

Sam dabbed at his eyes with his bandanna. "It's what it woulda wanted," he replied.

A few minutes later, everybody was harnessed back up and ready to go. Dusty trotted from one end of the convoy to the other, making sure everything was set. "All right, y'all. Let's kick up a li'l dust, shall we?" He stopped by the wreckage of his instrument, looking down at it with a grim expression.

Revka walked over to him. "That's a real shame, that is."

Dusty bit his lip. "It shore is," he said quietly. "But you gotta take the good with the bad in this world, and that ain't no lie." He reached back into his saddlebags and began to rummage around. "I suppose I can pick up another one when I get back. In the meantime," he pulled out a large oblong object. "I reckon I'll just have to go with the accordion."

* * * * *

On the distant mesa, the coyote watched them go. After a while, he carefully put out his pipe and got ready to leave.

"Well," he said to no one in particular, "that was different. I mean, myself, I'd go for the other guy. Got hero written all over him, he has."

A moment's silence, then, "Really? Well, I suppose it's your choice."

More silence. "All right. I'll see what I can do."

The coyote heaved his bag over his shoulder and turned. He reached out and tugged a piece of empty space, then disappeared.

Chapter Two

RED VALLEY LAY AT the edge of the desert, where the mesas and buttes began to give way to the titanic mountains of the west. These old stone giants, the Tandari (from the old Equine word meaning big and pointy) stretched north to south along the western edge of the continent. The Great Ridge separated the desert from the far-distant lands beyond. The trek across the Tandari was rough, with only a few trails allowing safe passage to the other side. The few towns nestled along the base of the mountain range were popular waypoints for traders. They were the last places to prepare before an arduous crossing.

Red Valley was one such place. Two long crescents of rock branched off from the mountain range and encircled a large, empty plain, before drawing back together at the mouth of the valley and the town of Red Valley. Runoff from the mountains had been harnessed through ancient canals into the town and through the cultivated fields which supplied the centaurs who, for centuries, had made this place their home.

The convoy crossed the city gate a little after noon and made a beeline for the Mercantile Company warehouse at the back of the town. There, the wagons were unhitched, inspected, and duly signed for. Finally, the wagon crew was paid and dismissed.

"There won't be a convoy back for a couple of days," Sam said as they wandered away. "Mostly we hang around until then, safer than trying to make the trip back yourself. Also, of course, it's another payday, so that's nice."

"Makes sense." Revka looked around. The main street—pardon her, the main stretch of dirt—was a long, broad avenue that cut straight through the middle of town. On each side, a variety of taverns, inns, and other such places vied for the passerby's attention. "Anything to do around here till then?"

Sam chuckled. "Well, the thing you gotta understand about Red Valley is this is a town that's gen'ly full of folks just passin' through, merchants and wagoners like us. In other words, a lot of folks with time and money on their hands, lookin' to spend a little of both as pleasantly as possible." He winked at the two women. "It's a poor sorta town in that situation that don't learn how to extract some of that money for themselves real quick. Personally, I intend to assist them in that particular quest in a variety of ways before we head back. I'd invite you along, but..."

"Right, right." Revka and Iyarra exchanged glances. "What I meant was, would there be any little jobs or anything we could pick up while we're here? Guarding, protecting someone, that sort of thing?"

"Naw. Any of that stuff is liable to be done by the locals. Somebody may start a convoy out across the mountains in a day or two if you're lookin' to head toward the Ridge. Other'n that, just stick around and rest ya hooves for a while. You honestly might as well hang around and take the trip back with the rest of us. Ya did good out there; I wouldn't mind havin' you two on as regulars."

"Well, I don't know about regulars, but taking the return trip sounds about as good a plan as any." Revka turned to Iyarra. "What do you think?"

"Sounds good to me."

"Now, if'n you ladies will excuse me," Sam rubbed his hands together. "I'm a-gonna go wash the dust off, get a clean change a clothes, and have myself a time." He tipped his hat at them and sauntered off. "See y'all later."

They watched him go. "Well," said Revka, "what do you reckon?"

Iyarra tapped a hoof. "I think we should follow his advice," she said.

"What, stick around and catch the return trip back?"

"Well yeah, that too, but mostly I was talking about the washing and clean clothes part."

"Oh. Yeah, that's probably a good idea."

"I mean, I didn't want to say anything—"

"Yeah, you don't really—"

"But it's been a *really* long ride. And with the hot sun, and..."

"Okay, okay!" Revka laughed. "Let's find a hotel room before they fill up, shall we?"

* * * * *

One thing a traveler in fantasy worlds tends to notice, after kicking around for a while, is the particular architectural peculiarities that are favored by the various races. For example, take the humans. With humans, it's all up, up, up. The higher they can build, the happier they are. Even the humblest woodcutter's hut will have a loft above the main living area, and the buildings in the larger cities go up a good four or five levels, sometimes even more. As for the kings and magicians and their mania for building tall pointy towers...well, enough said.

Now elves, they like their buildings sleek and aesthetic. It doesn't matter what it is, it's got to be clean and airy, and radiate elegance and grace from top to bottom. Show an elf an ordinary outhouse, and he simply won't be able to use it until it's been painted white, topped with a few spires, and graced with an allegorical stained-glass window depicting the Goddess Charmelle bestowing the secret of toilet paper to mortals. Of course, by the time you get through adding all this, it's too late, but at least he has somewhere nice for next time.

The Gratt, the gray-green, pinch-faced race of bureaucrats and career pedants, tend to go for blocky, gray buildings devoid of any decoration. They are particularly noted for their lack of windows, there being nothing outside a Gratt especially wants to see.

Then there's the centaur people. The main thing about centaur-designed buildings is their lack of any stairs. They tend to build out, not up. Centaurs like their space and are not, as a general rule, overly fond of heights. When they do build up, it's usually with a long ramp gently sloping its way up along one of the walls. Also, the straw on the floor tends to be rather cleaner than in human buildings.

Revka and Iyarra found a room in a small, but nicely appointed inn a little ways away from the main street, which had come recommended by a passing guard on the strength of it being the one place in town the constabulary didn't get called to every single night. The room actually was rather nice, with two centaur-sized mattresses, a chest to stow their goods, and even a large trench tub big enough for Iyarra to sit down in. There had been a bit of a wait while the washtub was filled, but now she was settled comfortably in the cool water, industriously scrubbing off a week's worth of trail dust. Revka busied herself with soaping up the horsewoman's mane. "So, do you know much about this place?"

Iyarra shook her head. "No, never even heard of it before we got the job."

"I just find it interesting, a town made up of centaurs. I mean, I thought you were all nomads."

"Well, certainly, it is generally the case for centaurs, but there are a few permanent settlements out there. To tell the truth, this is the first one I've ever been to."

"Well, we may have to find out more about it." Revka dipped a pail of water into the tub and hefted it up. "Close your eyes."

Iyarra obeyed, and Revka carefully poured the water up and down the centaur's mane, rinsing the soap out. She put the bucket aside. "Anyway, it sounds like we're not going to be able to pick up much work around here before the return trip. What do you think we should do?"

"Well, we could explore a bit. Or maybe just hang around the town. It's been a while since we had a few days off. It will be nice to be around my people for a while."

Revka chuckled. "Well, now that you mention it, I suppose we do spend a lot of time hanging around humans, don't we?" She leaned forward and gave her girlfriend a hug. "Well, this will make a nice break for you."

Iyarra nodded and leaned back, letting her eyes close. "Mm-hm."

They held the embrace for a moment.

"Revka?"

"Mm-hm?"

"Where is your hand going?"

"I, ah, thought maybe you needed some help washing?"

"You know I can reach there just fine."

"So, you want me to stop?"

"Well..." Iyarra moved Revka's hands. "You could try here."

Revka chuckled and scooted up against Iyarra's back. "Oh, really?" She kissed the base of the Iyarra's neck. "Gonna need more soap for there."

Iyarra turned to nuzzle at her girlfriend. "Oh," she said, "I think we'll manage."

* * * * *

An hour later—oh, all right, make it an hour and a half—the two women strode down the main drag looking for something to do. The sun was getting pretty low in the sky. Soon it would disappear behind the mountains. If Revka was any judge, this wasn't the kind of town to let a little thing like that slow it down. They wandered down the stretch of road that seemed mainly dedicated to taverns, casinos, and other means of parting a bored working man from his money. They stopped in front of a place that seemed to be having a lively time of it, if the sounds inside were anything to go by. The pair stopped to watch.

"Say Revka, how come these taverns all have those weird swinging doors?"

There was a sudden cacophony of voices, the sound of splintering wood, and a rough-looking man came flying out and landed at Iyarra's hooves. He scrambled rather unsteadily to his feet, grabbed his hat, and stormed right back in again.

Revka turned to Iyarra. "That answer your question?"

Iyarra nodded. "I think. Let's maybe try somewhere else, shall we?"

Revka gave Iyarra a pat. "Good idea." They turned and walked away down the road.

A moment later, the man came flying out again. This time he didn't get back up but merely lay where he landed, occasionally mumbling the odd threat or imprecation, until one of the town guards dragged him away to sleep it off.

* * * * *

The next spot Revka and Iyarra found seemed a bit more promising. Rather than an inebriated man, music came from the open doors. The two women exchanged glances. "Well, Iyarra, what do you think?"

Iyarra shrugged. "Up to you. I'm game."

"OK, let's check it out."

They pushed their way through the swinging doors. Inside, the place was...

Well...

Take your average western saloon. You know the type: a big room full of tables, a long bar the length of the side wall, and a stage along the back. Some guy in the corner playing a piano. Got it? Good. Now, nail a bunch of antiques to the wall, slip some booths all around the sides, hang a bunch of colorful glass lamps over the tables and insert a bored, teenaged centauress behind a podium, right up front. She wore a vest festooned with slogan buttons like, *Is it Friday yet?* and *We're Crazy about our customers!* Something about the girl's expression suggested that this was not, in fact, the case.

"Welcome to T. J. Wannamaker's, home of the Fintoozler." The girl regarded the two women with all the enthusiasm of a dead sloth. "How many in your party please?"

The women exchanged glances. "Er, I don't think there is a party." Revka turned around and peeked out the door, in case a lot more people had suddenly materialized behind them. "Yeah, just the two of us."

"Uh-huh." The girl looked down at a paper map on the podium. "And will you be dining with us today?"

"Er...yes?"

"Smoking or no smoking?"

"No, I guess?"

"Fighting or no fighting?"

"You mean we have a choice?"

Iyarra cut in. "No fighting. Definitely no fighting."

"And will you be wanting a children's menu?"

"Sorry? For which one of us?"

"Sorry. I have to ask." She picked up another bit of cardboard. "See? It's shaped like a hat. You got the food on one side, and then you can turn it over and wear it, see?" On the other side was a crude picture of a Stetson. Somebody had cut a long slit through the brim large enough to stick one's head through if that was one's idea of a good time.

"Tempting," said Revka, as diplomatically as she could, "but do you in fact get a lot of kids in here?"

The young centauress put the menu away. "Not so you'd notice," she said. "What we *do* have is a new owner, who has decided he wants to shake things up a bit and create a 'unique family dining experience.'"

"A unique dining experience? What does that mean?"

The girl shrugged. "Mostly, it means nail a bunch of stuff to the wall and jack up the prices on everything. Follow me, please."

The young tauress grabbed a couple of paper oblongs and trotted off without bothering to see if they were following her.

They were halfway across the room when somebody called out to them. Sam, fresh and clean, was hanging out with some other taurs and humans. "Come on over, you two! We'll make room." There was a shuffling of humans and centaurs alike, until the new arrivals were squeezed in.

"I'll introduce ya," Sam declared. "Everyone, these here are Revka an' Iyarra. Came with us on the last wagon train. They're good people."

There was a quick chorus of howdies and raised mugs.

"I was just tellin' 'em about the bandits we had a few days back," said Sam. "Say, you gals thirsty? They do a good house braw."

Braw, a traditional centaur drink, is made by fermenting bread and other ingredients in water. Once a way to use up stale bread, it had become a favorite drink for celebrations and socializing. Most herds have their own specialized variations with recipes they guard jealously. Braw had even begun to cross over to other species. Humans, in particular, favored a variant made from white bread and effervescent water, usually with one or more fruit flavors added. Centaurs were closemouthed regarding the odd recipe, unless someone was foolish enough to ask.

Revka smiled at Sam. "That sounds great, thanks."

Sam waved a couple of fingers toward a passing waiter, who nodded and bustled off. "So, as I was saying, they took right off after that. Poor ol' guy ran after them with one horn on and the other off,

'Wait fer me, fellers! I'm yer *leaderrrr*!' Dangedest thing I seen in a long time."

"That reminds me," said Iyarra, "is Thompkins all right?"

Sam nodded. "Saw 'em over to the infirmary. He'll be fine, though I reckon he won't be making the trip back. Speaking of which, how about y'all? You coming back with?"

Revka nodded. "I believe so. I mean, assuming nothing else comes up." Just then, the waiter returned with a mug of braw for each of the ladies. Revka took an exploratory sip and nodded. "Not bad at all."

"Also, that Mr. Steele gets a new guitar," Iyarra added. "I don't think I could take another week of *Lady of Penangua*."

The older centaur flinched. "Oh lord, don't remind me." He chuckled. "Yeah, you'll see. He probably picked him up a new one first thing he got here." He leaned forward. "I tell you one thing, though," he said. "I ain't never complainin' about his guitar playin' again."

Revka laughed, raising her mug. "Amen to that." She took a long draw at her drink. "So, does anyone here know much about this town? Me and Iyarra were talking, and I guess there aren't a lot of centaur settlements."

"Oh, I can tell you all about it." A centaur, who had been introduced as Other Sid, scooted forward a little. "As a matter of fact, I grew up here. Family's been here since the mountains were babies, as my grandma puts it."

"Do tell."

"Well, okay." Other Sid took a long swig and gathered his thoughts. "The stories say that this place was founded by Chief Zauk Proudhoof of the Pan-Yi clan. Apparently, they'd been grazing their way west, and the grasslands kept getting thinner and thinner. They didn't want to head back east because...well, because Zauk was so dang stubborn, if you want to know the truth. He kept insistin' that there had to be more grass if they just went a bit further.

"Well, by and by, the other folks in the herd started to complain, said that if they didn't see some proper vegetation soon, they were gonna have to give it up. So, he made a deal. They had just enough water with 'em to go one more week before they'd have to turn around. So, if they found no sign of things getting better by the end of the seventh day, they'd start back.

"The first six days went by, nothin' but dust. Everybody figures they're gonna be turning back. Sun comes up on the last day, and there's the mountains up ahead, just waitin' for them. Old Zauk, he figured

19

there had to be some serious water around to grow mountains that big. So he—"

Revka leaned forward. "Sorry. He thought what?"

Iyarra grinned. "Centaurs used to believe that mountains were like plants. They needed sunlight and water to grow."

"You don't say."

"Anyhow. They hustled on toward the mountains, and by noon they could smell water. Just as the sun was about to set, they came up on the valley and the little stream that was tricklin' out from the mountain runoff. Well, they made camp that night, and long story short, they never left.

"They quarried out stone from the mountain to build the first shelters and dug the little stream out into the canal that brings the water into town to this day. Eventually, the mercantile routes sprung up. We were one of the only places this far out. The merchants brought lumber and supplies. More people started showing up, and the town began to get big. We've been sittin' pretty ever since."

"Neat," said Revka. "But one thing I don't get. How come they followed this Zauk guy all the way out here in the first place? I mean, we were out there. There's just nothing, even if you are a grazer. I'd have turned around long before finding this place."

"Well," said Sam, "you gotta understand how it is with us centaur folk. A herd is...well, we tend to stick together. When a herd moves, it moves together. That's just how it is. Besides," he added, "he invoked *sta nawah kendah*, so they pretty much had to."

"Sta...?"

"It's an old custom," explained Iyarra. "Once a leader has said it, you're pretty much honor-bound to follow them. To the edge of the world, if it comes to that."

"Why? What's it mean?"

Iyarra coughed. "Well, it roughly translates to shut up. We're not lost; I know exactly where we are."

A brief silence, as those assembled at the table proceeded to digest this particular bit of wisdom, was cut short when a young colt burst into the saloon.

"It's the thungas," he shouted. "They're runnin' amok!"

The effect was immediate. There was a stampede, as everyone tried to get out the door at once. Sam downed the last of his braw and swore. "Come on, everyone!" He got to his hooves and beckoned to

Iyarra and Revka. "And you too, ladies! It's all hands when the thungas get out!"

Within a minute, the saloon was empty. Outside, there were the sounds of shouting and thundering hooves in all directions. Inside, the silence was broken when one lone human snuck back in. He looked guiltily about before grabbing one of the children's menus. He folded it carefully and left as quickly as he came.

Chapter Three

OUTSIDE, EVERYTHING WAS CHAOS. People were yelling instructions at each other at the top of their lungs. Everyone was getting in everyone else's way, and the thungas...well, they were everywhere.

Thungas were large, slow creatures, about the size and shape of a buffalo. Native to the desert, their thick, reptilian skin allowed them to thrive in the arid climate.

Some people found it odd that the centaurs had learned to tame the thunga and even farm them, but the creatures were exceedingly useful, even if you didn't consume their tough and flavorless flesh, which put people in mind of chewing on a wad of wet paper. Their milk was sweet and wholesome, and kept surprisingly well, even in the hot, dry climate.

The creatures shed their horns every year during the calving season. The centaurs gathered the horns to make cups, utensils, and various other household objects. Thunga scat made for excellent fertilizer, to the point where bags of the stuff were a minor industry in the town. Further, thungas would shed their skin once a year, leaving behind a lightweight but durable material that, when soaked in their urine for a while, made a very soft and comfortable fabric for clothing, once you did something about the smell.

All of the above were easily and painlessly extracted from the beasts, so there was always a reliable supply. From the thungas' point of view, they were basically being looked after all their lives by creatures who were willing, even eager, to feed them, groom them, and generally clean up after them.

As a matter of fact—and it is just as well that no human or centaur ever suspected this—the thungas were by and large a very religious species. They believed quite firmly that these strange servant creatures were created by the Great Thunga Chief for the specific purpose of looking after his beloved children. This may sound silly to an outside observer, but in all fairness, it's not much worse than most religious beliefs. Also, there's just the chance they might be right.

The only real problem was that, once each year, the laid-back thungas suddenly got very interested in finding the nearest thunga beast of the opposite sex and seeing how they felt about long walks and swapping cud. During these times, thunga tenders generally had to separate the sexes, occasionally with a crowbar.

Revka swung herself onto Iyarra's back as they hustled out of the saloon and surveyed the scene. Thungas were trotting up and down the road, nosing their way into shops, knocking over everything smaller than a building, and generally making a mess of everything.

Sam scowled. He hauled out a lariat and began to swing it over his head. "You two," he shouted, "you know how to throw a lasso?"

"A what?"

"Never mind." He threw the rope expertly, dropping it neatly around a thunga's neck. "Just rope 'em the best you can."

"Right. Got it."

"Pens are in the back of town, a little way past the mercantile. Just bring 'em there. Good luck!" Sam trotted off, leading the thunga behind him.

Revka watched them go, then leaned down to Iyarra. "So," she said, "do we have any rope?"

Iyarra shook her head. "Not me," she said. "Nobody said anything about rope."

"Crud, I guess we'll just have to improvise."

A few minutes later, the people of Red Valley were treated to the sight of a woman on centaurback galloping up behind a thunga (which had knocked over a fence and was contentedly munching someone's begonias) and flinging a bed sheet over its head. The beast stopped midchew and began to frantically waggle its head, trying to shake off the sudden fog.

Revka hopped off Iyarra's back and scrambled onto the beast. "OK," she said, patting it. "Turn around, you. Come on. Turn around. Go left. Come on. Left, will you?" She thumped the beast's side, but it just stood there, "Left. Giddyup already! Criminy." She hopped off its back and tried leading it away from the garden. No dice. She reached under the sheet and tried to tug gently on the horns, which nearly earned her a good kick.

Revka scrambled out of the way and stepped several paces out of range. She half squatted in place and began slapping her hands on her thighs. "Here, thungie," she singsonged. "Here, thungie-thungie-thungie. Come to mama. Here, thungie!"

"Uhm...Revka?"

"Come on! Who's a good thungie?"

"Revka?"

"Hold up. I think I'm getting through to him. Here—"

"Revka? Honey? No. It's not working."

"I—"

"Please stop. People are staring."

"Ugh." Revka straightened up again and got back on Iyarra. "Well, it was worth a shot, anyhow." She reached over and tugged the sheet off the beast. "Come on, maybe we can lead it."

Iyarra obediently began to amble toward the street. On her back, Revka shook out the bed sheet and started to fold it back up.

Behind them, the thunga looked up at the billowing cloth. It snorted. Its eyes narrowed, and its front hooves traced deep lines in the dirt. Suddenly, it was full of business.

Revka saw the change in the creature and reached back to tap Iyarra on the shoulder. "Uhm, Iyarra…?"

"Something wrong?"

"I think you might want to—"

The thunga bellowed as it charged. Iyarra just managed to bound out of the way, leaving Revka to fall face first across the centauress' back. The bedsheet billowed out behind them as Iyarra picked up speed. Behind her, the bull thunga broke into a trot, its eyes locked on the rippling white cloth.

"It's the sheet!" Revka shouted back. "It's following the sheet! This is perfect!"

"So what do we do?"

"What else? Lead it back to the corral!"

"Okay!"

They hustled down the side street, the thunga keeping pace with them. This part of town was mostly houses, cabins of stone and wood where the longtime residents lived. The crowd wasn't quite as thick here as on the main street, but more than one looked up as the centauress and woman trotted by.

Revka flapped the bedsheet once or twice, lest the beast lose interest. No need, it just kept coming. Indeed, a couple of the others in the street began to pay attention. By ones and twos, thungas began to follow, first at a wary pace, then breaking into a trot.

Revka grinned. "Hey Iyarra," she called back, "I think it's working! We've got another few following us! Looks like this is going to be easier than we thought!"

"Yeah?"

"Sure! We flag a few down, lead 'em back together, and we'll have this over with in no time!"

They reached the junction of the main street, keeping up an easy pace. By now, several thungas were trotting along behind them. Revka kept flapping the sheet at them, "OK," she called back, "City gate's to the left, so hang a right and we should be able to find the corral easily enough. Then we'll come back for another batch. Work for you?"

"I...suppose." Iyarra bit her lip, peering down the street full of thungas and people trying, with varying degrees of success, to restrain them. Something in her voice suggested she wasn't a hundred percent convinced, but if Revka noticed, she made no mention of it.

They made the turn onto the street and began to work their way along. The thungas on their tail followed obediently behind, muscling their way past the others. Of these, one or two turned, saw the sheet, and fell in line. A few more thungas, wanting to see what all the fuss was about, joined the group.

Iyarra trotted forward, weaving her way through the traffic. "How are we doing back there? Still got them?"

When Revka didn't answer right away, she tried again. "I said, are they still following?" Silence. "Er, Revka?"

"What? Oh. No, no we haven't lost them."

"Oh, good."

"Actually, we seem to have picked up a few."

"Oh? How many?"

Revka's voice was small and tinged with restrained panic. "Oh, about ten or twenty. Something in there."

"*Ten or twenty!?*"

"Uhm, actually, pretty sure we're north of twenty now. Do you think you could go a little faster?"

Iyarra risked a look back. Sure enough, there was a small mob of thungas trailing behind them. She yelped involuntarily and began to run. Unfortunately, a crowded street is not the best place to try and pick up speed. She was forced to weave in and out of the chaos, which only served to collect more of the beasts, which caused her to become more desperate to outrun them. Every thunga they passed suddenly found itself facing a solid wall of its fellow beasts, into which it was summarily swept.

Further down the street, several of the townsfolk were patiently leading lassoed beasts back to the corral. Iyarra and Revka's growing herd was making a rumbling racket. The townsfolk looked back. There was a moment, as is so often the case in these situations, when their brains tried to make sense of what they saw and confirm that, indeed, they were seeing what they thought they were. This was followed, naturally, by blind panic.

There is nothing quite like a solid wall of galloping beef coming at you to take your mind off other things. In the panic that ensued, the citizens of Red Valley took off in all directions, some darting down side alleys or inside buildings, several taking off down the street in hopes of outrunning the stampede, and one particularly startled individual proving, contrary to all expectations, that centaurs *can* climb trees. If properly motivated.

At the head of it all were Revka and Iyarra, the former hanging on for dear life while the latter waved her arms and screamed, "Everybody out of the way!" as they charged down the street. Behind them, the mob of thungas just got bigger and bigger.

* * * * *

Jack Hadok, aged eighty-seven, bald, stone deaf, and not at all up on current events, opened the door of his old cabin and took a long, deep breath. There was something about that dry desert air that put a thirst in a man. Specifically, it gave Jack a thirst for the beer they served down the street at a nicely disreputable tavern that was known for the potency of its libations and the eventful evenings that often resulted therefrom. Not that he minded that part. Jack had actually been rather glad when his hearing went. He liked a quiet pint or three, and the constant background of singing, shouting, and fighting barely filtered into his consciousness while he sat serenely at his favorite spot down at the end of the bar.

He stepped across the threshold and was about to pull the door closed, when some motion caught the corner of his eye. A centaur woman came around the corner, waving her arms as she galloped by. He smiled, removed his hat, and waved back. Some awfully nice youngsters out there, no matter what some people said, yes indeed.

A trembling sensation rose up from the ground. He looked down at his boots in mild confusion, half-expecting to see something come tunneling up beneath them.

He looked up again, just in time to see a mob of thungas come swinging around the corner and charging right toward him. He froze in place as a seemingly endless mob of thungas thundered past, inches from his door.

It couldn't have been more than a minute, but it seemed like forever before the last few stragglers trotted by. He watched them disappear into the distance, then turned to look at the dust clouds rising up from the road. If he squinted, he could almost see the other cabins across the street. For a moment, he watched the dust whirl and dance in the wind. Then, without a word, he turned around, went back into his house, and closed the door.

Maybe he wasn't that thirsty anyway.

* * * * *

"Over here!" A thungahand waved frantically at Iyarra, pointing to his left. "Lead 'em through the gate!" Sure enough, there was a gate leading into a large open pen surrounded by low, but very thick, stone walls. Thungas weren't much good at jumping, but what they did have was momentum. Iyarra steered herself toward the gate, digging into her last reserves of energy. "Get ready back there!" she shouted.

"Right!" Revka dug her heels in, keeping an eye on the stampede. She jiggled the sheet some more, just to keep them focused, though in truth she needn't have bothered. They were mesmerized by the thing and kept coming full tilt.

Iyarra cleared the gate and aimed herself for the far wall. Inside the pen, a few thungas that had already been caught were milling around. She weaved around them without slowing down. "Almost time!"

"Right!" Revka glanced over her shoulder. She gave the bedsheet one last shake and let go. It flipped and billowed in the wind before hitting the ground in a crumpled heap. "Sheet away!" she shouted.

"Great!" Iyarra shouted back. "Hang on back there!" She pumped her arms, going full tilt for the fence. Behind them, the thungas converged on the bed sheet, stomping and poking at it with their horns.

Revka wrapped her legs around Iyarra's back as best she could and tried to find a grip on the back of the saddle. She felt the centauress' muscles bunch up under her as they approached the fence, then the moment of vertigo as they went sailing up and over.

They landed hard. Revka's forehead bounced off Iyarra's haunch, and she nearly got a mouthful of tail in the process. Iyarra slowed to a stop and turned around.

Thungas filled the corral. Now that the sheet was gone, the beasts were no longer paying any attention to centaur and rider. "Well," said Iyarra, "looks like we did it."

"Yup. Tell you one thing, though."

"Oh?"

"The hotel's never going to give us back the deposit on that sheet."

Iyarra trotted her way around to the front just as the last few thungas were being led in. A command was shouted, and two handlers hustled the gate closed and locked it.

"Good job, people!" shouted a tall, lean centaur. He was dressed somewhat better than most of the others, with a vest and jacket and a broad black Stetson. His ebony mane was cut close, and his mustache had been carefully waxed into position. He strolled over to the gate and knelt down to inspect the latch. "Curly," he said, "any idea how they got out?"

"No sir," said the centaur next to him. "Lock ain't damaged, and nobody's been in that I know of. Don't see no signs of breakin' in."

The fancy centaur frowned. "Well," he said, "better post a guard up for the next couple of days, just in case. Can't have that sort of thing happening. I'll see about getting a new lock."

"Yessir."

The centaur turned to Iyarra and Revka. "That was a mighty clever trick you two pulled, luring them back here like that. Pretty reckless too, I got to say."

Revka grinned. "Well, clever is kind of our middle name," she said modestly.

"So is reckless," added Iyarra.

The stranger laughed. "Well, never mind. Come on, let me buy you a drink. Name's Fleet, J. Everett Fleet. Don't believe I've seen you two around before."

The three of them departed for the main drag and the taverns. Behind the corral, unseen by anyone, the coyote sat on a fencepost and watched them go.

* * * * *

In time, the white sheet came to be regarded as a holy relic, one of the gifts of the Great Thunga Chief bestowed during the Miracle of the Open Gate. Unfortunately, by the alchemy these kinds of things tend to follow, disagreement broke out as to the significance and purpose of the holy object. For years, there were frequent outbreaks of violence between the various thunga factions, which their centaur handlers put down variously to skittishness, bad diet, and croup. Eventually, the sheet—a cheap cotton thing so thin you could almost read through it—disintegrated, whereupon it was buried with great solemnity and remembered as an example of never taking the gifts of the Great Chief for granted.

Meanwhile, a couple of villagers watched the proceedings from a nearby window.

"Well," said one. "What do you think about that?"

"Interesting," said the other. "We may have to keep an eye on those two. They might come in useful. See to it."

"Of course."

"Good. And get the word out to the others. We meet tonight. I think we have matters to discuss."

Chapter Four

BACK AT T. J. WANNAMAKER'S, Mr. Fleet escorted the two women to a table near the back, somewhat quieter than the rest. There were already a few centaurs there, sipping their drinks with the relaxed air of people for whom problems were always Somebody Else's. They were all dressed in the kind of clothes that never got dirty, because people dressed like that had people to get dirty for them. Revka had once heard that people who have people are the luckiest people in the world. If she was any judge, the occupants of this table were very lucky indeed.

"Please have a seat, ladies." Mr. Fleet waved them to a couple of vacant spots. "Let me get you something. Glass of wine, maybe? A beer? Have you tried the Fintoozler?"

"Well, uhm, what exactly is the—"

"Actually, we had a couple of braws back at the other table." Revka pointed across the room. "I'll just run over and get them real quick."

"Nonsense! Let me get you two fresh ones." He waved to an attendant, who scurried off. "Consider it my thanks. Those thungas can be a real pain if they get loose during mating season. We have to bring them out a bit at a time and keep them under control. Beats me how they got out."

"I bet it was rustlers." The speaker was a youngish centaur, not dressed quite as well as Mr. Fleet. He was attired in a quiet brown suit with a trimmed-down mane and wire-rim spectacles. "I shouldn't be surprised in the least."

"I don't think so." Mr. Fleet shook his head. "Lock looked all right, and there was no damage that I could see. I suppose it might have been picked, but I doubt any thief is gonna take that subtle an approach."

A middle-aged centauress dabbed her lips primly with a handkerchief. "Well, I do hate to be the one to say it, but perhaps one of your young men forgot to lock up? Mistakes do happen, after all."

"Well, I suppose it's possible, but the latch should have held, anyhow. I can't help but feel someone was fooling around. Well, I'll give it a proper look later. In the meantime, I've got a couple of the boys standing guard till I get a new lock on 'er. We're just lucky these two were around to...oh, for goodness' sake, I haven't even introduced them!" He laughed, shaking his head. "Allow me. Let's see, you were...?"

"Revka."

"Right, and the young lady here is Iyarra. Did I get that right?"

"Yes, that's right."

"Everyone, these two helped corral them thungas just as neat as you please. I think it might be worth talking to them about our little problem."

"Oh?" Revka perked up. "You have a problem?"

"Indeed we do. Before we get into that, let me introduce you to our little group here. We are the Red Valley Citizens Protection Committee. We sort of look after the general welfare of the residents."

"Like the guards?"

"Well not quite, not quite. They're more to do with catching criminals, rounding up drunks, and such. We tend more toward the general well-being of the community as a whole. Anyhow, let me introduce you. This here is Mrs. Haroldina Wildberry, chairmare of the committee."

The horsewoman who had spoken earlier gave the two girls a nod. "A pleasure. Tell me, the name Iyarra...Fleetwind tribe, is it?"

"Yes, ma'am," Iyarra nodded politely.

"Thought it was." She smiled a little. "Always glad to see the old naming traditions in use. We have so many young people these days going around with names like Bill and Frank and Gladys. I mean, I ask you, a centauress named Gladys?" She shook her head at the sorry state of the world.

"Speaking of names," Mr. Fleet dropped a hand on the shoulder of the younger taur who had spoken before. "Allow me to introduce you to Master G Findswater. That's G as in the letter."

The girls looked at each other. "G? Just G?"

"I'm afraid so." G looked up at the older centaur. "Mr. Fleet, one of these days I'm just going to have to put the story on some cards so I can hand them out whenever I meet someone new. Goodness knows how much of my life has been spent explaining it."

"Allow me," said Mr. Fleet diplomatically. "See, our friend G here comes from a long standing and very traditional herd. One of the traditions involves naming a newborn after a beloved relative, generally whoever was most recently deceased. Now, as it happens, some months before G was born, both his maternal and paternal grandfathers had perished while trying to corral a group of stampeding thungas. Given that they had both gone at more or less the same time, there was something of a dispute as to who to use for the namesake. Obviously, each side of the family felt it should be their candidate. I'm sorry to say that tempers got rather hot over the whole thing.

31

"Before long it looked like there was going to be a straight-up feud over it all, until someone—I believe it was your mother, wasn't it?"

"That's correct, yes."

"Right. His mother pointed out that her daddy's name had been Groff, and the other fella's name was Gurun. She suggested they just name the boy G, and each side of the family could say it stood for whomever they liked."

"Good grief, really?"

"Centaurs tend to be very intense about traditions," Iyarra said. "Especially when it comes to naming."

"Amazing."

"That's certainly a word for it, yes." Mr. Fleet patted his younger counterpart on the shoulder and turned back to the table. "Now, where was I? Ah yes. To Mr. Findswater's left, Mr. Tarran. He owns the main bank in town."

A portly centaur with red hair and sideburns gave the girls a curt nod. "How do you do."

"Next, we have Miss Roe. She's a teacher at the common school and secretary for our little group." The youngish centauress appeared not much older than Revka and Iyarra. She was dressed in dark gray from head to toe, with her hair tied up in a bun secured by two pencils. Just looking at her was enough to bring back years of homework-related anxiety. Revka pegged her for the extra-homework-on-holidays type, the kind of teacher who always manages to call on you when you don't know the answer. Miss Roe gave the girls what she probably thought was a pleasant smile.

"And last but not least, our good friend Deacon Mushrat, Grand Hallowed Semiquaver at the Temple of Unremitting Pravity." The gray-haired old stallion in question gave the girls the merest glance before fixing his eyes back on the middle distance. He was dressed in a long, black frock coat and a flat-top hat. His face wore an expression of determined piety. Or constipation. It was hard to tell.

"Now then." Mr. Fleet took a drink and collected his thoughts. "As I was saying, we have a little problem here in town. It's a mite unusual, safe to say, and calls for people equipped to take an unusual approach. I should like to put the matter to you and see if it might be something you're willing to look into. That is, if the committee is amenable to the idea."

Revka glanced around the table. Nobody was exactly jumping up and down over the prospect, but no one seemed particularly against it, either. Judging by the looks of the committee members, the consensus seemed to be, what the hell.

Mr. Fleet looked around the table and rubbed his hands together. "Seems there's no objection. Well then, I suppose we'd better start with a little background. Miss Roe, would you mind?"

The schoolteacher sat up and cleared her throat. "Very well. The legend of the Blood Moon Beast goes back about as far as there have been centaurs living here. It is said that the first herd found living conditions rather difficult. There was a steady supply of water from the mountain, but there was scarcely enough food to go around. Naturally, having been nomadic up to that point, they didn't know much about agriculture or desert survival. Still, it was far and away the best place they had found since they had begun their trek west, so they were disinclined to give it up.

"They had been here a few weeks, more or less grazing the area around the runoff from the mountain streams. They had to go farther and farther from the water source each day. Some of the herd were beginning to grumble, and many were increasingly of the opinion that their situation was no longer sustainable. There was talk of heading back, even if it meant braving the desert again. The situation was becoming increasingly untenable.

"On the night of the next full moon, the moon was tinted a deep blood red, such as none of the centaurs had ever seen. That night, we are told, a 'great billowing thing like a dancing cloud' appeared, with a face white like bone and eyes dark as night. It told them they had been guided there, and that this land would be theirs to steward. The specter promised to teach them how they could thrive in this valley. They would learn the secrets of the land, how to tame the water, how to cause food to grow. They would learn the medicinal uses of the different plants around the valley. Best of all, the gift of the thungas would be bestowed upon them."

"What," said Revka. "You mean those big lizard things we just got done rounding up?"

"Quite. If I may be allowed to continue?"

"Sorry."

"Very well. As I was saying, the specter said it would teach them everything they needed to thrive in this environment. The stories say they learned this all in one night, but of course, the whole thing is clearly an allegory. Yes?"

Iyarra put her hand down. "I thought those only lived in swamps?"

"Only what lives in swamps?"

"The allegories. I didn't think you got them in deserts. They've got nowhere to swim."

"Sorry. Sorry." Revka held up a finger. "Iyarra, I think you might be thinking about alligators."

"Er...yeah, I might. Sorry. Carry on."

"What Miss Roe is saying," Mr. Fleet cut in helpfully, "is that it's basically a story about how our people learned to live out here. Or at least, up till recently we thought it was."

"Until recently, huh?" Revka leaned forward. "OK, you got our attention. Tell us about recently."

"Several months ago, some of the townsfolk began to report seeing and hearing something out in the valley, a billowy thing that glows blue in the moonlight. Apparently, it's been lurking around the grazing areas, spooking the thungas. Nothing you could really pin down, but sightings have started getting a little closer to home.

"A couple of weeks ago, Nil Hawkson came trotting into town, looking white as a sheet. He'd been poking around by the mountains when this thing came out at him. 'Bigger'n a house, an' all glowing blue,' he said. Nil described the head like a skull and said it talked with a kind of echo. The thing told Nil he wasn't to hang around there, that the mountains were forbidden, and he should get himself gone.

"Well, you'd better believe he did that. Nil came into town the next day and told us all about it. Some of us formed a posse and rode out to have a look. Didn't see the creature, of course, but there were some giant footprints. We traced them back to an old cave in the mountains, but there the trail stopped."

"Did you go in?"

Fleet shook his head. "No, none of the boys wanted to go in. See, that's another thing about this legend. You see, the Moon Beast gave the first people some rules to live by, as long as they should be here. First, they were to look after the thungas and treat them well. Second, they were to help the traveler in need, just as they'd been helped. The third rule was to never, but never, go poking around in the mountains. And I know what you're going to say, but that's a story that's been in our bones since birth. Superstition or no, there's damn few people around here that would undertake to explore one of the caves, for anything.

"Which brings us to you fine ladies. We would like you to head down into the cave, find whatever creature made those footprints and undertake to stop it from scaring townsfolk and thungas alike. Now, I don't know if I believe it's the Moon Beast, but that doesn't mean there's nothing down there. We'd be prepared to pay you two a fair bounty—say, fifty gold?—for going in and dealing with it. The cave's not far, just a few hours across the valley. We could show you the way there in the morning, if you like. Get in, get out. What do you say?"

The girls exchanged glances. "I don't know," said Revka. "We don't exactly have a lot of experience hunting down ghost monsters."

"True," Iyarra nodded. "That hardly ever happens."

Mrs. Wildberry leaned forward. "Well as far as that goes, I rather suspect it's some poor animal or other that's wandered into the caves. It happens from time to time, you know. There are bears and so forth in the mountains, and while it would be unusual for one of them to find its way down here, it is not unknown. I think people's imaginations are doing the rest."

"Couldn't have put it better myself," said Mr. Fleet. "How about you two ladies sleep on it, and let us know what you think? I'll be over by the thunga pens first thing tomorrow morning. If you decide you're interested, just come along there and seek me out. How does that sound?"

Revka finished her drink. "That sounds reasonable. We'll talk it over and let you know."

"Splendid." Fleet offered them each a warm handshake. "I hope we'll have good news in the morning, and once again, thank you for your help today. You folks have a fine evening now, you hear? Be sure and think about it. Thanks muchly!"

After the two had gone, Findswater coughed. "Excuse me for asking, sir, but why them? They seem a little...unpolished."

Everett Fleet just chuckled. "Tell me," he said, "you don't know much about mining, do you, boy?"

"Can't say it's ever come up, sir."

"So you don't know about canaries."

"Well, I mean, I know of them."

"It might not be a bad idea to educate yourself on their uses when you get a chance." Everett Fleet stood up and adjusted his hat. "In the meantime, I have arrangements to make. Take care, everyone."

Chapter Five

IT'S A CURIOUS FACT that the further west you go, the later the day starts. This has nothing to do with time zones, understand, but everything to do with lifestyle. In the middle of the kingdom, where the majority of the crops are grown, the day begins as soon as the sun comes up and ends when it goes down. As one moves west, the population is less rigidly bound to the demands of an agricultural timetable and tends to take a more relaxed view. There is a tendency to let the day break itself in a little before getting down to business. Further west is The Great Rift, the continent-long crevice that divides Kalazad from the western lands beyond, where the natives surf the hot updrafts that blow from the center of the world. The days there don't properly get started until almost noon, at least partially because everyone is recovering from whatever party they happened to be at the night before.

In Red Valley, things weren't quite that laid-back, but the dawn had burnt off the early morning desert chill by the time Mr. Fleet and his party collected at the thunga corral. They didn't have long to wait. Iyarra ambled up to the group, Revka on her back. The two had apparently been shopping; they were each sporting one of the large-brimmed hats that were practically the local uniform. Revka, in particular, seemed to be taken with hers. She kept fussing with the angle and fiddling with the tilt of the brim.

Mr. Fleet smiled. "Good morning, ladies. I had a feeling you two would be along. Nice to have you with us. We're just going to have a quick trot around some of the valley—check on a few things while we're out—and we'll work our way over to the cave. I trust that'll work for you all right?"

Revka tipped her hat at the group. Currently, she was wearing it down low, so her eyes were completely hidden. "That'll be just fine, suh," she drawled.

Mr. Fleet laughed. "Well, I do believe you two are goin' native! All right folks, let's go." He turned and led the way west and out of town.

"We'll follow the canal most of the way. I want to make sure it's all in good order." He pointed to where a stone waterway had been laid into the ground. "We use native stone to build the channel, quarried right from the mountains themselves."

Revka peered down at the water as it ran along the channel. "Nice," she said. "What keeps it from seeping through?"

Mr. Fleet smiled. "Show em, Clem." One of the other centaurs reached back into a bulging saddlebag and held up a handful of gray powder, which he let slip through his fingers. "Special mortar," Fleet said. "We make it with ash and ground-up thunga bones. Add water, and it seals up tight as you like." He pointed to a board suspended vertically in a frame over the canal. "See that? We have one of those every hundred paces or so. If there's ever a leak, we can cut off the flow where the problem is and repair it in two shakes."

"Clever," Iyarra said, clearly impressed.

"Well, when you've been out in the desert as long as we have, you learn the number one thing is making sure that water keeps flowing. Ain't that right, Clem?"

"Y'sir."

"We always bring a little mortar just in case, but breaks are few and far between these days." Mr. Fleet peered at the water level. "Yup, she should be fine."

A little further on, the canal began to branch into smaller tributaries. These went off into fields where green plants were growing in neat rows.

"Irrigation," smiled Mr. Fleet. "We grow all the food we need here, even a little grain. We've developed a breed of wheat that holds up right well in the desert. I mean, it won't exactly make for the lightest loaf of bread you've ever seen, but it will fill you up, no trouble."

"I bet." Revka looked around at the setup. The crops stretched off to her right, going a fair way, with little rivulets running from the canals to the plants. "So, is the soil really all that fertile?"

"Well, not at first, but fortunately thunga scat is just the thing. You sprinkle some of that stuff on a rock, and it'll have a crop of grass on it next day." Mr. Fleet laughed and winked. "In fact, I once knew a feller by the name of Karf Hardgreaves, the baldest man I ever knew. The Vitric Ocean has more hair on it than he did. He was courting a widow in town by the name of Sara Pointsnorth. He wasn't getting very far with her, on account of that shiny dome of his.

"One day, he snuck off and put a little thunga fertilizer on his head. He went to sleep that night and woke up the next day with as fine a head of grass as you ever did see. He got a gardener friend to trim it all up nice and neat, and style it real fancy. Off he went down to the widow

Pointsnorth's, with a bouquet of flowers in one hand, and another one up top of his head."

"Okay," Revka chuckled. "I'll bite. Did it work?"

"Nope." The centaur shook his head sadly. "Turned out that she had the hay fever. Couldn't get near him. He had to give up on the whole idea. Last I heard, he had a job going around luring bees away from peoples' gardens."

Revka leaned down and nudged Iyarra. "Hey you," she grinned. "How would you like it if I had grass for hair? You could have a snack whenever you wanted."

"Depends on where you grow it." Iyarra spoke before she could stop herself and flushed as she heard the words come out of her mouth. She blushed hotly as waves of laughter echoed out over the valley. Fortunately, they seemed to be too busy laughing at the remark to really think about it, and the group rode on.

* * * * *

The mountain range rolled across the landscape like a wave of stone, billowing ever upward. The sun was well up in the sky by the time they got to the base, which was covered in the dry pinkish soil of the desert and populated by clusters of sage and chamisa. Further up, they thinned out into bald, gray stone. Barely visible, the peaks sat draped in glistening snow. The girls regarded the sight with awe.

"Now *that*," said Revka, "is one hell of a lot of rock."

Mr. Fleet chuckled. "Never seen anything like it, huh? They really grow 'em big out here, no lie."

Revka pointed to the nearest peak. "Anybody ever climbed up there?"

Mr. Fleet shook his head. "Naw. A few people have tried. The lucky ones made it back down in one piece."

"We spent some time in the Icarines a while back," Iyarra said, "but they were nothing like this."

"The Icarines?" Mr. Fleet chuckled. "Yeah, I hear they aren't so much mountains as wrinkles." He gestured to the wall of stone stretching off as far as could be seen. "These are *mountains*."

The group rounded a hillock of stone. Tucked neatly into a small valley of its own, the cave's entrance was large and wide, more than easy to drive a whole wagon train through.

Revka felt the hairs on her arm stand on end, and Iyarra pawed nervously at the ground. This wasn't a natural rock formation. It was too regular, too perfectly placed. Too sinister.

As they came closer, a sound just on the edge of hearing increased their apprehension. By the time they stood in front of the cave's mouth, the sound had become a deep, mournful moan rising and falling like the cry of a god who has gazed upon his works and despaired.

Revka shivered. "What," she said quietly, "is that."

Mr. Fleet laughed, though perhaps with less enthusiasm than he'd had up to this point. "Oh, that? Oh, we reckon there must be an opening somewhere that lets the wind get in. If you stand up close, you can feel the draft come out." He pointed to a spot directly at the cave entrance, while making sure not to get too close himself.

"That ain't what I was told," the one named Curly spoke quietly. "My grandmama told me this mountain was the hut of the mother of Death. Grandmama said that mother sits up all night and all day, crying on account of she can't never see her son again—bein' as she's immortal, y'see. They say that anyone she ketches, they can't die however long they—"

"Curly!"

"Sir."

"That's enough of that." Mr. Fleet pulled himself together. "Silly, old story anyway." He turned to the girls. "As I said, it's just some wind blowing through, but this is where the tracks led. Now, all we need you to do is to go on in a way, far as you can. I don't reckon it can be that far. Keep an eye out for any lost critters or anything like that. Like I say, if there's anything in there, it isn't anything to worry about. Just see what's there and head on back." He nodded to one of the other men, who pulled out a couple of torches. "We'll wait here a little bit. I may have to leave, but at least a couple of the boys will stick around, so don't you worry."

Revka nodded. She carefully stowed one of the torches and lit the other one. "All right," she said. "We'll be back as soon as we can."

"Just one thing," Iyarra hesitated at the threshold, turning back to the party.

"Yes, ma'am?"

"What happens if we don't find anything?"

This time, Mr. Fleet's smile was genuine. "Then that would be the best news of all."

* * * * *

"Why do we always wind up in caves?" Iyarra grumped, holding the torch a little higher. The tunnel snaked to the left as they went in, and it wasn't long before they could no longer see the entrance or hear the thungahands. As they walked on, the path began to turn gently to the right, as if describing a gigantic circle.

"Well, you didn't have to agree to it." Revka had her sword out on her lap, carefully going over the blade with a whetstone. Moon Beast or bear, there was no telling what might be in a cave like this. "I did say we could skip it, but you said you didn't mind."

"Actually, I said I didn't mind if *you* wanted to."

"Hon, you know you don't have to if you don't want to. You can say no. It won't hurt my feelings."

Iyarra smiled a little. "Okay, it's just... Well, you know me. Never been very good at being assertive, but as long as we're here..." She looked around. There was only one path continuing through the stone. Not even a side passage. Other caves had stone formations or little branches going off into other places, but this one...

"Tunnel," said Revka.

Iyarra blinked out of her reverie. "Beg pardon?"

"Tunnel. There's no way this is a natural formation, something carved this passage out. And you know what else is weird?"

"What's that?"

"Pretty much every cave we've ever been in has gone down."

Iyarra looked around. Sure enough, the arced path was sloping gently upward, a subtle but unmistakable climb. "We're going up into the mountain," she said. "I've never heard of that."

"There's something else that bugs me," Revka said. "Actually, can we stop for a moment? I want to check something."

Revka dismounted and asked for the torch. She walked over to the nearest wall, which she proceeded to stare at very hard. Iyarra waited patiently, but as far as she could tell, it seemed pretty much like any cave wall she'd ever seen. "Revka? You okay?"

Revka didn't answer. She reached up slowly and brushed a hand along some faint grooves in the wall, worn down with time, but still visible in the torchlight. "Claw marks," she said.

"Claw marks?"

Revka nodded. "Big ones." She took a step back, biting her lips. "And you want to know something else?"

"Er, do I?"

"These claw marks? They're going the wrong way. I mean, they're starting here"—she demonstrated—"and raking back to like here. See? It gets shallower as it goes."

"Yes?"

"Yeah. You see?"

"Hon," said Iyarra patiently. "You say this like it's some kind of terrible thing. I have no doubt that it is, but I have no idea why. So, although I'm about 99 percent sure I'm going to regret this, could you please just tell me what's so bad about that?"

"Oh. Sorry." Revka pointed up the tunnel. "It means that whatever carved this tunnel was coming from there, to here, and on down. You see?"

"So wait. You're saying that whatever made this tunnel started inside the cave and tunneled its way out?"

"Looks like."

Iyarra threw her hands up. "Yup," she sighed, "I completely regret knowing that."

"Sorry hon."

"It's all right."

"Are we still good to go on?"

"Might as well, but hand me back the torch." They walked along in silence for a while.

"Iyarra?"

"Hm?"

"Do you smell anything?"

The centauress stopped. She tilted her head to one side and sniffed the air. "Well, I'm still picking up the breeze. Beats me where it's coming from, if this is a tunnel going to the middle. Haven't seen any air holes or anything like that."

"Yeah, weird. Say, you don't suppose that this thing goes all the way to the top of the mountain, do you?"

"What, all the way up?" Iyarra tasted the air. "Well, it might be my imagination, but now you mention it, the breeze does seem a little bit cool. Of course, that's caves anyway."

"True," Revka said. "And you're not picking up anything else?"

"Well, there's a faint animal smell. Not much of one, but now that you mention it, I am picking up a whiff of...sulfur?"

"Sulfur?" Revka wrinkled her brow. "What would sulfur be doing here?"

Up ahead, the tunnel opened into a larger space. As the two girls walked across the threshold, a sudden, sharp *crack* echoed around the room. Lurid, blue light flooded the chamber. Iyarra and Revka stood frozen in terror at the nightmare before them.

Reaching almost to the ceiling, wrapped in a tattered cloak that billowed around its skeletal form, a creature loomed up from behind the blue-green flame that had appeared out of nowhere. The gargoyle's twisted shape sent grotesque shadows all along the walls and ceiling of the cave. Not much could be seen of the body beneath its tattered robes, but there were definitely too many bones and not any skin at all. The figure lurched forward, its long, sharp skull looming way too close for Iyarra's liking. Its eye sockets were empty and black as pitch, but she somehow felt that this would be no impediment if it decided to hunt them down. One too-long arm reached forward, a skeletal claw pointing a single accusing finger at the two. The creature hissed.

The girls screamed.

And they ran.

* * * * *

Outside, the group had settled in. Mr. Fleet had slipped a slender book out of his saddlebags and was reading in a shady spot he had found. Some of the other men had brought out a deck of cards, and a spirited game of baker's bluff was underway.

One of the men looked up from his cards. "How long's it been?"

Curly sorted through his hand. "Mmm 'bout half an hour," he said.

"How long we gonna be out here, anyhow?"

Mr. Fleet put a finger on his place in the book and looked up. "Well, personally, I am going to wait until around noon, then I really need to be seeing to things back in town. However, someone will have to wait here for them, so thank you for volunteering, 'Somin.'"

"Aw, boss."

"Don't worry. I'll send replacements at sundown, if necessary, but I really don't think..." Something had changed in the noise of the cave. He studied the cave's mouth, then deliberately dropped a silken bookmark between the pages and carefully put the book away.

The others heard it too. The cards and things were put away, and the men grouped themselves around the cave. It was hard to tell quite what it was above the howling of the wind, but something was coming. And it was loud.

A minute later, the centauress and rider burst from the cave mouth going full speed and screaming their lungs out. Iyarra waved her hands frantically as she galloped through the small group. "Move, move, move!" On her back—or to be more precise, clinging to one side—the human held on for dear life. They bowled through the group and kept going, galloping off into the desert.

Curly turned to 'Somin.' "What was that the lady was yellin' as she went by?"

"Dunno. Didn't quite catch it."

Mr. Fleet sighed. "I believe it was 'keep the frigging money.'" He shook his head sadly. "Come on, gentlemen. We'd better catch up with them before they get lost."

It took only a few minutes to track the girls down. They were stopped in a small field of sagebrush, trying to pull themselves together.

"Oh, by gods! Did you *see* that thing!?"

"I mean, holy Krep! I nearly dropped my apples on the spot!"

"Iyarra, ew!"

"Sorry, sorry, but you know what I mean, right? That thing was just...and with the..."

"Ladies." Mr. Fleet and his group trotted up. He looked the two over, then clasped his hands together. "Now, I'm no expert in these things," he said dryly, "but I do find myself suspecting that you found something."

"Found...yeah," said Revka. "Yeah, I think we can say we definitely found something, yes."

"Big monster. Big. Very scary."

"Big, glowy—"

"Skull—"

"With the bones—"

"And like, no eyes—"

"Just...bad," concluded Revka. "It was bad."

"My word." Mr. Fleet clasped his hands behind his back and began to pace. "Well, this is worse than I expected. I had hoped it would be some trapped animal or suchlike. Well, I guess there's nothing for it. I suppose we'd best get on back to town, and you can tell us all about this creature that you saw."

"Okay, yeah," said Revka. "We can do that."

"And then we can discuss the next steps."

Revka looked up at Iyarra, who made a face. "Well, to tell you the truth, I think our next step is getting the hell out of here. You sent us in there to see what it was. We did that."

"Well, I was hoping you'd stick around, maybe help us get rid of that thing. We don't have much in the way of monster hunters coming through here, as a rule. Y'all kind of struck me as the kind who were good at that sort of thing."

"Okay, I'm not saying we haven't fought a few monsters. Actually, now that I think of it, kind of a lot, but still, I think we'd just as soon skip out on this one if it's all the same to you."

"Yeah," Iyarra nodded. "That was, like, *really* big and scary."

"Besides, the convoy is going back east tomorrow. We were kind of planning on going with it. So..."

The centaur put his hands on his hips. He shook his head and tutted. "Well, I don't know what this world is coming to," he muttered. "I had you figured as bona fide hero types. And you mean to tell me that y'all are just going to leave this behind and turn tail back east?"

"Yup."

"Definitely."

"Sorry."

Fleet threw his hands up in despair. "Well, I suppose I can't force you. "Let's get back to town. I can at least pay you for your time. We'll head to the saloon. What do you say? First round's on me."

"After what we've seen," Revka said, "I could sure use one."

* * * * *

The next morning, the girls set out with the rest of the wagon train back east, never to return. The citizens committee sent more people into the caves. Some didn't come back. The raids on the city began, and then the people started disappearing. And then...and then...

And then, in a place that was nowhere, The Lady held up a hand. "No."

Before her, the pattern stretched in all directions, the seven-dimensional matrix where the past, present, and future were woven into the ever-changing tapestry of now. She focused her attention on a thread no different from any other, unless you had the knowing of it. She leaned forward and, with a touch as light as a butterfly's kiss, she tugged.

The pattern changed.

The Lady nodded. Technically, what she had just done was impossible, at least for most of her kind, but she was no ordinary goddess. And there was no point being the kind of goddess she was if she couldn't raise a little hell now and then.

She watched with some satisfaction as the pattern reknit itself. After a while, she nodded and stepped away, off to watch things for herself.

Suddenly, this was a much longer story.

Chapter Six

DAWN TIPTOED GINGERLY ACROSS the sky like a latecomer hoping that if they just slipped in quietly enough, people would think they had been there all along. The streets were quiet, with only a few early risers up and about. The local blacksmith/haberdasher was busy getting his fire up and hot for a long day's work (in centaur settlements, the two jobs are often combined. You can go in for a new set of horseshoes and get a purse to match). In some of the taverns along the main drag, the process of cleaning up the previous night's debris had already begun in anticipation of the lunch rush. Overall, however, the town was a picture of calm and—

"Whzrrgl-fnffl...(snort)"

—a picture of calm and—

"Huh? Whsst? Whtimsit?"

—calm and—

"Ohhhhh, goddddddd."

Quite a bit has been written about hangovers and their place in the literary canon. The ancient scrolls speak of pink elephants, odd flying things, or woodpeckers on the head. There are even whispers of a mythical leopard who tiptoes into a drunkard's room in ballet slippers to do something positively disgusting in the sleeper's mouth. In truth, no poetic metaphor, no creation of animal whimsy can accurately recreate the gut-wrenching avalanche of regret that hits you the morning after with the force of the intruding sun. It is then one recalls that hangovers can be funny, but only when someone else is having one.

Revka staggered to her feet and managed to make it to the nearest wall. She braced herself, waiting for the room to settle down so she could hazard the trek to the water closet. After a moment or two, the room settled into a predictable rhythm. She was able to push off from the wall and let inertia propel her to the open doorway, which she only slightly clipped on the way through. This, unfortunately, caused her to trip and fall forward, landing across the seat and over the pit just as she was inhaling sharply.

The events that followed are best left out of a fine, upstanding piece of literature such as this. Suffice it to say that Revka emerged several minutes later, somewhat lighter and considerably more sober than she had gone in. She staggered back into the main room, and collapsed on the bed, which said, "Ow."

"Sorry."

Iyarra staggered to her hooves, shaking her head. "Wh'timezit? And why're green 'n' purple splotches everywhere?" She swiped at the air in front of her face.

Revka glanced at the closed curtains. "I dunno, 'bout midmorning? Somethin' like that."

"Ugh." Iyarra wobbled her way toward the bathroom. "Krep, how much did we have last night?"

"Can't have been that much." Revka sat up again, rubbing her temples. "We went back with the guy. You know, the guy?"

"Mustache guy."

"Yeah, him." Revka eased herself to her feet. "I remember he said it was a shame we weren't sticking around. And we really shouldn't go without trying the Fintoozler."

"Oh gods, the Fintoozler." Iyarra wiped her hand down her face. "What the hell was in that, anyway?"

"Beats me. It didn't taste like it was too bad. At least not the first one."

It is, of course, an acknowledged truth among the more civilized corners of the universe that while the majority of strong drinks tend to wear their effects on their sleeves (or labels, as the case may be), it's the ones that don't taste bad at all that you really have to watch out for. This goes double for ones with funny names, and triple if they come in eye-searing colors. If it has multiple layers, or another, smaller drink floating in it, it's best to have a friend on standby with a wheelbarrow to get you home and, if necessary, hose you down.

The Fintoozler was not quite as bad, but it did have a certain impact all its own. The cheery drink was all bright colors and flash, many pieces of fruit on sticks, and a small wind-up monkey hanging off the sugar-coated rim. The overall effect of drinking one was not dissimilar to being run over by an ice cream truck.

"Well, we'd better get straightened out," said Iyarra. "I don't think we want to show up at the…"

Iyarra trailed off. Revka looked up from where she had been splashing water on her face. "Huh? At the what?"

Iyarra cleared her throat. "Uhm, Revka?"

"Yeah?"

"What time were we supposed to ship out with the wagon train?"

"We're supposed to show up at the warehouse at dawn, and uh…"

Revka hurried over to the window and yanked the curtain aside. The sun was already well above the horizon.

"Krep!" She bustled around, throwing her clothes on as fast as she could. Iyarra followed suit.

The world has applied great ingenuity to the research and discovery of hangover cures, but somehow panic has always been chronically underrated, despite being extremely effective. Careful testing has shown that suddenly remembering an appointment you should have been at five minutes ago has the same potency as approximately three cups of coffee and works much faster. And yet, people going drinking seldom take the precaution of scheduling important meetings, final examinations, etc. for early the next morning.

Not on purpose, anyway.

Five minutes later, Iyarra skidded to a halt in front of the Red Valley Mercantile Company. There was very little going on, but the fresh hoofprints and wheel tracks on the ground told them everything they needed to know.

"Nuts!" Revka thumped a fist down on the saddle.

"Hey! Easy, there."

"Sorry! Sorry." Revka sighed, looking down the road toward the city gate. "I don't suppose there's a chance we could catch them up?"

Iyarra sniffed the air. "Feels like it's been a couple of hours, at least." She trotted up the street until they got to the front gate. Before them, the desert spread out, a vast sea of brown speckled with pale green.

Revka shaded her eyes, peering into the morning sun. "Nope," she said at last. "Can't even see their trail dust."

"You mean we're stuck here?"

"Until the next convoy out, I guess. Unless you feel like taking on the desert solo?"

"With those bandits and things out there? No way."

Revka nodded. "Yep." She sighed. "Okay. The second thing we do is find some work. Bound to be something we can put our hands to for a few days. We'll check the mercantile place first. Maybe they need loaders or something."

"What's the first thing?"

"The first thing," Revka grumped as they turned toward the main drag, "is we get something in our stomachs. And something to drink."

"But no booze."

"Damn right. No booze."

The lunch crowd began to filter into T. J. Wannamaker's about an hour later. The girls had a small table in the back, where they were picking disconsolately at their plates. Full stomachs had somewhat helped the hangover situation, but it hadn't done much for their mood.

"Pretty good salads here," said Iyarra. "Never seen purple carrots before."

"Mmph."

"How's your potato?"

Revka shrugged. "It's OK, could use more chili powder."

"At least the drinks are nice."

Revka groaned.

"Sorry, but it is pretty tasty."

"Yeah, I suppose." Revka glared ruefully at her glass. "I just thought that cactus juice was one of those cutesy names they give drinks sometimes."

"Then why did you try to eat the garnish?"

"I wasn't paying attention, okay?" On the table next to the glass was a small cactus pad bearing teeth marks. "I thought it was some kind of fruit."

"Well, it was nice of the owner to comp the drinks for us."

"It would have been nicer if he'd taken all the spines out before serving them." Revka's tongue probed the spot just behind her upper teeth; it would be tender for a while.

"Ladies, good morning to you." A familiar shape loomed above the table. Mr. Fleet smiled at them. "Not that I'm not charmed and delighted to see you two again, but I was under the impression y'all were heading out this morning?"

"Missed the convoy," Revka said.

"Ah, yes." Mr. Fleet helped himself to a seat. "I had a feeling last night that might be the case. Particularly after you started singing." He tipped his hat to Revka. "Though I will admit I liked the one about why wizards have pointy hats. I'll have to remember that one."

"Oh, gods," moaned Revka, clapping a hand over her face. "Not the wizard song. I didn't do the one about the miller's widow, did I?"

"Sung it *and* acted it out!" Mr. Fleet laughed. "I tell you what, if you ever think of going into show business, I think you'd do mighty fine. Though, to be honest, I'm a little surprised we didn't have the sheriff's men in here after that one. That bit where—well, you know. *That* bit was hysterical."

"I didn't...I didn't do the gestures, did I?"

"Ma'am, the gestures were the best part."

"Oh, *gods*."

Mr. Fleet just laughed and gave Revka a pat on the back. "Look, don't worry about it. You are far from the first person to fall prey to the Fintoozler, but anyway, does this mean you're going to be sticking around for a few days?"

"Looks like," Iyarra nodded. "Going out into the desert isn't really an option."

"Well, you aren't wrong, there. I mean, I wouldn't do it myself, and I was born and raised here. Still," his grin broadened. "If you need something to occupy your time while you're here, I could always use a little help."

"Well, if it's going to be this beast thing..."

"No worries there. You made yourself very clear on that. I had something a little less exciting in mind. Nothing glamorous, but it's good honest work. Pay's decent too."

"Is it?"

"Oh, yeah. You'll clean up."

"Clean up he says," muttered Revka as she dumped another load of manure into the bin. "Everybody's a comedian."

"Well, we've had worse jobs." Iyarra carefully carried a large shovelful to the bin and tipped it in. "And it is pretty decent pay, even without the free nose plugs."

"I suppose, but I guess it would have to be. Probably people aren't lining up around the block for this gig. Anyway, I thought 'thunga wrangler' would be more than this. He made it sound more..."

"Glamorous?"

"Well, no. Not glamorous. Just maybe not quite so crapcentric."

"Oh, well, it's kind of like Daddy says. There are three kinds of jobs in the world: manual work, service work, and mind work."

"Yeah?"

"Yup. You're either shoveling it, putting up with it, or making it up." Revka chuckled. "Okay, but what about management?"

"Dunno. I guess they supply it."

Eventually, they got to the point where the corral was about as clean as it was going to get. A gate separated the freshly cleaned space from the next one over, and the thungas were duly herded from one to the other. "You can go ahead and tackle the other one tomorrow," said Mr. Fleet. "But if that doesn't work for you, I do have another suggestion."

Revka clanged her shovel against the side of the bin, cleaning off the last bits of debris. "Oh yeah? What's that?"

"Just a little security detail." He kicked a hoof against the gate. "Since they got out the other day, I've had the boys standing guard just in case. Having another couple of people to rotate in would be a solid help. If you can take midnight to dawn, I'll pay you good night rates."

"What would we have to do?"

"Not much, not much. Just keep an eye on the critters, and make sure nobody tries to mess with the gate. I also expect you to do a circuit of the corral twice an hour. Just listen for the chimes in the clock tower up the street. Other than that, just make sure everything is OK and nobody tries anything."

"I'm game. Besides, the desert nights are supposed to be cooler than the days." Revka looked at Iyarra, who smiled.

"Actually, they are a mite chilly. May want to bundle up a little, but I take it you're interested?"

"I think so, yeah," said Revka. "Midnight, you say?"

"Yes. A couple of my regulars will relieve you at dawn. Sound good?"

"No monsters?"

"No monsters."

"No shovels?"

"No ma'am, no shovels."

"Mister, you just got yourself some guards."

* * * * *

Later that evening, in a small, dark room in a quiet corner of town, another meeting took place.

"Tonight, then?"

"That's correct, yes. The shift change is at midnight."

"Well then, it sounds all right to me. Is there any objection?"

"No."

"No, ma'am."

"We're good."

"Very well. And you two, will you be ready?"

"We got the stuff moved over this afternoon, miss. We can be ready any time."

"Good." Pause. "Those two, what are they doing now?"

"I believe they went back to the inn, ma'am. No doubt getting their rest before tonight."

"A good idea, I would say. I suggest you do the same. Now, do we have any further questions?"

"Er..." A younger, more hesitant, voice spoke for the first time.

"Yes? Go on."

"Are...are we quite sure we're doing the right thing? I mean, I know the stakes, and understand why and everything, but...well, this just doesn't feel like something good guys would do."

"No need to apologize; we quite understand. And yes, it's a bit unorthodox, but when all is said and done, we are a bodyguard of lies, and we have a job to do."

"I guess, but...why them?"

"They're not from here. They don't know the whole story. That means we don't have to worry about whether they have some kind of hidden agenda. Besides, they did so well yesterday. Really the ideal reaction. They're just what we need."

"As you say."

"Very well. Was there anything else?"

Silence.

"Very well, then. Tonight."

"Tonight."

"And good luck to us all."

Chapter Seven

IT WAS A DARK and stormy night.

Thunder rolled across the vast western sky, the limitless vista of stars smothered by a heavy blanket of clouds. Deep within the vaporous mass, lightning danced, occasionally breaking out and slamming onto the ground below. A scream rang out.

"Dammit Iyarra, that was my foot!"

"Sorry!" The centauress yanked her hoof away quickly and took a couple of steps back just to be sure. "Are you all right?"

"Yeah, I'm fine. Fortunately, I was standing in some mud. Well, I think it's mud." The downpour of the early evening had slackened to a slow-but-steady shower that had turned the entire valley into a giant mud pit. Revka's boots squished as she trudged back toward the gate.

"I thought it didn't rain out here in the desert." Iyarra tugged the hood on her oilskin a little farther forward. Mr. Fleet's warning of chilly desert nights was an understatement. Between the cold and the rain, she was beginning to think longingly of home. She shivered.

The two had been equipped with glowstone lamps, little more than crushed-up crystals in a glass jar with a handle on top. Their bluish light was faint and barely enough to make out details even a few paces away, but they were light and could be used in all weather. Revka set hers on the corral fence and looked around for a stick. Not finding one, she pulled out one of her knives and carefully scraped as much of the mud off her boots as she could. "Is it just me," she said, "or has every job we've taken since we got here been a complete lemon?"

"Certainly seems that way," Iyarra nodded. "I can't say I'm having much fun since I got here. Still, we've had worse gigs. Remember the time we were sparring partners for that gladiator?"

"OK, yeah, that was worse."

"Or when we were on the cleanup crew after that dragon got slaughtered? That was pretty nasty."

"Yeah, real shame too. I liked those boots."

"Or of course, there was the nove—"

"Hold it. No. Stop. The words, novelty wrestling act weren't about to pass your lips, were they?"

"...maybe?"

In the dark, Revka made a face. "I think I'd rather clean up another dragon."

"Well, look at it this way. The story probably hasn't got this far yet."

"You want to bet on that?"

"Well, not particularly."

For a while, there was only the soft patter of rain and the occasional rumble of thunder.

"Quiet night," Iyarra commented.

"Yeah. I suppose it would be, though, wouldn't it?"

"I suppose that's one nice thing about bad weather. I guess even thunga rustlers don't want to go out on a night like this."

"True that." Revka examined her boots, satisfied that they were as unmuddy as they were going to get. "Well, if nothing else, things should be pretty uneventful till dawn."

There was a loud, terrifying roar. Revka threw her hands up in the air.

"When?" she shouted. "When will I learn to keep my mouth shut? Come on, Iyarra. Let's go."

She vaulted up and into the saddle and hung on. Iyarra, her lamp held high against the darkness, galloped toward the point where the noise had been. It was a little farther down the fence, away from the main gate. Sporadic flashes of lightning in the clouds flickered momentary shapes across their field of view. There was the fence, stretching off into the distance. Inside the corral, restless thungas milled about. Far beyond, the outline of the mountains could be seen, sharp against the billowing sky.

Down at the very end of the corral, there was...something. Iyarra strained her eyes as she galloped forward, her hooves pounding through the mud and rain. Something was there, something tall and lean and eldritch, glowing blue against the darkness.

Another bolt of lightning shot across the sky. For a brief moment, the world was in stark relief, all silhouettes against the landscape. There, in the middle of it all, the beast was waiting.

"Revka!"

"I see it! I see it." Revka hooked her lamp on Iyarra's saddle horn and reached for her sword. "Get in close, girl! It's out in the open now!"

Iyarra stopped running and pawed at the ground. "Are you crazy? We're going to fight that thing?"

Revka growled. "OK, it kinda scared us last time, but dammit, I'm not going to let it do that to us again! Besides, I'm still smarting from what Mr. Fleet said when we ran away from it the first time. Well, not tonight, Buster. We ain't running away." She tugged the brim down on her hat and gave the distant creature a steely eyed glare. "We ain't the kind to run."

"Wait, we aren't?"

"Hell, no. We—"

"What about that time in Port South, when those guys were after us, and—"

"I mean we don't run from monsters."

"Well, there was that one in the cave, remember? We had to go in and get his overdue library book? We totally ran away from tha—"

"Okay. Sometimes we do run from monsters, but—"

"Actually, when you think about it, we run away a lot."

"Iyarra?"

"Yes?"

"Can we please just fight the monster now?"

Iyarra threw her hands up but complied. She resumed splashing her way forward.

As they approached, Revka sized up the creature. It was funny, but out here in the open, it looked different, somehow. Less scary. Something about the way it moved...a little bell rang in the back of her head. If only she could put her finger on it.

The monster, which by now had noted their presence, let out another guttural howl. It stopped whatever it had been doing and turned to face them. Now that they were closer, it was clear it was giving off the same bluish glow as in the caves. It began to shamble toward them, its grotesquely long arms raised high, ready to sweep down and strike.

As the girls closed with the beast, it brought one arm down and across, nearly knocking Revka right out of the saddle. Iyarra screamed and just managed to jump out of the way of the other arm. She tried to turn around for another pass, but the slick mud slipped out from under her. She hit the ground hard.

Revka yelped, waiting for the crunch of a broken leg, but the mud had taken most of the impact. She braced her free leg against the saddle and kicked hard. The slick mud beneath her gave way easily and she slid out and free of the centauress, who was having a little difficulty getting herself upright. Revka scrambled to her feet, brandishing her sword at the creature. "Yarra! Can you get up?"

"Just a—just a second, yeah." Iyarra scrambled for purchase in the slick mud, trying to roll herself upright. She kicked out, pushing up with her arm. "Just a little hard to—" Her hand slipped out of place, and she hit the ground with a splat. "Krep."

Revka risked a quick glance back, then put herself between Iyarra and the creature. "Back!" she shouted. "You stay back!" She swung her sword once or twice, hoping the creature would remain at bay. It was rather slow and unwieldy, but on the other hand, it had a hell of a lot more reach than she did. Maybe if she were quick enough, she could jump in and stab it before—

One of the arms whipped across her field of view. She felt the creature's claws rake against the side of her face and turned away fast. OK, maybe it was pretty fast after all. She swore under her breath and just managed to parry the second arm as it came across. The shock of the impact nearly knocked the sword out of her hands. It was more like hitting a rock than a living creature. *Good grief, this thing really doesn't have any skin on it.*

Revka felt herself being shoved to the ground just as the claw came whipping through the air, right where she had been standing. Iyarra brandished her twin daggers and scowled at the creature. "Back, you!" she screamed. "You stay *back!*" Revka managed to scramble out of the mud and back to her feet. The creature weaved back and forth, looking between them. Its movements seemed more hesitant now, more circumspect. Revka wiped some mud away from her face and watched the creature thoughtfully. No way they could get close, not with those arms, but if...

"Iyarra! Flank!"

The centauress looked back at herself. "What? What about it?"

"Not *your* flank, I mean *we* flank! Spread out! It can't attack us both at once!"

"Oh! Right!" Iyarra sidestepped quickly to the left, while Revka moved right. The creature kept looking back and forth, maneuvering itself to be equidistant from the two. It tried another swipe at Revka, but she was now well out of reach. It seemed to reach a decision and turned its attention to Iyarra. The centauress raised her daggers threateningly and tried not to think about how useless they were under the circumstances. "If we get out of this, I am so getting a halberd."

Revka gave a signal, and Iyarra nodded imperceptibly, then turned back to the creature. She made a face at it and forced some bravado into her voice. "Come on!" Iyarra waved her daggers again. "Come on you...you big dumb poopy butt! I dare you! Just try it!"

The creature lurched toward her, raising its long arms, preparing to strike. Iyarra moved to the side, keeping her eyes locked on the creature and waiting for it to strike. She could just barely see Revka scramble up onto a fencepost behind the beast. Revka leapt.

The creature lunged forward, sweeping a claw toward Iyarra's face. She instinctively leaped back and out of the way, her hind legs giving out under her and sending her haunch-first into the mud. Revka landed badly on the creature, scrambling up to attack. The cloak that covered the monster began to billow, moving in strange ways. Revka scrambled forward, grabbing at the upper part of the creature and trying to get a grip, but it was just too big around.

Something blunt and hard jabbed her right in the ribs. She felt one of her legs slip away from the beast, and the rest of her went over and down into the mud. And just as she hit the ground, a bolt of lightning tore across the sky, lighting up the scene.

On the ground, Revka blinked as the afterimage danced across her eyes. Had she really seen what she thought she'd seen?

The creature was still standing over her. Quickly, she rolled out of its path before it could tread her into the ground. She grabbed at the tattered robe and tried to haul herself up, but the fabric only tore away in her hand. She staggered back and out of the way, slipping as she tried to get back on her feet.

In the distance, back toward the town, there was the sound of voices. Revka could just see a few of the glowstone lamps bobbing toward them. There were other voices, too, but they were coming from...

The creature turned and began to run off into the desert night. Revka managed to get to her feet and run a few paces, but it was clear there was no way she could catch up with it.

Behind her, Iyarra got to her hooves and staggered over to Revka. "Should we go after it?"

Revka stood still for a moment, looking down at the thing in her hand. "No," she said quietly, "I don't think so. Let it go. By the way," she added. "Big dumb poopy butt? Seriously?"

Iyarra grinned sheepishly. "Okay," she said. "So, I'm not so good at battle cries."

A few seconds later, some of Mr. Fleet's men arrived. "We heard the noise," said one. Between the darkness and his heavy rain gear, it was hard to see his face, but Revka thought she recognized the one named Clem. "Was that the thing?"

Revka just nodded. "Yup," she said quietly, "that was it all right."
She turned and looked out into the darkness. By now the creature was
gone, even the faint blue glow was no longer visible.

Clem coughed. "Er, you two all right? Looks like it was a hell of a
fight."

Revka didn't turn around. "Iyarra?"

"Hm? Oh, just some bumps and bruises. Nothing serious. You?"

Revka shrugged. "Couple scratches."

"Ah. Well, if you like, you ladies can go ahead an' cut out. I'll have
some of the boys finish off the shift for ya. You know, just in case it
comes back."

Revka finally turned around to face the others. "I think we should
be good to finish out our shift if you don't mind."

"But the beast...?"

"The beast isn't coming back," said Revka flatly. "Not tonight,
anyhow." She looked down at the torn cloth in her hand, turning it over.
"And in the morning," she added, "We need to talk to your boss."

* * * * *

After everyone had left, there was a movement in the empty air. A
corner of the rain moved aside, and the coyote stepped out from
behind. He knelt at the spot where the fight had taken place, staring
long and hard. Then, shaking his head sadly, he got up and left the way
he'd come.

He just hoped the boss knew what she was doing.

Chapter Eight

THE MORNING SUN MUSCLED its way past the last remaining clouds and began the long climb to its accustomed place. Already the earth was baking back into the hard ground of the desert. In the office of Amos Trawler, apothecary and assayer, the plot was thickening.

"Thank you for seeing us, Mr. Trawler." Mr. Fleet doffed his hat as they moved into the back room, where the laboratory equipment was kept. "I hope we're not interrupting anything important."

"Not at all, my dear boy." The elderly human pushed up his glasses and led them to a workbench. "I was just consternating."

"Oh dear," said Iyarra. "Should we come back when you feel better?"

"What? No, no I mean I'd be defenestrated to help. What's the precise nature of your inequity?"

"That's kind of a personal question, isn't it?"

Mr. Fleet waved the girls into silence. "The beast struck again last night, Mr. Trawler. These two ladies were on guard duty. During the fight, they managed to tear off a bit of this cloth. I wonder if you could have a look at it."

"The beast, you say? Well, naturally I'd be abundant to help. Let's have a look at it, shall we?"

Mr. Fleet nodded to Revka, who handed over the scrap of cloth. The rough canvas was the type used for sacking or tents, or really anything where durability was more important than, say, comfort. One side had been painted over with what looked like thinned-out whitewash sprinkled with little blue specks.

The old man held the cloth up to the light, frowning. Then he put it on the table and picked up a giant magnifying lens. He held it over the cloth, studying intently for a long moment, before giving a grunt of satisfaction.

"Well," he said, "this is a very somnambulant bit of evidence. You see these little blue bits, here?"

The observers nodded. "Yessir," said Mr. Fleet. "You know what they are?"

"Abrasively." The chemist pointed to some of the larger specks. "You see these? That's glowstone. Ground to a fine powder and mixed in with a binding agent. The white paint is highly reflexive, so it makes the light shine right out. It's cheap to produce, and if you put it where it gets plenty of sun, it will last all night."

"You don't say?"

"Inscrutably. In fact, I hear tell that, in some towns, they even use it for the street signs so you can read 'em at night."

"And you're sure that's what this is?"

"I'm absolutely prostrate."

"Yeah, I thought you would be." Mr. Fleet folded his arms. "Well, I'll be," he said. "Play acting. All the time it was play acting."

"Would appear so, sir, yes." The old man chuckled a bit, laying the sample on a metal tray. "Actually, it's funny you should say that. I recall once going to a play, when I was a young man in St. Elucida. They had a fella done up as a ghost. His whole outfit was covered in the stuff, even his face. Made a hell of an imposition, I can tell you, the moment he came out on that stage. Best show I ever saw."

"Gosh."

"Yup. I heard it took him two weeks to get all the paint off." The old man took his glasses off, cleaning them reflectively. "Now, that is some dedication to one's art."

"Well," said Mr. Fleet, "be that as it may, I do believe our next order of business is to head over to see Sheriff Lestrange. I would like you two ladies to tell him what you told me. Between that and this scrap of cloth, I do believe we have enough to say that somebody around here is pullin' hijinks."

"But what could they be after?" asked the old chemist. "I mean, what does anybody have to gain? What's their mastication?"

"Could be just kids messing around," volunteered Iyarra.

Revka shook her head. "No, you forget I saw under the costume when I hit the ground during the fight. It was definitely a centaur with a man on his back. The man must have been the one working the arms. Definitely not kids."

Mr. Fleet nodded. "A man and a centaur, huh? That's useful to know. I suppose you didn't get a good look at their features or anything?"

"Not at the angle I was at, no. After all, I was on the ground looking up. About the only thing I can tell you is the human was wearing the same boots everybody around here wears and the centaur was a guy."

"Oh?" said Iyarra. "How do you know th—oh. Right."

"Anyhow," said Mr. Fleet, "Middle of the night? During a rainstorm? There's more to this than messing around." He carefully folded the cloth remnant and put it in his jacket pocket. "Somebody's up to something serious, and I aim to find out what it is."

* * * * *

A few hours later, Revka and Iyarra were in front of the sheriff's office, watching a crowd of centaurs and humans prepare to ride out. Mr. Fleet was there with his men, and quite a few members of the Citizens Protection Committee had come by to see them off. Mrs. Wildberry, in particular, was moving from person to person, making sure everybody was prepared.

"Everyone make sure you have plenty of rope! You can't have enough rope. I really can't emphasize that enough. Also, please make sure your canteens are full before we start. I see you over there, Silas Mitchell. If that's *water* in that canteen I'm a monkey's aunt! Go on, pour it out. For goodness' sake."

"Mighty exciting, isn't it?" Mr. Fleet strolled up to the girls, watching the organized chaos all around them. "Guess you've probably never done this before?"

Revka coughed. "Well," she said, "not *exactly* this."

"Eh?"

Iyarra smiled sheepishly. "We're not usually on this end of the posse," she explained.

"Uh-huh." The smile didn't leave Mr. Fleet's face, though it may have flickered just a bit. "Well. It's nothing too difficult. We just head out, track down whoever's pulling this stunt, tie them up, drag 'em back, and bung them in the jail, neat as you please. Not complicated at all."

"One question. How do we track them down? After the rain last night, even Iyarra couldn't follow the scent."

"Well, we know where they were scrapping with you two. And we know the general direction they headed in when they took off. I reckon we go back to the scene of the crime and see what we can figure out."

Up at the front of the mob, Sheriff Joshua Englebert Lestrange was pacing back and forth. He was a lean, black centaur with long sideburns and a mustache that almost completely covered his upper lip. He cupped his hands over his mouth and shouted. "All right, people! Looks like we're about ready to go, but it's still only twenty minutes to noon, so I need everybody to just sit tight for a li'l bit, a'ight? Don't go wanderin' off."

Mrs. Wildberry piped up. "Remember, people! Once we get started, there will be no rest breaks! If you need to use the biffy, do it now and come right back, you hear?"

Revka turned to Mr. Fleet. "So, if we're ready to go, why don't we just go? What exactly are we waiting for?"

Mr. Fleet chuckled. "You're still new here, so I guess you wouldn't understand. See, you must wait till high noon for any kind of important thing like posses or showdowns. I mean, who ever heard of a posse riding out at eleven forty-three? See what I mean?"

"Ohhhh," said Iyarra. "This is one of those code of the west ki—"

Right on cue, the entire mob doffed their hats at once. "The Code of the West!" they chorused.

"Okay. I guess that's a yes." Iyarra sighed.

Mr. Fleet strolled off, and Revka turned to Iyarra. "Do you think they practice that?"

* * * * *

Jack Hadok stepped out of his cabin and proceeded to saunter down the street. He had slept right through the previous night's storm and well into the morning. Jack was looking forward to a leisurely lunch. If said lunch had a significant liquid component, well, so much the better. He pushed his hat brim up a bit and surveyed the sky. Not a cloud left in it. He smiled and took a long, deep breath. Sure enough, there were just the last traces of that smell one got after rain. Rare as snail's teeth, as his momma used to say. Well, it was going to be a fine day indeed.

He was just about to take the turn onto the main road, humming a tuneless little thing to himself, when the posse swung into view. Dozens of men and centaurs galloped by at full tilt, headed for the outskirts of town. He couldn't hear what they were shouting, but they sure did seem heated up about *something*. In fact, if they didn't watch out, he... "Oh, hell..."

A few minutes later, he lowered himself down from the fence, grunting with effort. Jack was not the kind of old person that people refer to as spry. He took things slow and easy, and tended to avoid sudden movements on the basis they might make him spill his drink, but somehow, he'd managed to get up a fence taller than himself almost without noticing he'd done so.

Back on the ground, he leaned against the fence, panting. His unplanned vertical expedition had taken rather a lot out of him. After a minute or so, the landscape settled down a bit, but then his legs began to register their opinion on the adventure. He groaned. Lunch would have to wait. Moving slowly, and using the wall for support, he turned around and headed back to his shack.

Well, he could always try again later.

* * * * *

The posse came to a halt at the corner of the corral. It wasn't hard to spot the place where the fight had taken place. The tracks in the mud told the whole story. Iyarra spotted the place where she'd hit the ground and winced a little at the memory.

The sheriff trotted forward and knelt down. "Well now," he said, "let's see here." He squinted at the impressions in the now-dry mud, then stood back up. "Them girls what fought the thing," he shouted, "are they here?"

"That's us." Revka waved as Iyarra trotted forward.

"All right." Sheriff Lestrange looked around. "So, it looks like you tussled with 'em over here, and...yeah. All right. Ma'am, would you mind showin' me a hoof real quick?"

Iyarra obligingly raised her left front leg for him to see. He looked back down at the tangle of tracks. "So, these here would be yours, which means these other ones are our beastie's. You can put your leg down, ma'am."

Mr. Fleet stepped forward. "Very nice, sir. I don't suppose I could just point out—"

The sheriff waved him off. "Hold yer britches, son. I'm in the middle of an investigation over here. Gotta take things scientifical. Now then." He began to pace back and forth across the scene, muttering to himself as he followed the beast's prints. "Let's see. Staggered a bit here, kinda turned around this way, then back again—you can see on account a the print is over the older one—and then, yup. I got it."

Iyarra tilted her head. "You do?"

"Yup. It was a centaur."

Revka and Iyarra looked at each other. "Yes," said Revka patiently. "We told you it was. Remember?"

"Ah!" said the sheriff. "But now we know for *sure*. And furthermore, since we can eliminate your prints from the scene of the crime, I can logically conclude that the second set of prints here are definitely those of the perpetrators. Now, all we have to do is to make a plaster mold of the hoofprints. You'll notice there is a distinct scratch in this one, and what appears to be a loose nail. All we have to do is find out the exact size horseshoe, get a list of everyone in town that takes that size, and check 'em out. We'll have 'em in no time."

"Or," said Mr. Fleet quietly, "we can just follow their hoofprints. With the rain last night, they're about as clear as can be." He pointed. "See? They lead right off toward the mountains. Look."

The sheriff looked. Sure enough, a trail of deep, sunbaked hoofprints led straight for the distant foothills. His expression soured for a moment, then recovered. "Well, I suppose we can try that as well, long as we're here and all."

"All right folks!" He turned to the mob and cupped his hands over his mouth. "We're just gonna follow this trail and see where it goes. Everybody stay together, and don't wander off. Everybody still got your posse buddy?"

A sea of clasped hands rose into the air.

"Excellent. Then let's *git!*"

The group thundered out of town, the sheriff and the girls in front. Mr. Fleet came just behind with his men, and then the general mob of town folks, thungahands, and sheriff's men trailed behind like a comet.

The trail was, more or less, a straight shot out of town, only wavering from time to time to move around a boulder or other obstacle. Once, the tracks disappeared into a thick patch of sagebrush. A quick investigation found the tracks coming out on the opposite side, still following the straight line.

After about an hour, they were getting close to the mountains again. So far, the trail had been leading northwest, but it began to dogleg a little to the north, aiming toward a point where two mountains joined together. The sheriff snorted. "Well, I'll be damned," he muttered. "The Gap. That just about figures."

"The Gap?" said Revka, who did not like the sound of those capital letters. "What's that, then?"

The lawman waved vaguely at the wall of mountains before them. "Oh, there's this space between these two mountains, y'see, and well, it's kind of a maze. Like a canyon but cut through all over with little passages and trails all through it. A dandy place to get lost in, I can tell you. Supposedly used to be water flowing through from the mountains, and every so often it would change course, owin' to the ground movin' around or some boulder fallin' into the path or something. Anyway, the water's all gone now, but if you wanted to hide, that's a hell of a place to do it in."

A few minutes later, they arrived at a wide opening that tapered as one went in. The trail turned into a smooth, flat path surrounded by jagged towers of red stone. The group, which had been pretty chatty during the main run, fell silent as they filed in.

The posse began to pick their way along, following the hoofprints that were still clear on the ground. Revka noticed that several people had drawn their weapons and were peering carefully into every side path they passed on the way. Actually, now that she thought of it, this would be pretty much the ideal place for an ambush.

Revka reached back and pulled her crossbow into position, then slotted an arrow into the shaft. She nudged Iyarra, who nodded and drew her daggers.

An eerie silence fell as they trooped through the stone labyrinth. Nothing much lived there, except for a few birds who made their nests up on top of the stones. From time to time, one would call out, the cry echoing strangely through the canyon walls. The group drew closer together as they followed the path, eyes and ears pricked for any sign of trouble.

About ten minutes later, the group stepped into a large, open space deep in the heart of the maze. *It's almost circular...suspiciously so.* Revka noted a fire pit in the middle, long since extinguished. Some stones and even the occasional log from gods-knew-where had been dragged into a border around the remains of the pit. Men, centaurs, and even a few animals had left their tracks, scattering off into seemingly every passage that left the central area.

The sheriff put his hands on his hips and spat. "Stone me," he muttered, "there's a whole mess of 'em."

"Figures," muttered Mr. Fleet. He paced around, examining the tracks. "Well, what do you reckon?"

"Well, looks like they came here before the rain got too bad – notice how the prints goin' in are hardly there, whereas the ones goin' out are nice an' deep. Also, you can tell the ones going out are over the ones going in. Now, this allows us to conclude that they came before they left."

"Yes," said Mr. Fleet, exuding patience. "We know they came before they left, on account of they ain't still here. Can we hurry this along? We don't have all the daylight in the world, you know."

"All right, all right, young feller." The sheriff looked around, grumbling under his breath. "I suppose there's nothin' fer it. We're gonna have to split up. Everybody buddy up, find yourself a pair of tracks to follow and stick right with it. Now, there's all sorts of little mountain passes and things here, so if you find yourself hittin' rock you're to come right back, you hear? I don't want nobody wanderin' lost up in the mountains. Just follow the tracks as far as they go. If you find someone, holler. Everybody got that?"

Revka hopped down off Iyarra's back and began to work her way around the perimeter of the area. She crouch-walked along, examining each set of hoofprints in turn. She got about a quarter of the way around before standing back up and waving to Iyarra.

The centauress trotted over to join her. "What's up?"

Revka pointed. "See these tracks? The little line here in the right rear shoe? And this one here, you can see the loose nail."

"Yeah?"

"Yup, just like the sheriff said. That's our boy." Revka drew out her sword and began to follow the track into one of the many side passages that branched off from the main area. "Come on," she said. "Let's hunt these suckers down."

They followed the track out and along the passages that wound around the central area. It really was rather like a maze, with side branches breaking off at regular intervals. Occasionally, their path would cross another, or another group would go by, following a different set of prints.

"I'll tell you something," Revka muttered, as they went along. "There ain't no way that this was carved out by any river. It's too regular. I don't care how many times it changes course, there's just no way."

"So it's a labyrinth?" Iyarra asked. "Who would put a labyrinth out in the middle of nowhere?"

"Search me, but I bet if someone ever made a map of this place, it would definitely show it to be some sort of maze."

In fact, quite unknown to the girls, a map *did* exist, one that showed very clearly the layout of the place, and, for those with the right kind of knowledge, its purpose. None of those who currently traced their way through the various paths were aware of this, nor did they know what would happen as those particular paths were trod together. Of all the people of the valley, only a very few knew the secret.

Just now, one of them was sneaking up on the girls.

Revka stopped at a crosspath. She frowned at the ground. The tracks they were following went straight along. Another set of tracks cut through. She knelt down and examined the latter with a suspicious eye.

She turned and followed them with her gaze, turning her head slowly until she got back to Iyarra. "Huh."

Iyarra tilted her head. "What's up?"

Revka beckoned. "C'mere." She pointed off to the right, indicating the second set of tracks. "That look familiar?"

"Well," said Iyarra after a moment, "It might, kind of. Of course here, it's kind of hard to tell one way or another. It all kind of looks alike, you know?"

"Yeah, well, I'm prepared to swear we came this way a few minutes ago. We crossed that other pair of tracks, remember? Well, I think this is it. It looks like we looped around and we're going back across the way we came. What do you think?"

Iyarra moved Revka out of the way. She took a few paces down the other passage and sniffed the air. "Oh, yes," she said, "we went this way, all right."

"Knew it." She looked down at the two sets of tracks where they met. "So, why are they crossing over their own tracks? That makes no sense."

"Maybe they got lost?"

"Maybe, maybe, but that doesn't feel right somehow. It feels...deliberate." She looked along the trail, then made a decision. "All right," she said. "Let's keep going, but keep your eyes peeled."

"Gotcha."

They followed the track deeper into the maze. By now, it seemed to be going off on a very deliberate path. From time to time, they could hear the calls of the other members of the posse, but the voices grew fainter and fainter as they went.

After a few more twists and turns, the girls emerged in another open space. The dirt gave way to a smooth, flat stone. *Almost a perfect circle.* Faint markings, long since baked by time and sun, were just barely visible on its surface. Revka hopped down and knelt to get a closer look.

"Well, isn't this something?" She pursed her lips and brushed some of the dirt away. "Looks like circles going around each other. And there's a big path leading up from the bottom straight to the middle, and..."

"What, like here?"

"Yeah," said Revka quietly. "Exactly like here." She traced a finger along. "There are these paths...looks like four of them, each going out from the middle. And each winds around to a different spot, four corners of the place."

"Circles don't have corners."

"Okay, yeah, but you know what I mean, right?"

"Fair enough."

"And this one, yeah, this one here is the one we followed." Revka traced her finger along the weaving ochre line. "See? Here's where we went around that curvy bit. And over here is the place we crossed over the path, remember? And that brings us right to..." She looked around. "Here."

"So we're here?"

"Yup."

"Great." Iyarra looked around anxiously. "So," she ventured, "er, what happens now?"

"Beats me." Revka turned around and examined the area. The path came to a dead end, with only the stone map and a bit of random debris. "Seems a long way to go to get to something that just tells you that, yup, you're here all right." She frowned down at the map again. "And why the weird route? If this thing is accurate, you could go straight here from the central part in half the time. Much more direct." She looked up. "I wonder if—"

Iyarra turned around at the sudden silence. Revka was gone. Iyarra looked around, but there was nowhere else the human could have gone, no other way out.

"Uhm, Revka?" she called out. No answer. She moved around the open space, looking for any kind of hiding space or trap door. There was nothing but the bare stone.

The centauress hugged herself, her stomach knotting up in fear. She stumbled away from the walls, moving toward the center of the space, until she was standing on top of the maze.

The world went black. Then there was torchlight flickering against the walls of a dark place. A hooded figure stood silhouetted against the light, holding Revka's unconscious form.

Iyarra opened her mouth to scream, but there was movement behind her. Something hit her on the back of the head. The darkness came rushing back, and her body slumped to the floor.

Chapter Nine

REVKA AWOKE IN DARKNESS. The world was black as pitch. An old, musty smell filled her nostrils. She was lying flat on the ground, a dirt floor by the feel of it. Someone had bound her wrists and ankles, and unless she missed her guess, her sheath knife was missing. It wasn't her only weapon, of course, and some of them were rather well hidden, but it would be tricky trying to get hold of them in her present condition. Besides, she was not alone.

There were four, maybe five voices. A mix of male and female, as far as she could make out. Their voices were muffled, as if coming from another room, or as if there were a sack over her head (Revka realized, rather belatedly). She held still, straining her ears to hear what was being said.

"—don't care where they come from. The point is, they're strangers. Who's gonna miss 'em?"

"Don't be ridiculous. They were part of the posse. People will notice they're gone."

"Well, what are we supposed to do? They followed the path right here, didn't they?"

"All right, I'll admit that was our fault. We should have muddied up the trail a bit, taken a few detours before we completed the walk. I said I was sorry."

"Well, it's too late now. They're here, and we have to decide what to do."

"You know," said a new voice, "we could just dump them in the desert somewhere. A little out of town. If we do it before they wake up, they never have to know that they were here at all. Problem solved."

"That would be the easiest way," said another. "How long will they be out, do you think?"

Beside Revka, a familiar voice groaned. "Revka? Revka, you here?"

"Well, that's out," said another. "Any other bright ideas?"

Revka decided she might as well speak up. "Yeah, Iyarra, I'm here."

"Where are we?"

"Nobody answer that." This new voice sounded awfully familiar. *Someone in town, maybe?* It was hard to tell with the bag over her head muffling everything. "You're just...somewhere that you shouldn't be, and now we have to decide what to do with you."

Revka sighed. "All right, look." She could feel the weight of their gaze on her. "I don't...hang on." She tried to swing herself up into a sitting position but kept rolling back onto her side. "Sorry. I was just saying, I don't know what this is about, and we don't know where we are or who you are, so if you did let us go, there's nothing we could do or say."

"Unfortunately," said the first voice, "you know how to get here. That was our mistake, but you've seen the maze and you know the rite of passage. You could lead others. I'm afraid just letting you go is not an option."

"The rite of passage, what the heck do you—" Something inside Revka's brain went *click*. "The path," she said. "That's why it was all criss-crossy. You can't just go straight to that stone thing; you have to follow the exact route to get there. That's it, isn't it?"

"Very perspicacious of you," said one of the other voices. "I had hoped you wouldn't have put the pieces together quite yet, but I suppose that was too much to hope for."

Crud. "Well, I am fully prepared to forget all about it, if that will help."

"Not a chance we can take, I'm afraid." That voice again. Revka was seriously beginning to dislike this one. "I'm sorry," the voice spoke again, "but we have to protect ourselves. Even if it means...unsavory measures."

"There is another way." This voice was somewhat gruff, though not unpleasant, and off in a way Revka couldn't quite put her finger on. Further, the other voices so far had been muffled by the cloth bag over her head, but this one was clear as a bell. Instinctively, Revka tried to turn her head toward the direction of the voice, but it didn't seem to come from anywhere in particular; it was just there. "Why don't we let *Her* decide?"

Revka winced. Capital letters *and* italics? There was no way that was good news. Still, the idea seemed to be going over well with the others. "Yes, yes," said the first voice. "That might not be a bad suggestion at all."

"She can decide one way or another."

"Let *Her* handle their fate."

"Why get our hands dirty?"

"But the ritual—"

"I know, I know, but do you have a better idea?"

"Well…"

"One you would be willing to carry out yourself?"

"Oh."

"Right."

"Uhm." Revka made another attempt at sitting up. "Excuse me, but do we—"

"Shut up."

"Fine. Shutting up," she muttered. "You're not making any friends here, you know."

There was the sound of footsteps, and Revka felt someone standing over her. Her last thought before she was knocked unconscious for the second time was that she should never have gone west.

* * * * *

The sun was well up in the sky when Revka awoke. She and Iyarra were out in the middle of the desert, the mountains a distant shadow against the sky. She sat up—or tried to, but it turned out she was still tied up, securely. She managed to roll upright and get onto her side to get a look at the scenery. There wasn't any. Nothing stretched out in all directions, covered in sand.

A shape came toward her. For a moment she thought it was the beast, but as she focused the body resolved itself into a centaur wearing a hooded cloak that covered its entire body. The centaur knelt before her and took out a canteen, which it held to her lips. "Drink."

Revka suddenly became aware that she was thirsty—no, check that, absolutely parched. She licked her dry lips and took a big gulp.

The liquid was sickly sweet and a bit peppery, with some seasonings she couldn't place. She stopped in midgulp. "Hey," she managed to whisper, "what gives? This isn't water." Her eyes narrowed. "If this is poison…"

The figure sighed. "Think," it said. "If we wanted you dead, why drag you out here and *then* poison you? No." It shook its head. "You must drink this. Your friend has already had her portion. Drink it now."

"And if I do? What happens then?"

"That will be for *Her* to decide."

'Her' again. "And if I refuse?"

The figure shrugged. "I suppose someone will find your remains, eventually."

"Fine, fine." Revka sighed. "Go on, then."

"Very good." The figure guided the canteen back to her lips. "Now then, drink it down, that's the way."

* * * * *

It was hard to say how long she had been out. The figure had left after she finished drinking, explaining only that whatever it was would make them sleep for a little while. The sun was still up; or, at least, it was still bright. Something about the light seemed odd, different somehow.

Revka shook herself awake and stretched out, yawning. She rubbed her eyes, only then realizing that her hands were free. A quick check revealed her legs were as well. Well, at least they had the decency to untie her. Probably figured there was nowhere she could run away to, out here in the middle of nowhere. She rolled over to where Iyarra was lying and nudged her awake. "Psst," she muttered. "Hey. Yarra? You awake?"

The centauress gruffed a little, kicking a hoof as she woke up. She rolled upright and blinked blearily into the oddly flat light. "Whuzza? What's going on?"

"Dunno." Revka cracked her neck. "Last thing I remember, they dumped us out here and made me drink some weird-tasting stuff. They do that to you, too?"

"Oh, right." Iyarra looked around. "Yeah, I remember that. Did they tell you what was supposed to happen next?"

"Only that whatever it was would be up to her, whoever 'her' is." Revka sat up and surveyed the desert stretching out before them. Now that she looked, there was definitely something different. Everything she saw was slightly diffused, hazy, almost ethereal. The vista had that same unreal feel she associated with fairy gardens and other magical places. In the middle of a barren desert, it felt really out of place. "I wonder if—"

"Ahem." The sound came from behind them. The two girls turned to see a tall, beautiful woman, whose brown skin was strikingly offset by the silver hair gathered into a loose bun at the top of her head. She was wearing a classic, white chiton of the type one imagines gods and goddesses to wear. She was lounging underneath a giant, garishly multicolored beach umbrella. Her tatty green-and-white tartan, aluminum lawn chair was equally tacky. She held a tall glass of blue liquid with a novelty straw and a small, fruit salad impaled on a tiny plastic sword. Behind her, a coyote-like creature leaned against the umbrella pole. Its tall hat matched its lanky frame. Revka didn't like its smirking expression, not one bit.

The woman raised the drink to her lips and took a leisurely sip with the straw. She then passed the drink up to the coyote, who took it with a slight bow. The woman smiled and spread her arms out in a welcoming attitude.

"Behold."

Chapter Ten

REVKA STARED AT THE bizarre sight. "Who the hell are you?"

The mysterious woman smirked. "I'm the deus ex machina," she said. "Well, the deus part, anyway. Coyote, you want to do the honors?"

The creature behind her grinned and strode forward. He reached into the air and tugged down a short metal rod on the end of a long, black cord that reached up to the sky and that Revka could swear hadn't been there before. He held the free end of the rod toward his mouth, tapped it a couple of times, and began.

"*Ladies and gentlemen!*" his words echoed out across the desert until it seemed they would reach the very mountains themselves. "*Tonight, for one night only, we take great pleasure in bringing you the mistress of mayhem, the queen of chaos, that diva of disorder herself. Ladies and gentlemen, please put your hands together for Eris Diiiiiiis-CORDIAAAA!*"

The silence that followed was broken only by the coyote, who began to applaud wildly, cheering, whistling, and making excited crowd noises.

Revka and Iyarra looked at each other in confusion. "Uhm," said Iyarra, "should we be doing something, here? Do you think?"

Revka just shook her head. "I don't...I have no idea." She turned back to the coyote, who was now pumping one arm in the air while making whoop-whoop-whoop noises.

"Okay, that's enough." The goddess waved a languid hand at the coyote, who immediately shut up. "I am, indeed, Eris Discordia, the goddess of chaos, and this is Coyote. He's sort of my avatar in the mortal world."

Coyote doffed his hat and gave the girls a low, sweeping bow that only came off as slightly insincere. "Ladies."

"Hey!" Iyarra pointed at the creature. "The voice before, when they had us tied up! That was you, wasn't it?"

"Oh, yeah!" Revka nodded at Iyarra. "I think you're right!" She turned back to the coyote. "Hey mister, what gives?"

Discordia chuckled. "Yes, you've had something of a rough time of it, haven't you? Sorry about that, but it took some doing to get you here. Almost lost you a couple of times, in fact. And that would have been such a shame, seeing as I was so looking forward to finally meeting you two in person."

"Er, you were?"

"Oh, indeed." the goddess smiled. "I'm a big fan of your work, you know. Great stuff. You're naturals."

Iyarra's brow furrowed. "Our work? Like guarding thungas and escorting convoys and stuff? Because—"

The goddess waved her off. "No, no, not that. That's just stuff. It's not what you do so much as how you do it, you see?"

"Er..."

Eris stood up. "Look," she said. "Most people, you drop them into a situation fraught with chaos and disorder, and they will try to fix it. Fair enough, right? But they try to fix it with order. Reason. The logical thing. But not you. Oh, no. You fight chaos with *more* chaos. You," she smiled, "are my kind of people."

The girls looked at each other. "Well," said Revka, "I guess I can't really argue with that, but what gives? I assume you didn't bring us here just for a meet and greet."

"Well, no. I...actually, let's do this right." She cleared her throat. "I have manifested unto thee—"

"Sorry, what?"

"God talk. Now, please don't interrupt. As I was saying, I have manifested unto thee, because there are terrible things afoot, and I need a couple of extra pairs of hands if we're going to hold them at bay. Coyote here is, of course, very capable, but he is only one trickster. And the others...well, they just don't have the proper mindset. I mean, honest to goodness, dressing up as a monster? How hokey can you get? So, I brought you here."

"What others?" asked Iyarra. "You mean those people back when we were tied up? Are they, like, your followers or something?"

The goddess chuckled. "Not exactly, no. They know *of* me, of course. Though not by name. Mostly they know that there's some sort of divine presence keeping an eye on things and their 'holy work.' I don't generally manifest myself in person around them. I find a bright light and a big echoey voice does the job nicely."

"Uh-huh." Revka looked the goddess up and down. "And that happens often, does it?"

"Not very. The drink they gave you temporarily opens up your latent metaperceptions, so you can perceive multiple reality levels. Obviously, they only use just enough to allow direct communication with the ethereal plane. Trust me, you do *not* want to know what happens if you drink too much of that stuff. Human brains are not built to handle

11-dimensional multiverses, let me tell you. Saw someone try it once. Gruesome."

"Sorry, but what has this got to do with anything?"

"Absolutely nothing." Eris grinned. "Goddess of chaos, remember? I'm just explaining that I don't generally show myself, but desperate times and all that jazz. Humans don't generally come out well from direct contact with the divine. They tend to wind up either drooling vegetables or prophets. And it's anybody's guess which is worse." She began to pace back and forth, waving a hand in the air as she spoke. "No, the problem is that some of those numbskulls out there are going to wake the Sleeper, and all I've got to work with are Coyote here and a handful of civilians playing dress-up. I need ringers, people I can count on to rise to the madness. This is no place for rational thinking, me girlies. In short, I need you."

Revka and Iyarra exchanged glances. "Well," Revka coughed. "That's awfully, uhm, flattering. I think, but really, couldn't you, I dunno, give those cult guys a little more guidance, maybe shove them in the right direction?"

"Yeah," added Iyarra. "I mean, we already saved the world that one time. Shouldn't it be someone else's turn by now?"

"See? That just shows you've got experience. A very rare skill set. And frankly, the cultists—don't get me wrong, lovely bunch of folks, dedicated as anything—but about as flexible as a rock. And with the stakes as high as they are, well, I can't take chances."

"Just what *are* the stakes?" said Revka. "I mean, you mentioned something about a sleeper, but I still have no idea what any of this is about."

Eris snapped her fingers, pointing at the girls. "You know what? You're absolutely right. Here I've been prattling along, and you still have no idea what we're up against. Coyote, why didn't you say something?"

Coyote looked up from a bag of popcorn that had come from god knows where. "Just enjoying the show, boss."

"I think we'd better let these two in on the stakes, don't you?"

"As you like, ma'am."

"Then show them."

Coyote reached up into the air and pulled down a large white screen. There was a click, and the world went from day to night in the blink of an eye. Somewhere, a whirring, clicking noise started up, and the screen was suddenly illuminated with a silvery glow. Upbeat music floated in from somewhere, and *Red Valley — And You!* appeared on the screen.

The view switched to the interior of a well-kept home, all done in shades of gray. A young centauress, somewhere in her early adolescence, was reading a book by the fire. "This is Susan." The deep, sonorous voice produced an air of genial authority so pronounced you could practically hear the pipe in its mouth. "Susan is an ordinary girl, and like ordinary girls, she has a lot of questions about the facts of life."

An older centaur woman walked into the picture, dusting the furniture with a suspicious amount of enthusiasm. The girl looked up at her and put her book aside. "Mother?" she said. "Why is the Red Valley so barren and bereft of life? The rest of the world is green and full of happy creatures, but there's almost nothing here."

The older centauress sat next to her daughter. "Well, dear," she said. "You're getting older, and I guess you're ready to know. You see, it wasn't always like this. Once upon a time, the desert was just as lush and green as the rest of the world, but something terrible happened. Long, long ago, before any centaur set hoof in this place, there was a great battle between the gods and a terrible creature from another place far away."

"Golly!" said the daughter. "Did the gods defeat the creature?"

"Well," said the mother, "They did, sort of. It's a bit complicated."

"That's right, Mom," said the narrator. "You see—"

"Okay, that's enough." The goddess snapped her fingers, and the show stopped. The screen zipped back up into the air, and the world clicked back into daylight. She turned to the girls and cracked her knuckles. "Best if I just show you myself," she said.

A moment later, the skies were burning around them. An army of titanic beings—humanoid for the most part but with a thousand different variations—were charging across the desert landscape. Iyarra screamed and held her hands up protectively as a large, lizard-headed man with expensive taste in hats charged toward her...and right through. Eris and Coyote were still standing right where they had been, apparently unconcerned. "This is an illusion," the goddess explained. "Nothing here can hurt you. Don't be scared."

"If you say so." Iyarra watched in horrified fascination as the army of Titans pounded across the landscape. It was not a pretty sight. There were obvious signs of greenery, but most of it was either trampled or burning. The gods were hurling fire, bolts of lightning, and magic of all kinds, and all aimed at something behind the girls.

Iyarra gulped and risked a peek over her shoulder.

The thing was...well, there was no word for it. Titanic, but bigger than anything she'd ever seen, bigger than any living thing had any right to be. It looked like it could step right over the mountains.

Iyarra looked around, thinking there must be a mistake, but it was true. The mountains were gone.

The monster loomed against the sky like some twisted writhing behemoth, all arms and tentacles and bits Iyarra couldn't even begin to identify. The worst part, the part that almost made her lose her lunch on the spot, was the way it changed. Every time a part of it moved, it would take on a different shape, stretching and flaring and distorting in eye-watering ways. It stood at bay in the middle of the wasteland, hurling bolts of green fire at the attacking gods.

As the girls watched, the army of gods split and ran to either side of the giant creature. They kept their distance, giving the thing a wide berth as they charged forward. They were forming a circle around the creature. As the girls watched, more and more gods thundered past, gods of the old pantheon from stories heard long ago, and many unknown others. All sizes and shapes they came, fanning out around the titan monstrosity. At last, they closed the loop.

The fighting slowed, but a few clusters of gods still harried the creature with bolt after bolt of lightning, but that wasn't the real action. Up at the circle, something was beginning to happen.

Eris grinned. "Let's have a closer look, shall we?" With an uncomfortable lurch, the world moved beneath them, repositioning itself so they were just inside the circle. The assembled gods spread their arms (or whatever appendages served as arms). They appeared to be concentrating. The sheer amount of power being drawn into the scene felt like heavy waves.

Behind them, Eris leaned forward and pointed to a familiar figure farther down in the circle. "Oh, look," she said. "There's me. Hi, me." She waved to the shadow from the past, which turned and waggled a single eyebrow at her future self before turning back to the task at hand.

The magic was building up now, making the very air feel heavy. Iyarra tried moving forward, but it was like walking through syrup. She could feel every hair on her pelt standing on end. None of this should have had any effect on her. She just about understood that they were watching a memory of the past, so how could the magic affect them when they weren't really there? Something was obeying a very different set of rules.

Suddenly, a pale-yellow light flared up, hovering between the outstretched hands of two gods. More and more lights appeared, until the entire circle was illuminated. A bolt of raw magic raced around the circle, joining all the nodes together.

The magic seemed to launch itself out. The gods were mere vessels, conduits, as the magic leapt from one node to a distant one on the opposite side of the circle. It bounced to another and another still. Back and forth it went, weaving line after line of magic, slowly surrounding the creature who lurked in the middle.

By now the monster had noticed what was happening and was flailing desperately in its attempts to escape, but something was wrong: it couldn't move forward to attack the circle. The creature's movements became erratic, riddled with panic. The magic bolts it threw were harmlessly absorbed by the circle. Revka nudged Iyarra.

"It's a web," she said. "They're trapping it in a web."

"Full marks," said Eris. "It took just about every one of us, too. Now hush up, this is the good part."

The magic finished its weaving, every node connected all around the circle. The creature was in full panic, launching bolts of green fire in every direction. It tried to break the web, sever the enchantment, but it was already too late.

Revka jumped when a claw tapped her on the shoulder. Coyote smiled toothily and pointed upward. She looked up into the livid golden sky. The clouds were rolling and boiling. The sun hung high in the sky, larger than Revka had ever seen it. She felt like, if she looked too closely, she would fall right into it. That sun was a window into a universe of fire.

Unable to look away, Revka stared, as the sun...blinked?

A cone of light came down, trapping the creature inside. The ground beneath them began to tremble. In the distance, the very landscape began to rise up. As Revka and Iyarra watched, the web of light grew smaller and smaller, tightening the cone around the titanic monster. More and more ground detached itself from the surface. Great masses of stone freed themselves from the earth, drifting slowly upward.

There was an almighty clap of thunder, and the bottom of the web snapped itself shut. The creature tumbled backward in slow motion, its body spreading across the landscape for what seemed like ages. Giant clouds of dust that seemed to reach up to the very roof of the sky kicked up around the supine figure. The haze of the sun gave them a curious, eldritch glow.

The ground, ripped from the earth's surface, was magically moved over the enormous figure and dropped unceremoniously. The pace began to pick up. Vast amounts of dirt, stones, even giant boulders bombarded the monster. The crash of their impact echoed across the landscape. It might have been minutes, or hours; Revka could not say. At the end of it, the Tandari Mountains stretched from one end of the landscape to the other.

Behind them, Eris dusted off her hands. "Well," she said. "Any questions?"

Chapter Eleven

"WE COULDN'T KILL IT, you see." Eris had dissolved the illusion of the past, and was now expositing over tea and scones. "The thing—what you saw—was only those bits of it that fit in this world. Destroying it altogether was quite impossible."

"The bits that fit in this world? What's that mean?" Revka reached for another scone. "I mean, that thing was big, but I thought it was all there, wasn't it?"

The goddess shook her head. "No, it wasn't. And what's more, it couldn't be. Did you see the way its form changed every time it made a move? Different parts of it appeared and disappeared as they passed through our dimensional phase space."

"Ah. Dimensional phase space. Right." Revka nodded. There was a long pause. The girls looked at each other, then back at Eris, who sighed. "You have no idea what that means, do you?"

"No idea."

"Sorry."

"It's all right." The goddess collected her thoughts. "Let me explain. In this world, as you know, we have four dimensions: height, width, depth, and zepth." She demonstrated with her fingers, the last one causing them to momentarily disappear. "Now, the—"

"Wait, zepth?"

Eris looked down at her hands. "Oh, right. Right. Mortals. Okay, forget zepth. The point is, we have only a few dimensions in which we can understand space. That's how things work in our universe. However, there are other places, other universes, where they don't have the same set of dimensions. They may have more or even fewer. I'm not even going to get into fractional dimensions. Believe me, you are *not* ready for that."

"Uh, thanks?"

"Don't mention it. Now, that creature you saw, it came from another universe, one where the rules are...different. I mean very different. It is probably at least a seven-dimensional creature, based on our best reckoning. It was trying to rip its way into our world, but there's no way it could fit, you see? It would be like one of you trying to squeeze inside a piece of paper. You'd just wind up with some ripped-up paper."

"Oh," said Iyarra. "So, if it had pushed through, it would have torn the world up?"

"Probably not exactly that, but it would have made an almighty mess. We had to do what we could to keep it out. So, we trapped it—that is, the part of it that made it through to our world, then we bound it so it could come no further. We dumped a bunch of rocks on top of it and hoped that would keep it from getting out and running around."

"After that, the area was looking...well, pretty bad, as you saw. Something got into the land. It wasn't a good place for growing things anymore. In the end, it was decided to just leave it this way, hoping that nobody would come out here, or if they did, they'd at least have the sense not to hang around."

"How long did that work?"

"Oh, about five minutes." The goddess shrugged. "The thungas found their way here, and they flourished. And eventually, the first centaurs. Just a small herd, but they stuck around. When we saw they weren't going to split, I had Coyote here show up and teach them how to survive."

Revka snapped her fingers. "The Blood Moon Beast!" she exclaimed. "They were telling us about it in the town. That was you?"

Coyote bowed with that same toothy grin. He drew a pale mask out of the empty air and slipped it on, wiggling his fingers for effect.

"Anyway, we got them settled in and took the time to get the measure of them. See, most gods prefer to take an out-of-sight, out-of-mind approach to things. They're like babies, you know? If it's not in front of them right now, it doesn't exist. Most of 'em have forgotten all about the Sleeper, or at least they actively try not to think about it, but being that my beat is chaos, I have to take a more long-term approach. I know how thoroughly things can go haywire. And, well, there's chaos and then there's chaos. A world-ending catastrophe would end the party real quick. So I thought it might be nice to have a little backup. And that's why I created the Tex Arcana."

"The Tex Arcana?"

"It means very big secret. Think of it as a priesthood, but without the worshipping part. I manifested to some of the more sensible members of the herd and made them understand that the mountain contained a terrible secret that must never be uncovered. They were to guard it with their lives. Also, they were to pass the knowledge on to the more reliable and discreet members of the next generation, and so on. They have, for more generations than I care to count. I mean, occasionally things get a little muddy, and I have to whip a little magic show on 'em to get back on track, but generally, they just had to keep an eye on things and make sure nobody went poking around in the mountains. Up until now, that's worked just fine."

"And now they're dressing up in bedsheets and scaring people. So, what changed?"

Eris looked off into the middle distance, swirling the tea in her cup reflectively. "A few months ago," she said, "A villager was out inspecting the canal. He noticed something catching the light. Further inspection showed it to be a few minute particles of gold, which had come down from the mountain. Apparently, the water has worn down the rock enough to expose a vein somewhere. This villager brought the matter to the attention of certain members of the community, who went out and did a little exploratory work themselves. Since that time, someone has been carefully collecting the gold as it comes off the mountain, before anyone else can find out about it, and efforts are underway to start up an operation on the quiet."

"Ohhhh," said Iyarra. "And you're afraid they'll dig down and find the big scary monster?"

The goddess nodded. "That's about the size of it. Not that I think they'll be able to get it out from under those mountains, but that thing has powers beyond the physical. Besides, it's hard to see how uncovering even a bit of an extra-dimensional monster from before the dawn of time is going to turn out well. Nope, better to leave the damned thing alone. I told the Tex Arcana to do what they can to disrupt the proceedings, but I'm afraid they just don't have the hang of it. That's where you girls come in.

"When you go back to the town, take whatever work you can, stay busy, keep your eyes open. The Tex Arcana will be in touch. They may have little jobs for you to do, things to find out, that sort of thing. You'll know if something's from them, because they'll sign it like this." She drew a sign in the air with her finger, a blue light tracing the path. The result was like a cross where the left and upper legs were tied together in a loop. Below, a small line neatly subdivided the bottom leg.

"So, what are we supposed to do, exactly?" said Revka.

"What you do best..." Eris said. She poured herself some more tea from a dainty, china teapot. She lifted the cup to her lips and blew the steam toward the girls. Somehow it filled their vision, and the world went white. There was a sound like the last vestiges of water disappearing down a drain, but in reverse, and the world shifted.

* * * * *

...raise a little hell.

Revka blinked, shielding her eyes from the sudden glare of the noonday sun. She sat up, rubbed her eyes, and looked around. They were in the desert again. The jagged peaks of the present-day mountains loomed up in the distance. There were figures approaching, their shapes undulating from the heat haze.

"Found 'em!" somebody shouted. "That's them. Shake a hoof, people!" In a moment, a small group of villagers surrounded Revka and Iyarra, helping them to their feet and giving them swigs of blessedly cool, sweet water from their canteens. Iyarra managed to get to her hooves and looked blearily around. "Uhm, where are we?"

One of the centaurs shrugged. "Out in the desert," he said. "We checked all over The Gap for ya, and Hennessey swore nobody come out while they was guardin' the entrance. Beats us how you wound up out here, but Mr. Fleet, he said you couldn't have got too far and sent us out to look for ya."

Iyarra looked around. "Really?" she said. "Oh, wow."

Revka, meanwhile, managed to sit up and was waiting for the world to stop spinning. Somewhat belatedly, she realized there was something in her hands. She looked down at her hat and turned it over a couple of times, as if unsure of quite what to do with it.

She shrugged and stood with a stretch. She looked around, trying to get her bearings. "Been looking long?"

"Actually, not too bad at all. Maybe half an hour. Anyway, we should head back, let everyone know you're all right."

"Sure, right, of course."

Revka clambered up onto Iyarra's back, fanning herself with her hat before slipping it on her head. The group set off, turning away from the mountains and back toward the town.

"So tell me," said one of the men, "just how did y'all wind up out here, anyway?"

"Long story." *And I've got* till *we get back to town to come up with one that won't get us both locked up in the booby hatch.*

* * * * *

"So," said Sheriff Lestrange, "Lemme see if I got this straight. Y'all were following them tracks through The Gap, yeah, and started to get the feelin' as to how something or someone was tailing you. That right?"

"That's right."

"I see. And then you kinda blacked out for a time, yes?"

"Yup."

The lawman consulted his notes. "And the next thing ya knew, you were wakin' up in the middle of the desert." He looked up. "Well, it's just a theory, but I have an idea that maybe somebody done snuck up on ya and knocked you out."

"Amazing," said Mr. Fleet dryly. "How *does* he do it?"

Once the girls had been escorted back into town, Mr. Fleet insisted on taking them to the sheriff's office himself. There Revka gave the edited-highlights version of what had happened, which seemed to satisfy everyone. At least they didn't ask any inconvenient questions. The testimony was noted down and filed away, probably (according to Mr. Fleet) to gather dust until the end of time.

"Still," he said as they walked down the main street together, "I suppose the day wasn't a total washout. We know they're using that place as a hideout, whoever they are. We just gotta catch them at it, flush them out."

Revka exchanged glances with Iyarra. "Er, yes," she said. "Right. That sounds like a plan, right there."

"Glad you agree." He smiled and extended a hand. "I reckon you two will want to take the rest of the day to rest up after everything. I'll talk to the others. We'll see if we can come up with some sort of a plan. That sound good?"

"Uhm...all right."

"That's fine." He shook each of the girls' hands in turn, then turned and headed off down a side road. "Pleasure to be working with you, ladies."

They watched him go. After a moment, Iyarra turned to Revka. "So," she said, "is it just me, or did we just get recruited into both sides of this thing?"

"It's not just you." Revka kicked at a dirt clod, which disintegrated. "How do we get into these things?"

"I think we must have a special knack for it." She grinned a little at the human. "What can I say? Someone up there likes us."

"Yeah, and she's a nut." Revka started down the street again. "Come on," she said. "He's right about one thing, at least. I could definitely use some sleep."

"And then what do we do?"

Revka shrugged. "I guess we do what we do best."

* * * * *

85

In a dark, secret place below the town, three hooded figures gathered.

"I have news," said one. "It seems that She has accepted the two newcomers. They are to be of assistance to us."

"Those two?" another said. "But they're..."

"I know. I know," the first one replied, holding up their hands placatingly. "Nevertheless, the Lady has spoken. We must bow to her superior wisdom."

"Look, I quite understand about her being an all-knowing goddess and all, but...well, just how all-knowing is she?"

"You're not starting this again, are you?"

"Well, I'm sorry, but look, there's omnipotent, and there's omnipotent, you know? I'm just really concerned that bringing those two in is a big mistake."

"Damn it, Phil," said the third. "Do you want to be the one to go to the Lady and tell her she's a few hooves short of a thunga? No? Then let it be."

There was a sigh. "Fine."

"She says they will be useful," the first one added. "She said they have unique skills, which would be of use to us. I will contact them in the morning and see what may be done."

"It'll all end in tears," said the second figure.

"All right, Phil. That's enough."

* * * * *

That night, Revka slept fitfully. In her dreams, giant monsters in oversized cowboy hats stomped back and forth across the desert, throwing mountains at each other and riding giant thungas. Beside her, Iyarra lay still, swathed in a deep, dreamless sleep. Huddled up against the horsewoman and listening to her gentle breathing, Revka drifted off again and got some actual rest.

The morning came clear and bright, letting everyone know they might as well just get used to the idea the day would be a scorcher. Iyarra was doing her morning ablutions. Revka splashed a little cold water on her face. "So," she said, "these gold miners. We'll have to ferret 'em out somehow. Know anything about mining?"

"Not me. We're nomadic hunter-gatherers, remember? Grew up on the plains. Not an awful lot of mining going on."

"Well, I grew up in the mountains, and there *was* mining. Iron, mostly. That was the main business of the town, you know. I'll tell you one thing: a mining operation is a hell of a thing to try and keep secret. Even if you, I dunno, hide the entrance and everything, you've still got the refinery, the transport moving everything in and out, and manpower. Lots of manpower. Even a little operation is fairly easy to spot, but from what she was saying, it sounds like they're getting together something big. And that means there will be signs. Maybe the local toolsmiths have been busy. Or the wheelwright's been making carts. Maybe the assayer has seen something. We can swing by later and ask him."

"Makes sense."

"Right." Revka stretched, arching her arms over her head. "I reckon we go out, see if we can snag some odd jobs around those kinds of places, and keep our eyes and ears open. Start looking for pieces. If we get enough, maybe we can put something together."

"Sounds good."

"Right." Revka stood in the middle of the room, staring at nothing. "Now, that just leaves the question of where to start."

"Well, we could see what that note says."

"Yeah, the note. Good." Pause. "What note?"

Iyarra pointed. "The one somebody shoved under our door last night. It's just there. Look."

Sure enough, there under the door, was a folded-up piece of paper. She grabbed it and opened it up.

We believe T&F Mercantile Co involved in gold operation. Try and investigate. Underneath the message was the sign that Eris had shown them.

"Well," said Iyarra, "I guess that's as good a first step as any."

"All right." Revka carefully folded the note and put it away. "Then I suggest we get a little breakfast, then see if T&F are hiring. Sound good?"

"Works for me."

Outside their room, a figure had watched the protruding corner of the note disappear beneath the door. *Finally.* It stood in the shadow of a nearby building, almost completely blending in with the mottled gray wood. It nodded its head and disappeared around the corner.

The day is definitely going to be an interesting one.

Chapter Twelve

T&F MERCANTILE WAS LOCATED in the small industrial part of the town, right next to the warehouse they'd first come to as part of the wagon train. It looked like pretty much every other specimen of its type, being essentially a big box to hold things in with a few desks up front to keep things going.

Revka and Iyarra wandered through the front door, looking the place over. There was a fair amount of activity going on, most of which seemed to be carrying pieces of paper and shouting. The two threaded their way to the nearest occupied desk. A wan, dappled-gray centaur with premature baldness and pince-nez hanging off his not inconsiderable nose sat behind the desk, busy with his work. He gave the girls the briefest possible glance before returning to the paper on his desk.

"Can I help you ladies?" he asked in a drop-dead voice.

Revka removed her hat. "Yes, good morning. Is Mr. T here? Or Mr. F? Either would be fine."

The clerk fixed them with a look. His tail twitched irritably. "Mr. Tarran is generally at the bank, and Mr. Findswater is quite busy. Do you, in fact, have an appointment?"

Revka patted her clothes. "Appointment, appointment...no, I don't believe we do, actually."

"Then I'm afraid he really can't be disturbed at this time. Thank you. Good day."

"Well look, maybe we could talk to you instead?" Iyarra offered.

The clerk looked up at them. His expression did not change but managed to convey that there was nothing in the world he would want to do less. "I am very sorry," he lied, "but I don't have time—"

"Look," tried Revka, "we just want to see about getting a job."

"Oh, a job." The clerk jerked a thumb over to a human female sitting at a distant corner desk. "That's Miss Paulificate, then. Over there." Having exhausted himself in this prolonged bout of customer service, he scooped up the paper he was reading and buried his face in it, holding it up as a shield against any further interactions.

Revka nodded. "Than—eh, oh." She looked up at Iyarra, who just shrugged. The two of them turned and moseyed over to the corner desk. This was a somewhat nicer one than the clerk's, made of polished rosewood with brass trimming at the corners. The contents of the desk had been laid out carefully. Stacks of paper were lined up perfectly, everything squared off and equidistant. The front of the desk displayed a large sign. *PERSONNEL* had been crossed out and replaced with *HUMAN/CENTAUR RESOURCES*, which itself had been crossed out and replaced with *BIOLOGICAL ASSET MANAGEMENT*.

Miss Paulificate was perched behind the desk, sitting so rigidly that her back didn't even touch the rather plush office chair she inhabited. She was about fortyish and slim. Her face suggested it had not been grown so much as carved. As the girls approached, she put down her pen and looked up at them. "Can I help you two ladies?"

"Er, yes," said Revka. "The gentleman over there said we should come and see you about a job."

"Ah, I see." She cleared her throat. Her eyes took on a slightly glassy expression, and she began to recite. "The T&F Mercantile Company welcomes applicants from all walks of life to apply to be part of the T&F Mercantile Company family. We are an equal-opportunity employer. Please note that this is not a guarantee of any opportunity, either expressed or implied, but merely an acknowledgment that the possibility does exist. Your names, please?"

"Well, I'm Revka, and this here is Iyarra."

"Family names?" the woman chirped.

"Kenmason."

"Brings Plenty."

"Mm-hm." The woman had whipped out a clipboard holding a long, complicated piece of paper and was industriously filling it out. "Current address?"

"Well, we're over at the Dower's Inn if that's what you—"

"It will do. Now then." She handed the clipboard over. "Please fill this out, including your last nine employers, three previous addresses, any and all skills you may or may not have, as the case may be, and at least three character references, none of whom can be family, friends, or former coworkers. Please be aware that all employment with T&F Mercantile is at will, namely ours. You get one day off a week, sick days must be arranged three days in advance, outhouse breaks over four minutes will result in docked pay. We reserve the right to call you in on your day off, you reserve the right to complain about it afterward. We provide a safe working environment, so any injuries on the job are, by definition, your fault. Any questions?"

"Er..."

"Good. You can fill out the application over there." She pointed to a few depressing wooden chairs shoved up against a nearby wall. "Bring it back when you're finished, and don't walk off with that pencil, you hear?"

"I say! It's the ladies from the stampede, isn't it?" G Findswater bustled over to them, a small group of subordinates traveling in his wake. "What brings you here?"

Revka straightened herself up a little. "Well, we were just hoping to get a little work, sir, seeing as we'll probably be here a while."

"Oh, splendid." He turned to the woman behind the desk. "Sign them on, Miss Paulificate. I shall vouch for them myself."

"As you wish, sir." The woman took the clipboard back and put it away.

Findswater turned back to the girls. "Either of you experienced in construction?"

Revka shrugged. "I can swing a hammer."

"And I can haul stuff."

"That will do." He turned to a big, stocky centaur behind him. A walrus would have envied the guy's mustache. "Harry, can you use them on the site?"

The stallion touched the brim of his hat. "Always could use extra hands, sir."

"Fine, that will do. Ladies, wait out front, and Harry here will take you to the job site. It won't be long."

"Yes, sir."

"Thank you, sir."

* * * * *

Outside, Revka looked up at the sign. "T&F," she said. "Tarran and Findswater. Tarran was the banker guy, wasn't he?"

"I think so, yeah."

"They're both on that citizen's committee thing. Interesting."

"You think it means something?"

"Might do, might do." She looked around, searching for any telltale signs. There wasn't much to go on, just a bunch of nondescript crates and carts loaded up with random goods. Of course, if someone was starting up a mining operation on the sly, they'd hardly have their equipment in the middle of town, would they? Still, she'd keep her eyes open.

A few minutes later, the centaur who had been introduced to them as Harry came out the front door. "All right," he said. "Y'all two can start by helping me haul this stuff out to the job site." He pointed to a nearby cart stacked with timber and metal sheets. "Go ahead an' get hitched up. We'll start heading out that way."

Revka helped hitch Iyarra to the cart and clambered aboard herself. Harry led the way out of town, following the long road along the canal.

"So," said Revka after they'd left the city well behind, "what are we working on?"

Harry didn't turn his head. "We're putting up a storage shed. They're doing a little quarrying out by the mountains, and they want a place where they can cut and store the stone before bringing it into town."

"You don't say." Revka looked back at the contents of the cart. The timber and a few bags of supplies were laid on top of several large metal sheets.

"Well, at least it'll be nice and safe," she ventured. The foreman didn't rise to it but just kept on heading down the road.

They were almost to the mountains when he took a sudden detour. Just a little off from the canal, a smallish camp had been set up. A couple of tents were the only visible structures, though the skeletons of more permanent buildings were rising up beside them. Several centaurs and a couple of humans were busily working away, the sound of their hammers echoing against the nearby mountain.

"All right, this is it." Harry pointed to a spot where timber and other supplies had been neatly stowed. "Y'all unload the cart here. Hang on, I'll fetch the others." He put his fingers in his mouth and blew a sharp whistle. Three more centaurs stopped what they were doing and trotted over to the cart.

Harry gestured to the two girls. "All right, y'all, this here's, uh..."

"Revka and Iyarra."

"Right. Revka and Iyarra. They just come on with us. Ladies, this here is the team you'll be working with." He pointed to a large, stocky cowtauress with her black hair tied back in a tight braid. "This here's Maisie."

Maisie gave the girls a nod. "Howdy."

Next to her stood a bowlegged, dapple-gray centaur with a lanky, sunburnt torso and his hat on backward. He was shirtless and carried himself in a way that suggested he considered he was doing the world a favor. He regarded the two with a lopsided grin. "All right! More ladies. Excellent. You can call me The Tom Monster."

Maisie whacked him on the back of the head. "Krep's sake, Tommy, nobody calls you that and you know it." She turned back to the girls. "Sorry about that," she said. "He's been trying to make that be a thing since puberty."

The third worker was tall and thin, with long black sideburns and a face that had long since settled into a state of permanent deadpan. "This here is Gabby," the supervisor said. "Don't let his quiet demeanor fool ya. He really is like that."

He gave the girls a nod. "Ey."

"Gabby," said Revka. "Good name."

"Well," said Harry, "I will go ahead and leave y'all to it. Come an' find me when the cart's all unloaded, right?" He tipped his hat at them and sauntered off.

The wooden boards were unloaded easily enough, but the metal plates were two-person jobs. Revka and Maisie manhandled one over the edge of the cart and down to where several plates were already laid neatly in a pile.

"Krep," she said, "these things are heavy. What the heck are they wanting these out here for?"

"Well, as I understand it, they're gonna line the inside walls of the main structure with them."

"Main structure?"

"Yeah, over there." The cowtauress pointed. Someone had marked off a fairly large rectangle of land, dug it out, and lined the surface with mortar and stone. "Storage area, supposed to be."

"Storage area? You don't say?" Revka nudged the corner of a metal plate with her boot. "You think they're worried someone's gonna steal their rocks?"

Maisie wrinkled her nose. "Probably for tools and whatnot. Some of that equipment gets expensive."

The rest of the day was spent working on the smaller outbuildings. One was evidently meant to be an office. Revka couldn't work out what the other one was for. The foreman kept the crew busy, so there was no chance to nose around or anything.

The work party got back to town a little after sundown, worn out and covered in sweat and road dust. The girls headed to the inn to wash up and change before dinner, only to find another note waiting for them.

"Meeting tonight, nine o'clock, 14 Merrybone Lane, ask for Babs," read Revka. "Hm, Merrybone? Don't think I remember that place."

"Isn't that one of the side streets close to the city gates?" said Iyarra.

"That sounds right, I guess." Revka wandered over to the window and peeked out. "Well, looks like it's about sevenish now. Let's get cleaned up and then we can go have some dinner, what do you say?"

"Works for me."

"Great." Revka peeled off her work shirt, letting it fall in a sweat-soaked heap on the floor. "I tell you one thing; I hope this undercover stuff doesn't go on too long. Gonna wear a body out."

* * * * *

Fresh from a leisurely dinner, the girls located Merrybone Lane a little after eight thirty. It was, indeed, very close to the town's entrance and seemed, at first glance, to be the upscale neighborhood for the town. Certainly, the houses were large and ornate. Busy too, by the sound of things. Apparently, the people here loved to entertain. Laughter and music drifted out into the night air from almost every open doorway, and several establishments seemed to be populated entirely by young women who had nothing better to do than lounge around open windows in either too much or not enough clothing. By the fourth such house, even Iyarra got there.

"Ohhhhhh."

"Yup." Revka sighed. "I guess we know why they call it Merrybone. Anyway, Number 14, wasn't it?"

"Believe so, yes."

"OK, just making sure." She glanced up as they walked by a place painted all in black with what sounded for all the world like the crack of a buggy whip echoing out through the night. "This is *not* a good place to get your addresses mixed up."

Number 14, when they found it, actually seemed a bit more staid than the other houses. Certainly, it didn't have so many young women lounging around the windows. The ones that were visible seemed to, at least, be sensibly dressed. A sign out front proclaimed it to be the *Pleasant Evenings Social House for Refined Gentlefolk*. Revka paused at the foot of the walkway leading to the front porch.

Iyarra nudged her. "You okay?"

"Oh, sorry. Just...hesitant." Revka smiled weakly. "What if they think we're, y'know, customers?"

"Mm, I know what you mean. I've never been in a...you know." Iyarra's ears flattened slightly, and she gave an embarrassed smile.

"Yeah, me neither." Revka looked up and down the road apprehensively. "At least there doesn't seem to be anyone around here. Not anyone that knows us, anyway."

Iyarra reached down and patted Revka's shoulder. "It's OK," she said. "I'm sure they wouldn't have sent us here unless it was safe."

"Girl, I'm not sure anything around here is safe, but yeah, I take your point." Revka squared up her shoulders. "Okay. Let's go."

As they approached, the door was opened by a short, cherubic centauress in a frilly black gown that so matched her horse half it was hard to tell where one ended and the other began. She fixed the girls with a broad smile and beckoned them inside. "Well good evening, ladies! Come in, come in! I don't believe we've had you two here before, but you're most surely welcome! I'm Patsy, and it's my very great honor to welcome you to Pleasant Evenings, the social club with a difference! Don't be shy; come on in. That's right."

Inside, it was...well, it was a lot. Somewhere in the ancient, unwritten rules of the universe, it is dictated that establishments of this type, particularly your old west style, must be draped in red velvet and furnished with plush *chaises longues*, stained-glass lamps, and on and on and on. Revka found herself briefly wondering if they all had the same decorator, or if, perhaps, there was a Bordello Starter Kit you could order from somewhere and it would all show up at once. *Now, that would be an interesting catalog to thumb through.*

Iyarra glanced anxiously over her shoulder as the door was closed behind them. "We don't get an awful lot of ladies here." Patsy patted her hands together. "But we do get them from time to time. I assure you that we can accommodate you. Now, are you together or separate?"

Revka, who was still getting over the decor, tried to snap back to reality and form some sort of response. Fortunately, Iyarra had the presence of mind to lean in. "We're here for Babs," she said.

"Oh! *Babs.*" The lady laughed. "Well, I should have guessed. Of course, of course." She glanced at a tall grandfather clock in the corner of the parlor. "Well, it seems you're a bit early. The others ain't quite here yet. So how about I give you two the grand tour?"

"Well, I mean, I wouldn't want to put you out or anything."

"Not at all, hons, not at all!" Patsy grinned. "We so rarely get visitors, and I do love talkin' the place up. Tell me, are you aware of the services we offer?"

The girls exchanged glances. "Well," Revka cleared her throat. "I mean, I think we can kinda guess? I mean we saw the other places and, uh…"

"Oh, no, no, *no!*" Patsy laughed. "No, we're not like them at all, hons. We appeal to a rather more select clientele. One that prefers a more…stimulating experience."

Iyarra raised a tentative hand. "Uhm, is this going to involve leather? Because—"

"Oh heavens no!" The centauress laughed, playfully swatting Iyarra with a black lace fan. "Naw, nothing like that. I'm talking about intellectual stimulation. What we do is, we find you interesting."

"Sorry, what?"

"Interesting. You see, anyone can go somewhere and take care of whatever physical urges they may have. That's nothing, but emotional urges are an entirely different matter. Madam Lafarge—this is her house—she figures everyone likes to feel important, like they matter. You ladies may not believe it, but even at them other houses, a lot of what the girls do is just listening. The girls here just happen to specialize in it. We can make anyone feel important, valued, an' interesting to talk to. Why, we have a feller who comes in here once a week and spends the whole hour showing off his stamp collection. And I'll tell you what," she confided with a wink, "it ain't easy coming up with new ways of saying, 'yes, that's a nice-looking stamp' all night long, but our girls are professionals and danged if they don't do it."

"Amazing."

"Right?" She had led the two of them down a plush, carpeted hallway lined with rooms on either side. As they approached one, she stopped them and held a finger to her lips. She snuck over to the door and cupped a hand to her ear.

The two girls tiptoed over and listened. Inside, a man's voice could be heard. He sounded young, and terribly earnest in a slightly nasal kind of way. "And they've got a new-fangled adding-up machine, what's got like a hundred gears and things inside of it. And it even does division! But it don't work so good. Bert at the office, he tried to divide something by zero, and the whole thing went crazy, started spinning, and wouldn't stop no how. Had to send for a guy to come and fix it."

"Good grief! Really?" The woman's voice was bright and cheery and radiated genuine interest. "Well, if that don't beat all!" There was laughter and the sound of a hand slapping a knee. "And then what happened?"

Patsy led the girls away from the door, grinning. She took them down to the end of the hall, and through a door at the back. This area was much plainer than the rest of the house, clearly not intended for the customers. The room was a combination kitchen and pantry. "Come on down." Patsy led the way.

The cellar was dry and fairly well lit. There was a good-sized rack of wine bottles, several kegs and crates stuffed into the corners, and a big, chalk circle outlined on the floor. "Now, you all just make yourselves comfortable," said Patsy. "I'm sure the others will be along in two shakes. There's robes on the hook over there." She pointed to several gray cowled robes hanging against the far wall. "Coffee and pastries are on the sideboard. Go ahead an' help yourself."

"Well," said Revka, once they were alone, "this is turning out to be a weird night."

"Tell me about it." Iyarra wandered over to the sideboard and grabbed a cheese khelmish (basically the same thing as a Danish but they don't have a Denmark in those parts). "Good, though. I didn't know these kinds of things were catered. Do you think we ought to put on some robes?"

"That won't be necessary." The girls turned at the new voice. A few new people were proceeding down the steps. All centaurs, Revka noticed. Most of them had already donned the gray robes, though a couple in the back were tugging theirs on as they came. The one in the lead, who had spoken, stepped over to where the girls were standing. "Due to your...special status, you will not need them. Good evening, ladies. Please have a seat anywhere around the circle and we shall begin once the others are here. You may call me Babs."

Chapter Thirteen

A LITTLE WHILE LATER, the group had assembled itself inside the circle. The oil lamps had been turned down so that the fat, white candles between each of the robed figures provided the only real light in the room. There were eight of them, not counting Iyarra and Revka, who sat together feeling somewhat conspicuous. An expectant hush washed over the darkness as the leader raised her arms.

"Has the Way been barred to all who have no part in this evening's work?"

Another robe nodded. "Yes'm. Locked 'er up tighter than a gnat's—" The leader cleared her throat. "Er, I mean, yes, high mistress."

"Good. And the wards? They have been fortified?"

"Just wrapping up the second pass, ma'am."

"Second pass? What are you doing over there?"

"Well, you remember last week, when I went to do 'em, and we were all out of the special, colored chalk? And you said never mind, we could do it twice next time and it would even out?"

"Oh, right. Right. Fine, carry on. Where was I? Ah yes. Are all summoned gathered here tonight?"

"Debra couldn't make it, high mistress. It's her eldest's anniversary tonight, so she's got the kids for the evening, you know how it is. I told her I'd swing by later and tell her if she missed anything."

"Well, all right then. Bring her a couple of the doughnuts when you go, will you? You know the ones she likes. Anyhow. Be there anybody here not of our covenant? If so, speak now, for otherwise you shall not leave this place and will be seen no more."

Revka coughed. "Uhm…"

"No, not you, dears. You're fine." The circle sat quietly for a moment, on the off chance that someone might suddenly jump up and hurry out the door, but no such luck. "Very well. Then I declare the opening of the circle to be whole and good. Now, let us begin."

"I would first like to start with the newcomers in our midst. I know that some of you are concerned about bringing outsiders into our covenant, and I share your concerns myself, but the Lady has made it clear that this is what She desires." She turned to Revka and Iyarra. "Tell me, when you were out in the desert, I understand she came and spoke to you herself. What did you see? What did you hear?"

Revka opened her mouth to answer but stopped when a whispered *hiss* brushed across her ear. It sounded as if someone was just behind and to the left of her, but there wasn't anyone back there, surely? She risked a quick glance over her shoulder. Nope.

The voice came again, in hastily whispered words. A memory clicked. Coyote. Revka listened to the words being fed to her and dutifully repeated them. "We saw a great white light...and heard a voice that echoed over the mountains... She commanded us to aid her loyal sermons...what? Oh. Her loyal servants. Sorry. She said we were anonymous workers, and that—hang on—oh, that we could go where others might not. And that we must trust entirely in your wisdom. Uhm, that's all."

The high mistress nodded. "Very good," she said. "It is quite unusual that she appears in this form. You may consider yourselves privileged, indeed, that She has revealed herself to you thus."

"Oh, yes, ma'am." *Lady, if you only knew.*

"I suppose she knows what she's doing." This from another robed figure sitting, more or less, across from Iyarra.

Revka's eyes narrowed. "I remember you. You're the one in the other place, who was talking about how nobody would miss us and stuff."

"Brother Philip was merely looking out for the safety of this group," interjected Babs. "After all, given the nature of our trust, every precaution must be taken to ensure we avoid discovery. We are guardians of a great secret. One which, for the sake of our people, must be kept secret at all costs."

She pointed to the girls. "I want to make sure you understand this. I don't know how much She told you, but understand that everything you see and hear here must be guarded with your life. We are part of a sacred trust. On no account may any of our secret knowledge fall into the hands of those unprepared for it. We are the only barrier between this place and absolute horror, and now, you are too. Do you accept this grave responsibility?"

Revka nodded. "Yes, ma'am."

Iyarra joined her. "We do."

The robe named Phil shrugged. "Fine," it said. "Long as you're happy, I'm happy."

"Very well." The tension in the room went down a smidge. "Now then, to business. I must first report that the general fund is nearly depleted. If you haven't paid your dues, I need you to get them to Debra by the end of the week, at the latest. I think we're doing a good job keeping expenses down, all things considered, but the recent spate of activity in the mountains means we will have to step up our efforts. I need hardly tell you that that will take funds we currently do not have. We are fortunate that Sister Lafarge has provided this place to meet in town free of charge—" She was interrupted by the sound of galloping hoofbeats upstairs and loud, raucous laughter. "Even if it does have its occasional disadvantages," she continued. "Nevertheless, we do need to bring in additional funds."

"Well, you know my answer to that," spoke up another robed figure.

The high mistress sighed. "Margaret, for the hundredth time. We are a secret society. We move in the dark, our existence known only to a select few. We are *not* going to have a bake sale."

"Well, we don't have to tell 'em what it's for! People buyin' pies ain't generally long on questions, from what I've seen."

"Yes, yes, I quite understand what you are saying. Nevertheless, I think we should hear some other suggestions. Anyone?"

As the discussion went on, Revka found herself tuning out. Secret societies had never figured much in her imagination, which was generally occupied with visions of her running around and being heroic. If she had ever given them any thought, she probably would have expected there to be more, well, conspiring. *You get a bunch of hooded figures together in some candlelit basement, they should be exchanging terrible secrets and making cunning plans, not arguing over whose turn it is to pay for the coffee.* She found herself wondering if all secret societies were like this. Maybe there was a smoke-filled room somewhere in the kingdom where a handful of elites, jaded with money and power, sat around arguing about what color ashtrays they should get. It was an intriguing thought and one that provided an interesting few minutes of speculation, until someone called her name.

"Huhwha?" Revka shook her head, trying to mentally rewind the last few seconds of conversation.

"I was asking," said the high mistress, "whether you two had had any luck getting on with T&F. I believe brother Sam left a note for you earlier."

"Oh, yes. Right. Sorry. Uhm, we did get a job over there. Fortunately, Mr. Findswater had met us already, so he got us set up all right. They took us out to the middle of nowhere, over by the mountains. Looks like they're setting up some sort of camp."

The robed figures listened, as Revka and Iyarra related everything they had seen and done. "Very interesting," said the high mistress when they had finished. "I must say it, more or less, falls into place with our suspicions thus far. A tool shed with steel plates, you say?"

"Yes ma'am," said Revka. "We figure it doesn't make much sense for a quarry, but if you were storing gold in there..."

"Yes, yes." The horsewoman seemed thoughtful, drumming her hoof on the floor reflectively. "Well, I suppose the best thing now is to keep at it. Go on and continue to work there. I won't tell you to sabotage the job, but if you can occasionally arrange for things to go slower than they otherwise might, well...just let your imagination be your guide. Mostly, just keep your eyes and ears open for anything that might be helpful. It sounds like you already have the ear of Mr. Findswater, so we may be able to leverage that. See if you can cultivate him, get him to take you into his confidence. Make yourselves useful, that sort of thing. We will continue to meet here on a regular basis. Do you have any questions?"

"Not at the moment, ma'am."

"I do." It was Brother Philip again. "Are we still gonna do the beast thing?"

"I think that's very unlikely," said the high mistress. "I'm rather afraid that they're onto us on that one."

Revka nodded. "Yeah, they know about the glow paint. Sorry."

"Well, just as well. Petty acts of sabotage were not accomplishing much. I rather feel it was beneath us, honestly. Best to retire the beast for now. At this point, it's only going to garner closer attention from the authorities."

"Well, I mean, you can't blame them," said Revka. "I mean, running around and scaring people is one thing, but the stampede, that was a bit much."

The high mistress tilted her head. "I beg your pardon? What stampede?"

"When y'all let the thungas out. Somebody could have gotten hurt, you know?"

There was a moment of bemused silence. Finally, Brother Philip cleared his throat. "That wasn't us. We never let them thungas out, whatsoever."

"Wait, that wasn't you guys?" asked Iyarra. "You sure?"

"Well, I'd reckon we'd known if we'd done it." He looked around at the group. "Less'n somebody went out and did it on their own?" This was met with a chorus of denials. "Yeah, we wouldn't do nothin' like that."

"Interesting," said the high mistress. "I hadn't given it much thought, but now you do have me wondering."

"Oh!" Iyarra brightened. "I bet it was—" but Revka jabbed her urgently in the side. "Uh, probably just some kid," she finished lamely.

"Hm. Well, I think that covers everything for now. Remember your instructions and we will meet again in a few nights. Good luck to us all. Any other business? No? Very well. Let the circle be closed, the way be unbarred, and someone go up and let them know we're ready for the ham rolls."

* * * * *

Some time later, Iyarra and Revka walked back through the city streets to the inn. Several of the saloons were still open and doing a brisk trade. The sounds of fighting and singing wafted out into the desert night, though sometimes it was hard to tell which was which.

Neither spoke until they got back to their room, each lost in her thoughts. It wasn't until they closed the door behind them that Revka shook her head and blew out. "Whew. Man."

"So that was a secret society, was it?" Iyarra sat down on the bed. "Are they all like that?"

"Search me. Never seen one before." Revka went over to the water closet and pumped a little water into the sink to splash her face.

"That was...not what I expected," Iyarra said. "When that goddess lady said she had a secret priesthood working for her, I thought they'd be more...well, mysterious, you know? All spooky and being like, bring forth the sacred such-and-such, but these guys were like, like..." she waved a hand vaguely, trying to find the words.

"Like a club. Yeah, I noticed too. Actually, it was kind of like my dad."

"Your dad? He was in a secret society?"

"Well, sort of. I mean, they called themselves The Ancient and Mystical Order of Iron, but honestly, anyone who worked in or around the iron mines was in it. And in our town, that was darned near everyone. Dad told me all about it, you know. They have a lot of stuff about sacred, time-honored secrets handed down through the ages, and you swear on the bones of your ancestors not to reveal what goes on at the meetings, and all like that."

"Gosh."

"Yeah. It turns out it's mostly just charity work and parading around in silly hats. Dad mostly joined it to be sociable, but yeah, this feels like the same thing, you know?" She wandered over to Iyarra and sat on her back, futzing with her mane. "It's like, they're supposed to be protecting the world and all, but they treat it like a hobby. I mean, that costume? The beast one? Who does that? Sounds like something some old coot would come up with to get people to stay off his land or something."

Iyarra snorted. "No kidding. And then the first group of kids that were even a little bit curious would figure out what was going on in, like, ten minutes. If that."

Revka giggled. "Exactly!" She shook her head. "All I know is, I am more than a little bit sure we're going to have to do most of the heavy lifting with this bunch."

"I hear you there." Iyarra sighed. "Still, it kind of makes sense when you think about it."

"Oh, how do you figure?"

"Well, they're a secret society, getting their orders from a goddess of chaos, but they don't *know* she's a goddess of chaos. I mean, what else are you going to get?"

"Interesting point." Revka mused, taking out a brush and brushing Iyarra's mane out a little. "Come to think of it, maybe that's not even on purpose. On her part, I mean."

"Oh?"

"Sure. Can you imagine a chaos goddess creating an efficient, competent group? Doesn't fit. Probably even if she did set out to create a group who had their heads screwed on straight, she'd wind up with a bunch of...well..."

"Interesting point." Iyarra leaned back a bit, closing her eyes and lowering her ears. "Well, I guess we're stuck with them either way. Funny thing, though, to think about it, bringing us in to shape things up. You'd never think we'd be the competent ones."

Revka laughed. "Now, that is scary!" She sighed and hugged her arms around Iyarra from behind. "Well, I suppose we'd better call it a night. Back to work in the morning and all that. Shall I get the light?"

"Yes, ma'am."

"All right." Revka slipped off Iyarra's back and wandered over to the lamp. She turned it down until the room was dark, only the filtered moonlight around the window curtain providing any light at all. She padded back over to Iyarra and tossed a blanket over her back against the cool night air. "Good night, sugar."

"G'nite."

Outside the inn, a shadow watched the light go out in their room. It nodded, stepped back into the deeper darkness, and disappeared.

Chapter Fourteen

MORNING, AND ROSY-FINGERED dawn did lightly caress the sleeping town, brushing away the shadows of recalcitrant night and tinting the world with a dance of gold. It washed across the valley, gently coaxed the citizenry from their dreams to meet the new day, and hit Revka square in the eye. She growled and yanked the blankets over her head.

Iyarra gave her a nudge. "Come on, you. We gotta get up and get ready for work, remember?"

"Whfzzl."

"Now, come on. We've got to get along to that construction site and find out what they're doing." The centauress grinned, tugging the blanket away. "I know you're not the biggest morning person, but we've got a job to do, right?"

"Grnph."

"Good."

* * * * *

They arrived at the site with the rest of the work party a little over an hour later. They were put on the construction crew for the big building, the stone floor having been set sufficiently for the real work to begin.

The girls had never actually worked on a building site before, it being one of the few jobs they somehow hadn't taken at some point in their wanderings. Frankly, Revka had always just assumed you started at the bottom and built your way up, but apparently, this was not the case. The crew laid out several planks to form the outline of one of the walls, which they nailed together into a kind of frame. They brought over several other planks that were placed inside the frame about half a pace from each other, going vertical from the bottom to the top, and secured these in place as well. The end result rather reminded Revka of a giant, barred window.

Over the course of the day, they managed to do all four walls, each laid out neatly around the foundation where they would be ready to be lifted into place and joined together the next day. As they worked, the crew kept up a steady stream of chat and gossip. A lot of it was to do with locals the girls didn't know, and was of the who's-doing-what-to-whom-and-for-how-much variety. There was also some talk about a new entertainer over at the Red Boa Club who, if her coworkers were to be believed, had quite a unique act. Revka liked to think she was a woman of the world, but if the comments of the crew were to be believed, then centaur exotic dancers were *really* exotic. Almost eye-wateringly so. A couple of times, she glanced at Iyarra to see if they were turning her on, but the centauress merely shrugged.

"So, never built a building this way before. Any of you guys?" Revka hoped to move the conversation to less awkward topics,

Tom fanned himself with his hat. "It is mighty peculiar," he said. "Though I suppose they know what they're after."

"Yeah, I didn't know they built places this way. I mean, doing the walls flat and all."

"Oh, that ain't the odd part." The centaur pointed. "That's just how you do timber frame buildings. Nothing unusual about that. Naw, I mean as how they ain't any windows."

Revka looked. Sure enough, Tom was right. The front wall had a big gap for the opening doors, but the other walls were all the same, not an opening to be seen.

"Barn," said Gabby.

Revka turned. "Do what?"

"Barn. That's how they used to do 'em back home. Put the walls together an' haul 'em up. Big doors, no windows. Barn."

Revka looked down at the wooden slats. "Well, now that you mention it," she said, "I can kind of see that."

"You think that's what we're building out here?"

Maisie shrugged. "Could be. I reckon one storage building is pretty much the same as any other, get right down to it."

The sun was beginning to work its way down, as the group packed up their tools and started the journey back to town. "So listen," said Maisie, as they trooped along the road, "some of us we go 'long to Mactingle's Saloon after work, for a cool-off drink. Y'all can come along if ya wanna."

Revka looked at Iyarra. "What do you reckon?"

"Well, I don't mind if you don't. Frankly, a drink would do me good."

"A'ight." Maisie grinned. "It ain't the snazziest place in town, but it's cheap, and they don't short ya."

"Sounds good."

* * * * *

Mactingle's was on the cheap end of the main drag, in the low-rent area where the tourists didn't go—or at least, didn't go on purpose. The one-story saloon was low-slung and catered mostly to centaurs, generally blue-collar workers who spent their days in the sun and were looking for something cheap and cold to unwind with at the end of the day. Revka tried to imagine Mr. Fleet and his bunch sitting around one of the rough, unwashed tables. She couldn't. There was something about the place that would naturally repel any attempt at gentrification. Any drink with a paper umbrella would spontaneously combust before you got it through the door.

"Careful," said Maisie as they claimed a table near the back. "Place can be a little rough, especially after workin' hours."

"You don't say. Er..." Revka looked around. "Where are the chairs?"

"Ain't got none." The cowtauress settled herself down, then grinned at Revka. "We don't get much in the way of humans around here, and the chairs don't last long anyway."

"Don't worry, I've got you." Iyarra repositioned herself so that Revka could perch on her back.

"Thanks." Revka settled down, then tugged a little at the table. It didn't budge. "Huh." She craned her head downward, peeking under the table. "Hey, Yarra," she said. "Table's bolted to the floor."

"Yup," said Tom. "All of 'em are like that. Also, they got iron bands underneath as holds 'em together. Otherwise, they'd get broke up and splintered all to pieces." He chuckled, using his hands to mime a centaur taking a crash landing onto a table. "*Boosh.*"

"Uh-huh." Now that Revka looked around, the place definitely had a different sort of atmosphere to it. The space behind the bar where the bottles were kept was enclosed in a series of wooden cabinets protected with chicken wire. A similar construction surrounded the piano player in the back corner, the result being that he looked like some sort of zoo exhibit. There was an overall stripped-down aspect to the decor, as if someone had taken pains to remove anything breakable and nail down the rest. Revka found herself wishing they'd taken a table nearer the exit.

Iyarra made a face. "Uhm, just what kind of place is this again?"

Maisie laughed. "Aw, it ain't that bad. Mostly it's all right. Just you get a lot of folks comin' in after a long day, looking to cut loose a little. Can get a little bit rowdy, but if I'm honest, it's not much worse than most places around these parts. Ain't that right, fellers?"

Tom nodded. "Yeah, pretty much."

"Yup," said Gabby.

"Anyhow. Let's go ahead and get the first round in. Braws all around? I believe it's your turn, Mr. Thomas."

"Aw, man. Natchally it'd be my turn when we got two new people along."

"Oh, don't worry about us," said Revka hurriedly. "We can cover ourselves. Come to think of it, since it's our first time, how about we get the first round, what do ya say?"

"Oh well, shoot!" Tommy brightened up. "In that case, I'll have me a Château Lahoof Wraithchild '83, or I guess an '84 would be acceptable too. If it's from early in the year. Oh, and one of them bendy straws. I like those."

Maisie clipped Tommy on the back of his head with her palm again. "You gonna take braw like the rest of us and you'll like it." She nodded to the girls. "Much obliged."

"No problem, I'll run and fetch 'em. Won't be long." Revka got up from the table, only to feel Iyrra's hand on her arm. "I think it might be better if I get the drinks," she said.

Revka blinked. "Whassat? How come?"

Iyarra nodded her head toward the room. "Look around."

Revka did so, wondering what she was looking for. The place was beginning to fill up a bit. True to what the others had said, the customers seemed to be working-class types. Most of them gathered in groups at their tables, but there was no shortage of lone drinkers. Seemed like pretty much any bar she'd ever been in. *What did Iyarra...?*

"Wait, am I the only human in here?"

Iyarra nodded. "Looks like it. I'm not super sure it would be a good idea to call attention to yourself."

"Well, that ain't wrong," said Tom. "I mean, we get humans in here from time to time, but they tend to keep to themselves, you know? Stay out of everyone's way."

Maisie nodded. "Probably best if ya don't call attention to yourself. Iyarra, girl, you go on ahead. Miss Revka can hang out with us."

"Okay."

* * * * *

Iyarra got up and wandered over to the bar. The bartender was getting through the line pretty fast. Most of the customers wanted whatever was on tap, anyway, so it wasn't like he was going to be tied up with any complicated cocktail orders. She and Revka had been to bars where they had special, custom cocktails with names like Liquid Sunset or Toe Curler. She found herself wondering what kind of cocktails a place like this would have. Probably, they'd have names like Concussion, or What Are You Looking At?

Her reverie was broken when the saloon door burst open. A large, heavily muscled figure filled the doorway, blocking any light from outside. All around the bar, conversations trickled to a halt. In his cage in the corner, the piano player stumbled out a couple of bum notes before stopping and glancing back toward the open doorway.

The bulltaur strode into the room and surveyed the crowd. "Just what the hell was *that*?" he bellowed. "That was sloppier'n hell, is what that was! Now. I'm gonna go out and back in again. Let's see if we can get it right!" He turned around, and stormed back through the doors, grumbling.

After a few seconds, the conversations around the tables tentatively picked back up where they had left off. The piano player started back up again, and Iyarra, more than a little bemused, turned her attention back to the bartender.

The saloon doors crashed open again. This time, the effect was immediate. Every conversation stopped, every head turned, even the piano player stopped midnote, which is no easy trick. Silence washed over the room as the bulltaur strode in, his thick, heavy hooves thumping against the floor. He looked around the room, then grunted. "All right," he said. "That's better. Try an' have some standards around here."

He strode over to the bar, pushing through the other patrons as if they weren't even there. Iyarra backed away quickly, staying out of the newcomer's way. Something about him struck her as awfully familiar. "Whiskey," he snarled.

The bartender gulped. "C-certainly sir," he stammered. "What kind?"

The bull's eyes narrowed. "Whaddya mean what kind? Whiskey!"

"Well, I mean, s-sure, but there's different whiskeys. You got your Caledonian, your Tarshish, your oat, your artisan, handcrafted, fennel-and-sugar beet..."

The barkeep trailed off as the bulltaur leaned over him. "I want," he said, "The cheapest, nastiest, rot-gut whiskey you got. Gimme the stuff you use to clean the sink with. And if you ever use the word artisan in front of me again, I'm gonna—"

"*Stumpy!*" Revka's voice rang out from the back. The entire crowd turned to look at the woman, who was grinning in mild disbelief.

The bulltaur's head whipped around, "WHO SAID THAT!?" he bellowed. Off to the side, Iyarra gulped. Oh dear, he did look familiar.

Revka smirked at the bulltaur and waved. "Hey there," she called out. "I see yer not wearin' your horns today."

Big Jake, for indeed it was him, scowled, his eyes narrowing. "*You*," he snarled. "I got kicked out of my own gang cuz of you! I'm gonna cream you!" He began to stride his way across the room toward Revka's table with murder in his eyes.

"Whoops," whispered Revka. She stumbled up to her feet, holding her hands out placatingly. "Easy there, man. I didn't do it on purpose. Things just happen, right? Come on, let me get you something. On me, what do you say?"

"I say you better say yer prayers." He got to their table and leaned down to the woman, pounding a fist into his hand. "Now," he growled, "any last words?"

"Yeah," said a voice. "Why don't you pick on somebody your own size?"

Iyarra stood behind the bulltaur, her voice almost steady as she issued the challenge. She pawed at the floor, her large hooves digging a rut in the hard-packed earth.

Big Jake looked over his shoulder at her and sneered. "I remember you," he said. "Well, I reckon I can take ya both on. Two against one ain't too bad when one of 'em don't hardly count at all." he grinned menacingly at Revka.

"Five to one." Maisie stood up, rolling back her sleeves. Gabby and Tom joined her, the latter raising a hand hesitantly. "Actually," he said, "I kind of have an appointment later and…" Maisie clapped him on the back of the head again. "Aw, dangit."

The whistle's shriek was really loud. "All right, people," the bartender called, hands cupped over his mouth. "You know the drill. Come on, now." There was some grumbling among the crowd, but those with drinks filed up to the bar and handed them over, receiving a numbered tag in exchange. A couple of centaurs made a circuit of the room, collecting up any breakables which were brought behind the bar as well. Iyarra cast an enquiring glance toward Revka, who just shrugged.

In less than a minute, the whole thing was over. The barkeeper reached up and pulled a metal cage down in front of the bar, latching it in place. "All right, folks," he called, "On your mark!" He ducked down behind the bar, out of sight. A second later, the whistle sounded again, and the fight was on.

Revka had just enough presence of mind to duck out of the way before Big Jake's first swing. She hopped back onto the table. High ground, that was the ticket. Big Jake was burly and strong. A blow from him would probably knock her flat. Fortunately, he was slow. She had that going for her. She kept him moving by dancing back and forth, wondering how long she could keep him going. More important, how the heck was she ever going to lay a blow on him?

A fist came flying across Revka's field of vision. Maisie, who had moved to the bulltaur's left, gave him a walloping crack across the jaw. This sent him staggering to his right and straight into Gabby, who elbowed him in the ribs, hard. Jake snorted, pulling back a fist to hit the centaur. Revka saw her chance. She leaped onto the bull's back and grabbed his horns. These weren't the detachable type. Jake roared, shaking his head and groping behind him, trying to dislodge the bulldogger. Gabby gave him several rabbit punches to the gut before he could grab her, then took a couple of quick steps back, leading the bull.

Behind him, Iyarra circled the bulltaur warily, looking for an opening. She had one hoof raised, poised to give him one in the lower ribs. Someone tapped her on the shoulder. She turned to see a big, burly centaur with a fat, unshaven face and a crooked grin. He tipped his hat at her, revealing a greasy tangled mane. "Pardon me, ma'am. Is this a private fight, or can anyone mix in?"

Iyarra bit her lip. "Oo," she said. "Uhm, well we *do* all kind of know each other."

"Oh, well that's all right then." He put his hat back on and moseyed over to another pair of centaurs who were duking it out at an adjacent table. This time his question elicited a different response. The two men looked at him, then each other, then one pulled back and punched him in the face. This answer seemed to satisfy him, and he gleefully plunged into the fray.

Iyarra shook her head and turned her attention back to the fight. Revka was now hanging on to Big Jake's back, kicking his upper torso with her boots whenever she could. Maisie was keeping Jake occupied, matching him punch for punch, with Gabby hanging off to one side and distracting the bulltaur's attention when necessary. Tom, for his part, had elected to hang back on the other side of the table, throwing punches from a safe distance and keeping up a nonstop litany along the lines of "Yeah!" and "How you like that, huh?"

Iyarra rolled her eyes. She shook her head and turned her attention back to Big Jake. He was big, and nearly all muscle, but three against one was starting to tell on him. She whistled at Revka, who nodded and leaped from the bulltaur. Revka landed, more or less, on Iyarra's back. She scrambled upright and clapped a hand on Iyarra's shoulder. "Clear!"

Iyarra brought both of her rear hooves crashing against Big Jake's side. He went over sideways, landing hard on the table. He bellowed in agony, flailing around as he tried to regain his hooves. The group stood around him. Even Tom moved into place with the others.

Revka glared at Big Jake from the safety of Iyarra's back. "Now, get outta here, or you'll get more."

Big Jake eased himself upright, grunting at his aching ribs. He glowered at the girls, his breathing ragged. "One of these days," he scowled, "Ah'm gonna catch y'all...without yer friends to back you up...then you gonna get it."

"Yeah, whatever." Revka grinned. "Now, beat it. Or next time we're bringing the barbecue sauce."

"Oh wow," said Iyarra.

The bulltaur hobbled away, pausing occasionally to glare back at them. Revka caught his eye and glared back. "Just keep walking."

"Yeah, man!" said Tom. "More where that came from! Woo!"

"Shut up, Tom."

"Geez, sorry."

The group turned back to their table and settled down. It looked like the rest of the bar was beginning to wind down a little. Certainly, a fair number of combatants were out of the fight one way or another, and the remainder didn't seem as enthusiastic as they had been.

"Well," said Maisie. "Y'all know Big Jake? He's a mighty rough customer."

"Yeah, we kinda had a run-in with him on the way to town. He was leading a bandit gang, and they tried to rob the wagon train."

"You don't say. Haven't seen him around town in a good while. Guess the bandit biz ain't going so good for 'em."

Revka grinned. "Yeah well, that's kind of on us. I'll tell you the story if you're interested."

The whistle blew again, and the barkeep emerged from his hiding place. "All right, y'all, that's enough for tonight. Come on up an' get yer drinks, them as has 'em." There were a couple of disappointed groans, but the fighters obediently stopped and began to file toward the bar.

Iyarra smiled back at Revka. "Tell you what," she said. "Go ahead and tell them the story, and I'll get our drinks." Revka nodded and hopped off the centauress' back, settling herself down at the table again.

"Okay," she said, "So, we were coming west with the wagon train, you see, and we came to this canyon. Everyone's all on edge, and I turn to Sam and I say—What's this piece of paper?"

Tom tilted his head. "Do what? What piece of paper?"

"This piece of paper right here." Revka plucked a folded sheet of paper off the table. "Is this anybody's?"

"Not mine."

"I ain't big on readin' material."

"Nope."

"Huh." Revka looked down at the table. "You know," she said, "this is about where that hunk of beef landed. I wonder..." She opened up the paper and read.

We have work for you. Be at the office of the T&F Mercantile Company at midnight tonight. Don't tell anyone.

"Well," she said, "ain't that one hell of a note."

Tom shrugged. "Looks like a perfectly ordinary one to me."

"No, it's just..." She looked back at the bar, where Iyarra was patiently waiting her turn. "Tell you what," she said, "I think we're just gonna have the one round, me an' Iyarra."

"That so? How come?"

Revka folded up the paper. "We got plans for tonight."

Chapter Fifteen

MIDNIGHT, AND THE TOWN of Red Valley slept.

Actually, that's not at all true. For one thing, several of the bars were still open, plus the hard-working ladies and gentlemen of Merrybone Lane were just gearing up for the late-night rush. A few places were still getting swept out, or guarded, and the local free hospital run by the Sisters of Perpetual Remonstration was looking after the slow-but-steady trickle of bar fighters who came in second. Or in pieces.

"I tell you what," muttered Revka, as they plodded through the nearly empty streets. "This town is playing hell with my sleep schedule. When was the last time we got a good night's sleep?"

"Last night."

"Oh. Right. Feels like longer." She looked around, the darkness only punctuated by the occasional oil lamp. "I mean, we didn't used to go creeping around all hours of the night like this."

"Well, at least the night air is nice and cool. Not like during the day."

"Well, sure, but at least if we get too cool back at the hotel, we could throw a blanket on. I don't think that's an option out here."

"Well, I brought your cloak. I thought it might keep you warm."

"Which one?"

"The dark green one."

"The one with that stain on it?"

"Revka, hon. It's dark out. Nobody's going to see it. Besides, it's a cloak. You can always flip it inside out."

"Yeah, but then the stain will be touching me."

"So?"

"So? Eww!"

"Oh, good grief." Iyarra rolled her eyes. She leaned forward a little, peering down the street. "That's the place up there, isn't it?"

"Yup, that's the warehouse. Think we'd better duck off the road?"

"Yeah, I think so."

They slipped along behind the adjacent building and crept up on the warehouse. In the dim light, Big Jake's silhouette could just be seen waiting around the side of the building. Revka signaled Iyarra to get low and gave her a gentle nudge. "The cloak," she whispered, "which pouch?"

"Left front."

"All right." Revka opened the bag and drew the cloak out as quietly as she could. It was a cotton one with a built-in hood, was not the warmest thing in the world, but better than nothing. Also, it made no noise as she slipped it on and pulled the hood over her head. She patted Iyarra's shoulder, whispered, "Stay here," and began to creep forward.

The yard at T&F was a working area, filled with crates, wagons, and all kinds of other items, so it was quite simple work for her to sneak her way closer to the building. She kept herself low, only moving from one cover to another when she was sure he wasn't looking her way. Before long, she was crouched behind some barrels, not twenty paces away from where the bulltaur waited.

Presently, a group of three figures emerged from around the back of the building. The centaurs were completely covered in hooded robes. Revka blinked. *The Tex Arcana? Here?*

They passed the light of a nearby window, and Revka saw that these robes were a dark crimson. *Okay. Different bunch, then.* On the other hand, just how many secret societies could a town this size even have? She shrugged it off and hunkered down into position, finding a space between two barrels where she could see.

Big Jake grunted as the trio approached him. "Took ya long enough," he muttered. "Been standing here since the bells went off."

"Our apologies." The thin voice was somewhat reedy. Revka cocked an ear, cupping her hand to hear better. "We had to finish the preparations. Nevertheless, your patience is appreciated and will be compensated appropriately."

The bulltaur snorted. "Whatever. What's the job?"

"Quite simple, really." The lead figure held out a hand. One of the figures behind it drew out a small, cloth pouch, tied with a drawstring at the top. "Take this."

Jake weighed the bag in his massive hand, frowning. "What is it, anyway?"

"Never mind. It's nothing you need to concern yourself with. Now, here are your instructions. You are to take the trail out of town going along the canal up to the mountains. When you get there, you'll find another trail, just a bit to the right, leading up the mountain itself. It's a fairly good trail, not the easiest thing in the dark, but I'm sure someone with your experience should have no trouble. I assume you have a light source?"

"Course."

"Very good. The trail will take you up to an area where the water has collected into a large pool. You will undo the cord on the bag, and throw it into the water, just in the middle will be fine. Then you will come back here. Someone will be waiting with your payment. Do you understand?"

Big Jake looked down at the bag. "Yeah. Uh listen, this stuff in the bag, it ain't poison, is it? I mean, I do a lot of stuff, but..."

The hooded figure laughed softly. "Oh, dear me, no. No, it's quite safe, I assure you. It's nothing you need to worry about on that account. No," the leader resumed, "your job is just to dump it and come back. Do not open the bag until you get there. Do not examine the contents. We are paying for your discretion and your ignorance. Be assured, it is in your best interest not to know any more than you have to."

The bulltaur grunted. He tossed the bag lightly a couple of times, then stuffed it into a saddle bag. "Fine."

"Very good. There will be someone here until dawn. Have it done and be back here by then."

Revka watched the three hooded figures turn and walk back around the corner of the building. Big Jake shrugged and muttered something under his breath. He turned, heading for the road.

Revka waited until he was out of sight, then crawled back to where Iyarra was waiting. "Well?" Iyarra asked. "What was that all about?"

"Beats me," Revka muttered, slipping off her hood. "But I tell you one thing, I wish I had the hooded robe concession in this town. It is lousy with secret societies."

"So, what did they want?"

"He's supposed to go up to the mountains, where the canal is, and dump some bag into a pool. According to them, it's not poison or anything, but they wouldn't say what it is. Weird, huh?"

"Should we follow him?"

Revka glanced into the darkness. "I dunno. I mean, it's dark out, but there's not a lot of cover between here and there. If he were to glance back just once, that would be it. Plus, it's like an hour each way, and it's already late."

"Ugh. Good point."

"Actually, the construction site they have us at...that's pretty close to the canal, isn't it? I bet we could head up there tomorrow, maybe over lunch. Could you follow his scent trail?"

"Him? Oh, lord, yes. Once smelled, never forgotten."

"Oof. OK, we'll do it that way, then. Meantime, I don't know about you, but I'm ready to get some shut-eye. Let's head back." Revka moved toward the street and made sure no one was about. She nodded to Iyarra, who joined her. After a moment, satisfied that they had the street to themselves, they crept out and started working their way back to the inn.

A few minutes later, three shadowy figures emerged from behind the mercantile building. They spoke briefly in whispers, then went their separate ways into the darkness.

* * * * *

The next morning, the girls were back at the construction site again, listening to the crew relate how the rest of the night had gone. Apparently, things calmed down considerably after the girls left. A couple of guys started a fight later on, but when no one else joined in, they lost interest and left.

The four walls having been completed, the crew hoisted them upright, one after another. Using temporary support boards to prop them up, they set to work fastening the walls together until they had a nice solid framework to build on. This operation took the better part of the morning. By the time it was done, they were more than ready for lunch.

Revka and Iyarra sat with the rest of the group, chatting as they ate bread and cheese. After she was done eating, Revka stood up and stretched. "Well, we got a little time before we get back to work. I think I'm gonna take a quick walk and stretch my legs a little. Iyarra, you want to come with?"

"Yeah, I think I will." Iyarra nodded to the others. "We won't be long."

"No problem," said Maisie. "Just be careful, you hear?"

"We will."

It was a quick walk to the where the canal met the mountain. Revka squatted down, peering at the stream for anything suspicious. "Looks all right to me. Can you smell him?"

"Hang on." Iyarra paced along the foot of the mountain, eyes half-lidded the way she did when she was letting her nose do most of the work. After a dozen or so steps, she stopped and pointed. "There."

Revka had a look. Sure enough, if you pushed some of the brush aside, there was a small but visible trail winding its way up. Now that she looked, there were a couple of places where the brush had been stomped down by something good and heavy. She nodded to Iyarra and pushed some more brush away. "After you, hon."

They began to work their way up the trail. It was clear the narrow path hadn't seen a lot of traffic, but it was fairly well marked out. Between that and Iyarra's nose, they were able to find their way along.

Revka looked down at the path behind them as the trail switched back on itself and wound its way upward. "Boy, imagine trying to follow this in the dark."

Iyarra shrugged. "Honestly, if you had a torch, it wouldn't be too bad," she said. "You can kind of see where the dirt's pounded down. It's an old trail, but still pretty usable."

"Yeah? I wonder why. Seems a bit out of the way."

"Well, didn't you say there's supposed to be a pool or something up here?"

"Oh, right!" Revka looked up at the centauress. "You reckon the settlers used to come up here for water? Like before they had the canal and stuff?"

Iyarra grunted a little as she scrambled over a steep spot in the trail. "Well, I wouldn't swear to it, but I mean, it sounds logical, you know?"

Revka pursed her lips, then nodded. "You know, I think you're probably right."

Iyarra preened a little. "Neat."

It took about ten minutes, all told, before they found the spot that they were looking for. Two different mountain streams met, where time and water had carved out a natural depression about the size of a house. Revka peered at the crystal-clear water. "Let's see, that looks to be about knee-high in the middle, maybe a little more. Okay, give me a second." She sat down on a nearby rock and began to tug her boots off.

"Going in? Are you sure?"

"Well, I can't see the bag from the shore, and he probably threw it toward the middle, so I'm thinking that's our best bet." Revka set one boot aside. She got the second off and rolled her trousers up as far as they would go. "All right."

Revka walked over to the water and dipped a toe in. "Wow! That is *cold*."

"Snow runoff." Iyarra nodded. "I imagine it would be."

"Okay, here goes." Once Revka was in, it was actually pretty nice, certainly a welcome contrast to the heat of the day, which had gotten an early start and was well on the way to being a scorcher. She moved forward, nice and slow, trying not to stir up any more dirt than necessary. She kept her eyes locked on the bottom of the pool. *Somewhere around the middle. Just a little further, and...*

The bag lay next to an old beer bottle (there's always one), its drawstrings waving listlessly in the currents and the mouth hanging wide open. A little of the contents had spilled out already. Revka blinked. She peered closer. "What the hay?" she muttered to herself.

Gingerly, she scooped up the bag and pulled it out of the water. It was a little one, fitting easily in the palm of her hand. She shook a little water off it, then peeked inside. No, it wasn't her imagination after all.

Back on the shore, Iyarra craned her head. "Did you find it?" she asked. "What's in the bag?"

Revka didn't answer right away. She studied the bag's contents. There wasn't much, maybe a handful, if that, but that was enough.

Reaching in, she gingerly extracted a pinch of gold dust and let it trickle through her fingers back into the bag.

* * * * *

"There they are," said Maisie as the girls returned to the worksite. She got up and stretched herself. "Y'all have a good walk?"

Revka nodded. "Pretty decent, yeah."

"Scenic," added Iyarra.

"Well, that's fine." She nudged Tommy with her hoof. "All right, folks, let's get back to it. Gotta see about covering them walls."

A stack of wide, wooden planks had been hauled to the site. The afternoon was spent cutting them to size and nailing them into place, all along the outside. They divided into two groups. Maisie and Iyarra started on one wall, Tom and Gabby on another. The centaurs would get the plank into position and nail the bottom and middle points, then Revka would come along with a ladder and take care of the top. It went pretty quickly that way. By the end of the day, they had most of the walls covered, even if Revka was sore from having to haul the ladder back and forth.

"Good day's work, people," said Harry as the team got ready to head back to town. "Also, just to let you know, I'm bringin' some temporaries in tomorrow. Humans, mostly. Time to put the roof on the thing. No reflection on y'all, but they really are better for scramblin' up there with the ladders and whatnot."

"No objection here, boss," said Maisie. "They can have it, for all I care. Ain't that right, fellas?"

"No kidding," Tommy said. "Keep my hooves on the ground, you know?"

"Yep," added Gabby.

"All right. Well, that's all. Meet at the warehouse tomorrow so we can haul the roofing stuff over. See you then."

* * * * *

The evening went by quietly. There was a fight at Mactingle's again, but tame compared to the one the night before. Revka told some of her favorite stories, which went over well with the rest of the group. The girls headed back to the inn in good spirits and made an early night of it.

Revka dreamed of a river of gold flowing through an otherwise empty landscape. Then it wasn't a river anymore, but the vein inside a giant monster. The dying beast lay on the ground as its body turned to stone. Revka stood on top of the stone. The golden river returned, and she could see where it flowed.

Later, when she woke up, she tried to remember what she had seen, but it wouldn't come back at all.

Chapter Sixteen

THE GIRLS WERE UP at the crack of dawn, just in time to catch the last bit of evening coolness burning away. The crew met at the warehouse, where another group was waiting for them. Half a dozen humans were lounging around a cart loaded with supplies. Revka went over to Maisie and nodded her head toward the other humans. "Those the roof guys?"

"Ayup," she said. "They're kinda the resident specialists around here, if you see what I mean."

"Oh?"

"Yeah," said Tom. "They like, just do roofs and that's it."

"Well, not *just* roofs," said Maisie. "I mean, any kinda ladder work, but yeah, mostly roofs."

Revka gazed over at the other cart. The crew was leaning against the cart, generally doing a lot of nothing. Occasionally, one of them would say something, but mostly they kept to themselves and silently waited. "Friendly bunch."

Tommy laughed. "Yeah, they ain't exactly much on talk. I've tried to, like, be sociable at 'em before, but it weren't any use. These guys, they even give Gabby a run for his money. Ain't that right, Gabby?"

"Ayup."

A few minutes later, Harry came out of the office. He had a brief word with one of the roof guys, then signaled for everyone to head out.

Once they got to the site, the roofing crew went straight to work. Without a word, they started unloading their cart, pulling out lumber, tools, and several collapsible ladders. By the time Revka and the others had unloaded their cart, the roofers already had their ladders up and were building supports. The six men scrambled all over the building, up and down the ladders, like ants over a half-empty bag of potato chips.

"Wow," Iyarra exclaimed.

"Tell me about it," agreed Revka. "These guys mean business."

"OK, enough gawking," said Harry. "Y'all can work on the office building while they're doing that. Revka, you OK to roof it?"

She looked at the small, squat building and nodded. "Yeah, that shouldn't be a problem."

"Great. It's all yours. Get to it, people."

The morning passed quickly, the office being pretty far along and not much more than a glorified shed in any case. During lunch, the two groups ate their lunch separately, the roofers clustered inside the almost completely covered warehouse. By the time the day was done, the building sported a brand-new, hammered-tin roof, and the crew had packed and left, all without saying a word to anybody.

Revka watched them go. "Well, I can't fault their work, but I have to admit I feel a little..."

"Slighted? Yeah." Maisie turned to the girls. "To tell the truth, I don't think they like centaurs much."

"Oh?"

"Yeah," said Iyarra. "You get humans like that, sometimes."

"Well, huh. But they seem OK with working for y'all." Revka gave the centaurs a puzzled look.

Tom rolled his eyes. "Oh yeah, they like our *money* all right. They charge enough, too, from what I've heard. Probably got paid more today than we will for yesterday *and* today."

"What, for real?"

Maisie nodded. "Yup. No kidding. They know they can put a roof on a place way faster than we can, so they can pretty much charge what they damn well please. Nice racket, if you can get it."

"You don't say." Revka looked thoughtful, then turned to Iyarra. "Say, I wonder where we could pick up a ladder around here?"

Before Iyarra could answer, Harry came strolling up. "All right, folks, day's over. Everybody head back. Iyarra and Revka? When we get back, step into the office real quick. Boss wants to talk to you. Everybody else, that's all for today. Good work."

It has been previously noted that "the boss wants to see you" is one of the three most terror-inducing phrases in any known language (the others being "How bad could it be?" and "Hey, watch this"). This is irrational and frankly unnecessary. Most bosses have to communicate with their employees on a regular basis and discuss all manner of issues, good and bad, but somehow, logic flies out the window when those words hit the ear. The brain kicks into panicked overdrive, scrambling through every possible misstep over the last six months. This reaction, irrational though it may be, is one of the great fundamental constants found among intelligent life forms. Even in distant worlds where the inhabitants have long since shed their corporeal forms, entities composed of pure intellect will frantically speculate about whether they've spent too much time on their enrichment chamber breaks, or looking at humorous cat pictures on the collective mind net (the presence of cats is also a fundamental constant of intelligent life, even on those worlds where feline life would not theoretically be sustainable. No one knows why).

The girls looked at each other in surprise. "Did he say what it was about?" said Revka, giving the time-honored response.

Harry shook his head. "Nope. Just mentioned he wanted to talk to you after work today. He didn't seem angry or anything, if it helps."

Iyarra's ears, which had lain flat at the news, untensed a little. She turned to the other centaurs. "Does he often talk to you guys?"

The crew shook their heads. "I don't believe I've ever had two words with the guy," said Maisie.

"He told me to watch where I was going, once," said Tommy. "Dunno if that helps."

Gabby just shook his head. "Nope."

"Well, huh."

Maisie smiled and patted Iyarra on the back. "Don't worry, if y'all get fired, the first round's on me tonight. Kay?"

"Oh, good," said Revka. "A win-win."

* * * * *

The sun was just beginning to sink below the mountains, when the crew trucked back into town. Revka and Iyarra broke off from the rest, promising to meet up at Mactingle's later.

The offices at T&F Mercantile were pretty quiet. A few workers were finishing up the business of the day. The girls were shown to an office in the back corner of the building, where G Findswater was in discussion with another centaur.

"Yes, all right. Just let me know when that shipment comes in, will you? If they're not on the next wagon train, there will be hell to pay."

"Yessir."

"All right, that's all." The other centaur left, and the girls were ushered in. Findswater looked blankly at them for a moment. One might imagine him to be mentally filing through the day's business. He brightened. "Ah, yes. The two ladies from before. Please sit down."

The girls sat, Revka on a short stool put there for human visitors. She folded her hands on her lap, looking across the desk at the centaur. "You, ah, sent for us, sir?"

"That's right, yes. Mr. Fleet and the others have been talking, and I understand that you have agreed to help us with our little problem."

"Your prob—? Oh, you mean the people who have been running around, dressing up as a monster and causing trouble."

"The cult, yes."

"Cult?" The girls exchanged glances. "You don't say," said Revka. "Er, we didn't know it was a cult."

"Oh yes," said Findswater. "I'm afraid I don't know much about it myself, but some of the others on the committee assure me it's been around for quite a long time. I believe Miss Roe once mentioned that it is some sort of secret society started a long time ago, possibly almost as old as the town itself. I find that rather unlikely. It seems they worship some sort of monster or something. I guess that's what that costume is all about. Anyway, it's pretty obvious they're a dangerous lot, so we really ought to do something about them."

"I see. So, er, do we have a plan?"

"Indeed. I think we'd like to go back into the cave."

"The cave? Which cave?"

"The one you tried to explore when you first came here."

"Oh, geez, that one? The freaky tunnel one with the mon...oh, I see."

"Correct. Now that we know that the monster was a fake, we should like to have another look at it. We were thinking tonight, in fact. We'll meet here at midnight. I hope that we can count on you two?"

"I..." Revka looked over to Iyarra, who just shrugged. "I guess," she said. "I mean, we've been there and all that, sure, but I mean it's just a big tunnel, after all. Do you really need us?"

"Well, we're using a small group. We want to limit this to a few people we can trust. We *can* trust you, yes?" He peered over his spectacles.

"Well, sure, but—"

"It's just that we've got to be back to work in the morning," Iyarra supplied. "May not be at our best if we've been running around all night."

"Well then," said Findswater, "I suggest you go and get some rest now."

* * * * *

"Well, how do you like that?" Revka heaved a sigh as they walked away from the warehouse.

"So, what do we do?" Iyarra trotted alongside. The sun had set behind the mountains, and the Red Valley nightlife was just rolling up its sleeves preparatory to some serious roistering.

"I dunno. Do you think we should tip them off?"

"Uhm, might be a good idea. I mean, if we're really working for Eris and all, only..."

"What?"

"How do we? I mean, we don't have any contact information for any of them, do we?"

"Oof. Yeah, that is a problem. Well, maybe we could, I dunno, run out there real quick?"

Iyarra snorted. "I beg your pardon? Run out to the place that's an hour away, in the dark, and get back again so we can do it again in a few hours?"

"Okay, forget that. Uhm, think, think, think...we don't know any of the people in the group, do we? I mean like their actual names or anything?"

"Well, there was that one guy, Phil."

"Oh yeah, Grumpy. Don't know his last name, though, do we?"

"Don't believe so, no."

"Well, that's no good. Can't just go door to door like, 'Hi, anyone here in a secret society and named Phil?' Can't see it working."

Iyarra snapped her fingers. "Oh!"

"What?"

"We do know someone."

"Do we?

"Oh, yes."

"Well hello, girls!" Patsy beamed as she ushered the girls into the lounge. "So good to see you again. Just come right on through." She escorted them through the lounge and into the kitchen, away from prying ears. "I don't think there's a meeting tonight," she said. "I mean, unless y'all ain't here on business?" She gave a knowing grin.

Revka shook her head. "Look, we have to get a message to the group. It's kind of important. Is there a way to do that?"

"Oh!" Patsy furrowed her brow. "Well, I could pass the message on to Madam. I suppose she could get the word to them, maybe. That's probably y'all's best bet if it's urgent."

"Okay. Great. Will you please let her know to tell them that there is a group going out to explore the cave tonight around midnight? It's the one where we first saw the beast. They'll know what we mean. Just...make sure they don't find anything, right? Or anyone."

Patsy nodded. "All right," she said. "I'll go right up and take care of it." She patted each girl on the arm. "You just head on out, and I'll make sure she gets the message." She escorted the girls back out of the kitchen, down the hall, and through the lounge. "All right, ladies," she trilled, "thank you both for coming by, hope to see you again soon."

Outside, the girls began the walk back to the main road. "What do you think?" asked Iyarra.

"Dunno." Revka shrugged. "Maybe it'll work. I hope so. In any case, it's out of our hands now, unless you have any other ideas?"

"Sorry, nothing, no."

"All right." Revka took a deep breath. "Then I suggest we head over and let the gang know we weren't fired, grab a quick bite, and get some sleep. I have a feeling it's going to be a long night."

* * * * *

Midnight.

A crescent moon hovered over the valley. Iyarra and Revka approached the offices of T&F Mercantile. A few others, all centaurs, were milling around in front of the building and talking in low whispers. One of them saw the two approach and came forward to intercept them.

"Hello ladies," Fleet drawled. "Thank you for joining us this evening. Do you have everything you need?"

"I guess?" Revka shrugged. "Couple torches, flint and tinder, that sort of thing."

"Also brought some snacks." Iyarra fished out a paper bag, holding it up.

"Uh-huh." Mr. Fleet smiled. "Well, that's all very nice, but I was referring to weapons and such. You got any?"

"Oh. Er," Revka patted her belt pouches. "Don't think I have anything heavy on me, no."

"We didn't think people used weapons around here," supplied Iyarra. "Code of the... Well, you know."

"Oh, *that*." Mr. Fleet chuckled. "Well, it's true enough we observe a certain etiquette when it comes to fighting in these parts, but as this is an...unofficial sort of thing, I think we can set the rules aside. Have you got anything at all?"

"Well," said Iyarra, "I think I have my small daggers in my bag. Hang on." She rummaged about and took out two thin, sharp stilettos. "Revka, you need one?"

"Yeah, if you don't mind." Revka took the proffered weapon and tucked it carefully in her belt. "Okay, we're good."

"Fine, fine." Mr. Fleet rubbed his hands together. "Well now, let's be on our way, everyone. Make sure your glow lamps are open. Does everyone have a posse buddy?" There was a chorus of yesses. "All right. Let's get moving."

Revka hoisted herself onto Iyarra's back and gave the centauress a pat. "Ready."

Iyarra nodded and fell into line behind the others. A procession of dim, blue lights snaked its way out of the town and into the surrounding darkness. Up ahead, the mountains were a jagged line of black against the star-filled sky.

Chapter Seventeen

THE POSSE SNAKED A silent path across the desert night. There was little enough moonlight, so the stars were in full force, blanketing the cloudless sky above them. There was no sound but the tread of hoof upon ground and the occasional snatch of conversation. After the heat of the day, the coolness that came with night was welcome. Really, if it weren't for the all-pervading feeling of terror, it would have been quite nice.

As they made their way across the empty desertscape, Revka tried to reason with Fleet. "So, this cave. It's the same one we were in before. Right?"

Mr. Fleet nodded. "That's right, yes."

"The one with all the scary legends about it."

"That's the one."

"The one where those people were hiding out."

"Yep."

"People who are probably, for example, really desperate and determined to do whatever it is that they're after? Possibly to the point of violence?"

"That's how I figure it."

"And, knowing this, that is where we are going."

"You got it."

Revka sighed. She tried another tack.

"Okay," she said, "but surely they've found out we know it was a costume, right?"

"Yes?"

"Which means they must realize we're on to them, right?"

"Probably."

"In which case, I can't imagine they stuck around. Probably hot-hoofed it out of there as soon as they could."

Mr. Fleet sighed. He reached up to rub his temples for a moment, then turned to the girls. "Listen, I know you ain't fond of this whole idea, and I guess I can't blame you after what happened last time, but I'll be danged if I'm gonna let myself be scared off from that cave ever again. I don't believe they were in there playing monster for the fun of it. They were hiding something, guarding it. And I aim to find out what it was. Now, are you with me or not?"

"All right, all right," said Revka, "we're with you. What the hell, we're already out here anyway. No sense in turning back now, right?"

"Darn right." He smiled at them. "Now listen, there ain't no shame in being afraid. I'll tell you one thing; nobody here is looking forward to this expedition. Anyone who grew up around here spent their life hearing tales about the caves around here, but the way I see it, those stories are spread just to keep us out of there. Which means that there's something in there worth knowing about. I'm not leaving until I know what it is." The blue light from the glow lantern caught the gleam in his eye. "I'll go in alone if I have to, but I'm going in. All the way."

The group marched on in silence, the mountains drawing ever closer. In the darkness, they looked like giant jagged teeth frozen in the middle of devouring the sky. Revka found herself glancing upward to look for another set coming down.

The wind stirred just the faintest suggestion of noise, like a storm far away. Revka felt her stomach begin to knot up and felt Iyarra's muscles tensed beneath her. All around them, the group got quiet. Even the sporadic attempts at conversation had petered out. Everyone just kept moving forward, lost in their thoughts.

By the time they came up to the very foot of the mountains, the moan of the wind coming from the cave mouth was fully audible. Was it Revka's imagination, or was it louder than before? In the dark it seemed so, and even more eldritch. She remembered what Mr. Fleet had said the first time they came out, but somehow it just didn't sound like mere wind. It was too...bestial.

A few minutes later, they stood peering into the cave's mouth. The howl had an unnatural quality. Revka could almost imagine there was more than one voice, groaning like the souls of the damned. The gooseflesh on her arms stood up. All around her the others fidgeted and pawed at the ground, their tails flicking nervously.

Mr. Fleet cracked his knuckles. "All right. We're here, people, and we're going in. Tucker, you and Mason guard the entrance in case someone shows up. Anybody does, you holler, got that?"

The two centaurs sagged with relief. One of them nodded. "Oh, you don't have to worry about that, boss."

"All right. I'll go ahead and take the lead. Rest of y'all just file along. Ladies, you can take up the rear or be up front with me, your choice. There may be nothing there, but there may be some of the cult people in there waiting for us. So, it's up to you I guess."

Revka and Iyarra looked back at each other. "I think," said Revka, "We'll guard our rear flank, if it's all the same."

Fleet chuckled. "All right. Don't blame you." He turned toward the mouth of the cave, squaring his shoulders. "Okay," he said to himself. With only the slightest hesitation, he began to walk into the dark tunnel. The rest of the group fell in line behind him.

It was just as Revka remembered it. They made their way along the tunnel in single file, no one talking at all. A steady stream of air blew past them, even as the moan from the mouth of the cave faded away.

The others in the group muttered to themselves when the path started to climb. Someone began to whimper until Mr. Fleet turned and shushed them.

The rest of the climb proceeded in silence, every member of the group occupied with what might be waiting for them around the next turn. Revka tried to remember as much of the previous expedition as she could. They had wound around the tunnel. There had been the smell of sulfur, and they'd come into the big chamber. She shivered. Somehow, knowing it was a costume didn't make it any better. She leaned forward to Iyarra and tapped her on the shoulder.

"What?" Iyarra whispered.

"Remember last time?" Revka whispered back. "You said there was a smell of sulfur. Do you smell it now?"

Iyarra shook her head. "Not so far," she replied. "But I don't think we're quite where we were yet."

"OK, just let me know if you do."

"You got it."

A few minutes later, Mr. Fleet stopped and held up a hand. He gestured to the closest person behind him to step up and whispered something in his ear. The centaur moved back to the next member of the group and passed the message down. "Air changing up ahead. Shutter your lamps and get your weapons ready. We're going in."

The group moved together as close as the narrow tunnel would allow. They turned the sharp corner that Revka remembered from the last time, and slipped into the chamber as quietly as they could.

It was empty. Revka nudged Iyarra, who took a couple of steps farther into the room. Revka unshuttered her glow lamp and took a good look around. Yes, it was the same place they had met the monster. The sickly blue glow as the others opened their lamps was all too familiar. She pursed her lips, pacing it out. *Yes, we would have been right here, and the beast...*

She pointed. "It was right here. We came round that corner. There was some sort of noise, and there it was." The spot was bare now, just an empty stone floor betraying not the slightest evidence of anyone or anything ever having been there.

Mr. Fleet peered. "Interesting. They were probably igniting some glow tubes. That would have been the sound. So, what happened then?"

"Well, it made this horrible roaring noise and pointed at us, and then we just kind of..." Revka trailed off.

"We ran away," Iyarra supplied.

"Yes, Iyarra. Thanks."

Mr. Fleet chuckled. "Well, I can't say as I blame you. Probably would've scared the apples out of anyone. So, you didn't get past this point at all?"

"No, sir."

"Which means you didn't get to see the other room?"

Revka looked. Sure enough, on the opposite end of the chamber was an opening into another space. She and Iyarra looked at each other in surprise. "Er, no," she managed. "It must have escaped our notice."

Mr. Fleet nodded. He led the way, the others slipping in after him.

This room was...well, for a start, it was not a room. It was the bottom of a deep shaft, ten paces across and almost perfectly round. Above, an opening let in the stars and the cool night air. All the way around the walls were symbols. Some were carved deep into the rock, some painted with ochre or long-faded suet. Over these, someone had painted new glyphs, apparently using the same glowstone paint that had been used with the beast costume. The eldritch characters wound their way up the wall and over a fair amount of the floor.

In the middle of the floor, inside a design of several shapes nested inside one another and more incomprehensible glyphs, there stood a large stone. It was clearly not a part of the mountain, for it was perfectly black and smooth as glass. The stone was about half Revka's height, and long enough for her to lay out on. Something about it nagged at her mind. *Something familiar...*

Mr. Fleet paced around the chamber, frowning. "So, this is what they were guarding. Well. I don't like this at all. Anybody got an idea about these signs?"

There was a general consensus that they were completely unfamiliar. Fleet took out a notebook "Well, guess we'll have to check around. I've got a couple of people who are good at book stuff. Let me just jot some of these down."

He worked his way around, studying the glyphs on the walls and copying them down. Revka could feel the tension in the room; everyone seemed to be on edge. The other centaurs milled around, carefully making sure not to step on any of the painted parts of the floor. Revka wondered how long they were going to stay there.

She sidled up to Iyarra and gave her a nudge. "Smell anything?" she whispered.

The centauress shook her head. "No chance, not with the wind, you know."

"Oh, right." Revka slouched around the room some more, looking for something, anything familiar. The symbols that decorated the walls and the floor had a vaguely sinister, occultish air to them. She wondered if it was a real language. If so, it was pretty clear that someone had designed it specifically for writing eldritch warnings, dire curses scrawled in one's own blood, that sort of thing. It wasn't the kind of language you could imagine someone using for, say, a muffin recipe. Certainly, you wouldn't want to try any baking that came from those markings.

The giant stone block in the middle kept drawing her attention. Something about it bothered her. It wasn't just black. It was almost...she shook her head. She was being silly. Still...

Revka moved back to Iyarra and unhitched the glow lamp. Treading carefully so as not to step on the painted symbols, she got right up close to the block. Even without touching the surface, she could feel the coldness coming off it. She held the lamp up to one side and peered.

"Well, there's a thing," she said quietly.

One of the other centaurs looked up. "What's that, now?"

"No reflection," said Revka. "This thing looks perfectly smooth, but no light reflects on it at all. In fact..." She moved the lantern back and forth a couple of times. "Okay, that is just weird. Look."

She moved aside, then brought the lamp back and forth a couple more times for the others to see. Each time the lamp was brought closer to the block, it dimmed. Not much, but enough to notice. She swung the lamp back, and the light resumed its ordinary glow.

"Good grief," said Iyarra. "How does that...I mean, what even *is* that?"

"Search me, but I ain't touching it, that's for sure." Revka backed away a step.

Mr. Fleet stood quietly, studying the block. He put his notebook away and opened his glow lamp. A double handful of crushed glowstone gave off their blue-white light. He pinched a few granules out of the light and tossed them onto the block. The fragmented rocks rattled across the top of the stone, their lights dimming almost immediately. In a matter of seconds, they were completely dark.

Mr. Fleet turned to one of the others. "Clem? You got a stick or something you can knock them off there with?"

The centaur nodded and fetched out a long-bladed knife, which he carefully used to shove the pebbles off the stone and onto the ground. He picked a few of them up and handed them back over to Mr. Fleet. Their light did not return.

Mr. Fleet frowned at the small stones cupped in his hand. "Very curious. Very curious indeed." He put them away carefully, then looked around. "I think we've seen all we can here. It's clear they were guarding this, though heaven only knows why. In any case, I have a feeling they won't be back."

He yawned. "Let's get a move on back home, folks. It's been a long one. I don't know about the rest of you, but I gotta get right back at it tomorrow. Let's git."

The group filed out of the room and down the spiraling passage. They moved quietly, not out of fear of detection anymore, but with each member of the party absorbed in their own thoughts. It seemed they had found more questions than answers, and heaven only knew what questions *those* answers would lead to, assuming they ever found them.

By the time they found their way out of the cave and into the cool, desert night, the mood had lightened a little. Even the moaning of the wind didn't bother them too much. They left the cave behind, trekking across the valley to home. Up ahead, the warm glowing lights of Red Valley welcomed them. Their fear melted into the traditional after-the-fact bravado. It was just lucky for those creepy cult guys that they weren't there, by gods. Why, they'd have shown them a thing or two. Running around in dumb costumes and scaring the thungas. Boy, if they ever got their hands on those varmints, they were gonna wish they weren't never born. Damn right. Woo.

A little while later, after the men had disappeared into the night, three shadows slipped from around the rocky foot of the mountains. They peered carefully at the cave mouth, then at the valley stretching out into the night.

One said, "Was that all of them?"

A shadow nodded. "Seven went in, seven went out. We're good."

"Right." Pause. "You got the thing?"

The third one patted its robe. "Right there."

"Good, good." The first shape turned to the second. "You stay out here and keep an eye out in case they come back. We'll run up and put it back."

"Will it be all right?"

The first shadow looked up at the night sky. "Well, we waited until after sunset, and we've got a while till sunrise. Yes, we should be fine." It hesitated, then nodded to itself. "Yes," it repeated. "We should be fine."

"All right." The second shape sounded doubtful. "If you're sure."

"It's all right, brother." The first shape patted the second one on the shoulder. "We have plenty of time."

"I just worry about what would happen if—"

"All *right*, brother. We know the stakes as well as you. Now, wait here. We won't be long."

Chapter Eighteen

THE NEXT MORNING CAME too damn early, if Revka was any judge. Long days of hard work in the sun followed by nights creeping around in spooky, glowy caves was doing nothing for either her energy level or her attitude. Fortunately, there was coffee on the boil at the office, and everyone was allowed a quick mugful before they began the trek to the worksite.

Some people were already there, and there was some sort of hubbub going on in the little site office. Harry kept going in and out on one errand after another. The group spent the morning hauling the large metal plates into the warehouse and attaching them to the inner walls. This was done using a special tarry substance that looked awful and smelled worse. The tarry stuff was slathered on the inner walls, then a metal plate would be pressed and held firmly for several seconds. After two choruses of "Don't Cry for Me, Mama, I'm Just Peeling Onions" the plate would be securely in place.

Revka eased her weight off the latest plate. "This stuff, is it really that good at sticking?"

Maisie grinned. "Try it. Give it a yank. Put your weight on it if you wanna."

"Well, okay." Revka shrugged. She gripped the edge of the plate with her fingertips and tugged. The plate didn't budge. She tried to get a better grip, but it made no difference. She brought a leg off the ground, hanging sideways for a moment before she dropped away.

"Wow, that stuff really sticks. What is it, anyway?"

There was a sudden chill in the atmosphere, one of those moments of conversational awkwardness that can throw a whole discussion off the rails. The centaurs looked at her like someone who had just wondered aloud what kittens taste like.

"Er, rule number one when it comes to glue. Never ask what it's made out of." Even Iyarra looked at her like she'd said the kitten thing.

"Especially around centaurs," Maisie added.

"We don't talk about it," Iyarra added.

Revka coughed. "Oof. Okay, sorry. Didn't know." She gave the metal plate a kick. "Well, it works, anyway." She gave the others a sheepish grin. "Shall we get back to it?"

The morning progressed smoothly, with the team getting into the flow of things. Gabby and Tom would haul the plates in and the girls would get them fastened to the walls. By the time lunch came around, they had finished the first two rows going all the way around. The plates covered the walls to a height just a little taller than Revka. They had even gotten a start on the third row, though the going was rather slow. Revka had to do most of the gluing and sticking while standing on Iyarra's back. Still, they were making decent progress, and everyone agreed they were on track to finish things up by the end of the day.

During lunch, Iyarra excused herself and wandered off to stretch her legs a bit and, as she put it, "get the glue out of her nostrils." Revka was laying out on some of the rocks to catch a bit of sun before retreating to the darkness of the shed. She was just beginning to doze a bit when Iyarra tapped her on the shoulder. "Psst."

Revka opened one eye. "Hm?"

Iyarra tilted her head in the direction she had come from.

Revka lifted her head a little, furrowing her brow. "Huh?"

Iyarra did it again, this time wiggling her eyebrows and clearing her throat.

"What? Something over there? Something on my face? Is it a bug? Oh Krep, it's not one of those big juicy ones, is it?"

Iyarra blew out through her lips. "Will you just come with me?" she hissed.

"Oh." Revka swung her legs onto the ground. "Why didn't you say so?"

They headed toward the small office, moving around toward the back. As they got closer, Iyarra put her finger to her lips. Revka nodded.

The two crept forward, going slow and keeping out of sight of the lone window. From inside, they could hear the sounds of conversation.

Revka concentrated but couldn't quite pick out the words. She motioned Iyarra to stay put and crawled her way over to the wall. Crouched against the back, just around the corner from the window, she held her breath and listened.

"...guarantee at least fifty for the first batch. I figure their first job will be to cut a path round the back, so we don't have to bring 'em through town. That'll make it easier to move things in and out."

There was a chuckle. "About time we had a back door to this place. Any idea when?"

"Just as soon as we give them the go-ahead. Oughta take a couple-three weeks to get 'em here. We'll have some of the boys go out and set up a camp on the outside of the valley for the initial path. There's a nice little place where you can't see it unless you're basically on top of it. Boss showed it to me once. Anyway, once the path is done, we can just route 'em straight through to here and into holding."

"Nice. Though I gotta say, fifty of 'em in that thing is gonna be kinda tight."

"Well, bear in mind, only half of 'em are gonna be in there at any one time. Between the digging and the...other stuff, we're gonna keep 'em occupied."

"Rather them than me, I'll tell you that much." Pause. "Say, who are these fellers, anyway?"

"War spoils, supposed to be. Humans captured off south somewhere. There's more where they came from too."

"That's good. I have a feeling we're gonna need 'em."

Laughter. "Yeah, I reckon the boss is gonna work 'em pretty hard."

"Well, not just that. I mean...when we actually *find* the thing..."

"Yeah?"

"Well, it might be hungry. Know what I mean?"

"Oh, man. You think so?"

"Well, it's a possibility."

There was a low whistle. "That's pretty nasty. Glad it ain't me."

"I hear ya there."

Revka's head swam. What in the world was going on? It sounded like they were going to sneak in a lot of people for...well, that was the question. Digging for gold, most likely, but there was something else going on, wasn't there...?

She crawled back over to Iyarra. "Did you hear that?" she whispered.

Iyarra flicked her ears. "Some," she whispered. "Enough."

"Okay, let's just sneak away and get back to work, pretend none of this happened. We can talk about it at home."

They crawled back the way they came, keeping down and out of view until they got back to the others. There were no shouts, no sounds of pursuit, but the girls didn't truly relax until they went back to work a few minutes later.

They were inside the big shed again, fastening more of the metal plates to the inner walls. It was rough work, and getting the plates up along the top row was unwieldy as anything, but at least it was out of the sun.

* * * * *

Harry wandered over to the building and had a quick look inside. Satisfied that everyone was busy, he hurried over to the office and went in. The brief conversation was mostly in whispers, but a passerby might have heard "that human" and "under the window," among other things. A few minutes later, one of the centaurs left the office, heading back to town as fast as he could.

* * * * *

Revka put her weight on the metal slab, standing spread-eagled and on tiptoe in an attempt to get as much leverage on the plate as possible from her position on Iyarra's back. "Is it time yet?" she called down.

Maisie held up a hand. "Just about...hang on...okay. Go ahead. Should be good." Revka pulled her hands away from the metal sheet and moved back. The plate stayed in place.

"That's it." Maisie grinned. "Hop down."

Revka lowered herself onto Iyarra's back and slid off. "Whoof." She shook her arms out. "I'm not gonna be good for anything tomorrow." She wandered to the middle of the room and looked around. She had to admit, space was pretty impressive. The metal plates went around all four walls and straight up to the roof line. She put her hands on her hips and nodded. "Not bad," she admitted.

"Yeah," said Tom. "Kinda like being inside a bank vault, you know."

"Or prison," said Gabby.

The others looked at him in surprise. He just shrugged.

"Come to think of it, did they ever say *what* they're going to put in here?" Iyarra asked.

Maisie shook her head. "I think it's meant to be a tool shed, or equipment, or something. Maybe a machine room?" She trailed off. "That's what the boss said, anyhow."

"You know what I heard?" said Tom. "I heard that's just a cover story. And they're really gonna be mining for quartz. A friend of mine told me he heard they found a seam, and some people are setting up a whole mining operation right under everybody's noses. He said the government hushed it up."

Revka and Iyarra exchanged glances. "Interesting," said Revka. "We've, ah, heard something similar."

"Bet that's it," said Tom. "Gonna be a quartz mine. We should go to them and demand a cut, you know? I mean, we built the thing."

Maisie wrinkled her nose. "I don't know if that's a good idea. Maybe we oughta keep our mouths shut for the time being." She took a few steps around the large empty room, looking it over. "Though, I think I would like to talk to the boss about what exactly we're building here. I ain't at all sure we're bein' told the truth."

Revka nodded grimly. "You and me both."

"Well," said Maisie, "it can wait. For now, let's get the site cleaned up and everything put away. Getting pretty close to sunset, I reckon, and a cold drink is calling my name."

The group packed up in quick time, so they were ready to go as soon as Harry called time. On the way back, Revka let her mind wander back to the conversation they'd eavesdropped on. *So, they're bringing in lots of manual labor to work the mine. Fine. Why the secrecy? Why go to all the trouble of cutting a path out so they didn't have to go through town?*

She remembered what they'd said about war spoils. *Probably prisoners. Enemy combatants or whatever they called them. That would probably be it.* She'd heard of soldiers being enslaved if they were caught, which she supposed was better than being stabbed through the gut, but still not anything to look forward to. Thank goodness she wasn't a soldier. She didn't think she could live like that. Following orders, being marched around...

A memory tickled at the back of her mind. Hadn't there been something, a few years ago, some kind of scandal? There was...yes, there had been some lord or other, and he'd been leading his own regiment. Word got out that he was actually fielding two sets of soldiers. The first bunch was fighting the battles and so forth, but the second group was finding isolated villages and conducting raids. They'd take any food, whatever valuables were around, and pretty much all the people. Women, older children, men too old for a sword but not for a shovel. They'd cart them all off and chuck a match on whatever was left. Turned out he had been selling them off on the sly to people who needed cheap labor. There was a big stink about it, of course, but then everything had just sort of gone quiet. Revka supposed the whole thing got hushed up, and the lord probably had to go into exile, or pay a big fine, or whatever counted as punishment for those people. Maybe he had to write *I will not enslave entire villages* a hundred times or something. That sounded about right.

So. A bunch of slaves were being brought into the valley and hidden away at the camp, being put to work in the quarry—or, more likely, the mine. She couldn't imagine they'd be able to keep it under wraps forever. Surely, somebody would work it out at some point. She couldn't imagine a major industry like that making use of forced labor would go over well with the townsfolk. They'd almost certainly have something to say about it.

Around her, the group traveled on, only the occasional sporadic burst of conversation separating the long stretches of thoughtful silence.

As they neared the city, Revka noticed there seemed to be something up. A few centaurs were hanging around the back entrance to the town. There were no buildings of note out there, so no reason anybody would want to stick around. But there they were, three of them that she could see, standing by the road where a break in the split rail fencing allowed egress to the town proper.

Revka felt her hair stand on end. There was something about the situation she didn't like. Even at this distance, she caught the impression that they weren't there to pass the time of day. These men were on business. Guarding, she thought. Or waiting.

As they drew closer, she recognized the one in the middle. It was the sheriff. The two centaurs flanking him didn't look familiar, but she could see their badges glinting in the waning sun. She felt her stomach knot up. The authorities always made her nervous. It wasn't a guilty conscience—not *exactly*—just that low-grade terror anyone feels when one is suddenly confronted with members of the law enforcement community. She reminded herself that no, they hadn't been up to anything a policeman might regard as untoward for quite a while. In fact, they had been helping the law. *So, there's nothing to worry about. Right? Right.*

Now if she could just convince her stomach.

It wasn't hard to see the group coming. By the time they got to the fence, the sheriff and his men were standing in the middle of the road. He held up a hand as they approached. "Hold it, folks. Sorry about this, but Miss Revka? Miss Iyarra? Need to talk to you two."

Revka hopped off Iyarra's back and tried to make herself sound bright and helpful. "Sure, Sheriff. Got some more questions? We'd be happy to help."

"Er, yeah." The lawman coughed. "This might actually...we should go somewhere more private."

The little voice in Revka's mind whispered, *here it comes.* "Uhm, okay? I guess?" She turned to the rest of the group. "Y'all might as well go on ahead. We'll catch you later."

Maisie nodded. "A'ight. If you need help or something, send someone over to Mactingle's and we'll come a-runnin' quick."

"You bet."

Once the others had ambled down the road a bit, Sheriff Lestrange and his men guided the girls off the road. He took his hat off and rubbed his head, seemingly unsure how to begin.

"So, what exactly can we help you with?" Iyarra prompted.

"Well, it's ah...well, let me first say, you two have been mighty helpful the last few days. I mean helpin' us track down that there beast and all. An' for what it's worth, I personally got nothin' against you, whatsoever. Er, that being said..." He trailed off again, looking down at his hooves.

The girls exchanged glances. "Yes?"

The old sheriff sighed, his ears drooping somewhat. "This town...well, we're kinda traditional around here. Honestly, old-fashioned is what I'd say. And, well, we've had information that you two have been engaging in an unnatural relationship, having unlawful knowledge of each other, an' generally encouraging degeneracy. This isn't me saying it," he added hurriedly, "it's just that the laws are on the books, y'see. Once an accusation has been made, well, I gotta take you into custody until such time as an inquest can be made. You understand?"

"Are you...are you seriously arresting us?"

The sheriff sagged. "Got to," he said. "Somebody said they heard p'ticular noises of a distinctly carnal nature comin' out of your room the other night. And also, we've had reports of you both being seen entering a known house of ill repute together." He held his hands out, palms up in a gesture of helplessness. "It's not so bad as it sounds," he added. "Honestly, if you take a plea, we can skip a trial. Generally, the traditional punishment is banishment from the town, but I don't reckon you'll be wanting to stick around here, anyhow. Maybe we can get this taken care of? Nice and quiet? I don't want any trouble."

"Well," said Revka flatly. "That's good to know. You hear that, Iyarra?" She turned. "He says he doesn't want any trouble."

"Well, I certainly feel better."

The old stallion waved an arm. "Come on, the jail's that way. Burt an' Conroy here come along in case you weren't cooperative, but I hope it's not going to come to that. Er, is it?"

The women exchanged glances. Revka looked at the street, then at the two centaurs flanking the sheriff. She considered their options. It didn't take long.

She threw her hands up in the air. "No, no, it's all right. Lead on."

Chapter Nineteen

THE JAIL, TO REVKA'S surprise, was actually pretty decent. The cell was clean and relatively spacious, and there was even a window to let in sunlight. The bench wasn't the comfiest, but there were two thin, feather-stuffed pads on the floor for them to rest on, and the straw on the floor was fresh. As these things went, it was downright ritzy.

Revka slumped on the bench and reflected that she was altogether too much of an expert on jail cells. Since the time she'd left home to seek out adventure, she'd found herself hauled off to a variety of lockups by a variety of people. Sometimes it had been the good guys, sometimes it had been the bad, but somehow, people just kept wanting her to stick around.

It must be my magnetic personality.

She found herself wondering if there was any way she could put her unfortunately extensive knowledge of jail cells to some sort of financial advantage. Was there any such thing as a jail critic? Maybe she could be the first. Come up with a rating system, get her name out there a little. Could totally be a thing. *This bijou sylvanian slammer is just the thing for the mendicant wishing to spend thirty or so days surrounded by woodland splendor. The mush is unpretentious, almost jejune, but one cannot argue with the quantity. Sadly, the experience is marred by irregular service, with the slop bucket only being emptied once a week. Reservations not required.*

Her reverie was interrupted when one of the deputies arrived. "Dinner," he announced. "Got hot oats and coffee." He slid a couple of bowls of mush and two tins of hot coffee through the bars. "I'll warn ya, the coffee's kinda strong. Most of what we get in here is drunk & disorderlies, so we tend to sober 'em up as quick as we can."

"Thank you." Iyarra took her bowl.

"Yeah, thanks," said Revka.

"Don't mention it." The deputy looked around, then leaned forward. "Sheriff says to treat you two all right, at least as long as you behave yourselves. So y'all just sit tight and don't make no trouble, and everything will be just fine, okay?"

"Thanks."

"Sure thing." The centaur hesitated, then leaned even closer. "Uhm…"

"Yes?"

"Is it true? I mean, do you two really...?" He trailed off, waving his hands around vaguely.

Revka regarded him coldly. "Do we what?"

The deputy hesitated a moment, then caved. "Nothin' at all," he muttered. "Never mind." He slouched away, back to the main part of the office.

Revka glared after him. "Can you believe that guy?" she growled. "What does he expect us to do, tell him all about it? I suppose he'd like it if we drew him a picture or something."

Iyarra patted her shoulder. "Now, now. He was probably just curious, that's all. I'm sure he wasn't going to go asking for details."

Revka snorted. "Bets? I know guys like that. They'll act all concerned and stuff, but they just wanna hear all the sticky details, the creeps. And now we're crammed in here because some 'concerned citizen' couldn't mind their own damn business." She sat back on the bench, sulking.

"What a world," she muttered.

After a while, Iyarra gave her a nudge. "Hon?"

"Mm? What?"

"If you don't eat your mush pretty soon it's gonna get cold. You know you don't like it when it turns into a big lump."

"Ugh. Okay." Revka grabbed the bowl. It was already cooling down a bit, so she forced herself to get some down.

"Needs salt," she muttered.

The door to the front area swung open again. The deputy stuck his head around the corner. "Got a visitor. Ya decent?"

"Not according to some people," Revka grumped.

"Do what?"

"Never mind," said Iyarra. "We're fine. Go ahead and let them in."

Mr. Fleet strode past the deputy and stopped in front of the cell. "Ladies, ladies. I just found out about all this a little bit ago. This is just...well, I can't apologize too much, and that's the truth." He doffed his hat and gave the girls an embarrassed smile. "I talked to the sheriff, and he is sympathetic, but he reckons his hands are tied. Law's been on the books since the olden days. I don't reckon most people give a damn about it these days, but once it's brought to the attention of the police, well, they can't hardly ignore it, can they?"

"Well, somebody clearly gives a damn about it," said Revka.

"So it seems. Again, I am most awfully sorry." He studied the girls thoughtfully. "I don't suppose you can think of any particular reason

143

why someone would go after y'all? I mean other than just being a bluesnout?"

"Well," said Iyarra, "They might be worried about...er..." She cast a worried glance at Revka.

"About what?"

"Sorry," said Revka, "We aren't exactly sure who to trust just at the moment, you see? There's all these factions and secret societies running around—well, you've seen the same stuff we have, at least some of it. Maybe someone's worried about what we've found."

Mr. Fleet sucked his teeth, nodding. "That's very much a possibility," he said. "I hate to say it, but you may be right." He looked around the jail with obvious distaste. "Damn silly way to go about it," he muttered as if to himself. "Well. If that's the case, they probably just want you to get out and not come back. I'd hate to think what else they'd have in mind."

"The sheriff said it would probably be banishment, yeah."

"Sounds about right, but frankly, I don't think y'all should be kicked out of here regardless of who's scared of ya. As I recall, we're in the middle of a job, and I've got work yet for you both. You two just sit tight and keep your noses clean. I'm going to see what I can do to make things better. I know people around here. I've got a little influence, and you've got more friends than you know."

"Do we?"

Mr. Fleet smiled. His right forehoof began to scratch along the dirt floor. Without breaking eye contact, he drew a symbol in the dirt. It was a looped cross, with a bar splitting the bottom stem. The girls boggled.

"The—" Revka dropped her voice to a whisper. "You're with the...you're with them?"

Mr. Fleet didn't answer. He just swiped his hoof across the symbol, wiping it away. He gave the girls a wink. "Now then, you two just sit tight. I'm gonna go make some arrangements. Okay?"

The girls looked at each other. "Uhm," said Revka, "Okay, sure. No problem."

"Right," said Iyarra. "We'll be here if you need us. Er, well, obviously, but you know what we mean."

The centaur chuckled. He slipped his hat back on and touched the brim in salute. "I do indeed. Don't you worry now," he added as he headed out the door. "This will all be over before you know it."

A muted conversation filtered back from the front office, then the outer door opened and closed. Revka looked at Iyarra and shook her head. "Wow, the plot thickens, huh?"

Iyarra gave her a lopsided grin. "Personally, I thought it was plenty thick already."

Revka snorted. "No kidding." She wandered back to the bench and endeavored to make herself comfortable. "So, I guess we just wait, then?"

"I guess."

"Humph." She swung her legs disconsolately, staring at the opposite wall.

"Uhm, Revka?"

"Yes?"

"Speaking of things being thick?"

"Yeah?"

"You may want to check your oatmeal."

Revka looked. Sure enough, it was stone cold. The mush had congealed into a homogeneous beige lump. She tried standing her spoon up in it and was glumly unsurprised to see it stay upright.

She ate it anyway.

* * * * *

A little while later, there being nothing much else to do, she and Iyarra lay down and tried to get some sleep. This was easier said than done. Revka, in particular, spent quite a while staring up at the ceiling, wondering about who had ratted them out and why. Eventually, her tired body overruled her mind, and she managed to drop off.

A light flared in the otherwise darkened cell. She looked up with a start. There on the bench was a figure, human in shape, wearing an orange jumpsuit. The figure calmly lit a cigarette and took a deep, leisurely drag before leaning back against the cell wall.

"So," they said, "Whatta ya in for, bud?"

Revka sat up. "Eris?" she whispered. "Is that you? What are you doing here?"

The goddess chuckled. "Well, I'm not really here, not per se. This is a vision. You're still asleep. Look." She pointed.

Revka turned. Sure enough, she could see her sleeping form stretched out on one of the mats. "What do you know about that," she said quietly.

Eris grinned. "Pretty neat, eh?"

"Yes, very neat. So, what's happening?"

"Oh, I just thought I'd better drop in and see how things are going."

"Well, let's see. We've spent the last few days working in the hot sun while trying to work for both sides of this conspiracy. We've got a bunch of pieces that don't fit together and may not even be part of the same puzzle, and on top of everything else, we're in jail and about to get kicked out of town. So yeah, everything's just going great, thanks for asking."

Eris blew a stream of smoke into the air. "You see?" she said. "Perfect. You two were just what the goddess ordered."

"Perfect!?" Revka shouted. "Are you out of your *mind!?* It's a mess! We're no further than we were, everything's gone loco, and all we've got for our trouble are sore backs and sunburns. Krep!"

"Now, now. Calm down." Eris waved her hands placatingly. "You're actually doing extremely well. Believe it or not, you're further along than you think. Your quick thinking saved the key, after all."

"The key?"

"Sure. You didn't think that cave in the mountain was there for nothing, did you? That's where the key is kept. It's a kind of a...hm. You don't know what a solar battery is, do you? Well, the important thing is that the light shines down on it and it stores energy which goes into the heat si—the big black rock thing. Basically, it keeps the creature asleep and everything nice and sealed. Thanks to you, the Arcana were able to sneak it out of there before your posse showed up. It would *not* have been good for them to get their hands on it."

"Oh. Well, er, glad to hear we managed to be of help."

"Oh, undoubtedly. You've been so much help. I'm gonna let you in on a little secret. That key? It's not just a key. It's also a failsafe device.

"See, we always knew there was a chance the thing would get out one of these days. So, we got a little insurance. If Big Scary is ever successfully roused out of its sleep, we would need a way to stop it." The goddess took another drag of her cigarette and blew out a stream of smoke. The puff formed into a shape that looked like a pyramid with the tip made of some sort of smoky crystal. As Revka watched, the tip rotated clockwise, causing the four bottom corners to unfold and rotate until they were pointed upward and toward the center crystal. A stick figure of a man appeared, holding a pole. He stuck the pole in the bottom of the pyramid and brandished it like a halberd.

"If worse comes to worst, this will take the energy it's collected and concentrate it out and back. You can aim it at the beast, and it will get a nice hard blast of energy. Probably one shot won't be enough to stop it, but if you keep at it, it may at least slow it down, or even stun it. If you can do that, we can see about sticking it in the ground again or…I don't know, something. Anyway, just hold it up until the tip turns bright blue, and then aim it at the monster. Easy-peasy. Got it?"

"I…guess."

"Good. Hopefully, it won't come to that, but keep it in your back pocket, just in case. Now," she stubbed out her cigarette butt on the bench. "Time I called it a night. It's been fun, but I've got a long day ahead and so, I think, have you."

"Wait!"

"What?"

"What do we do next?"

Eris smiled. She blew a cloud of smoke into the girl's face. Revka felt herself getting woozy. The world swirled around her. She stumbled backward, falling onto the sleeping mat where her physical form still lay dozing.

* * * * *

Wake up.

Revka was snoring gently on her mat, directly under the window, when a few pebbles landed on her face. She didn't wake; she merely brushed them off with a hand.

A moment later, another handful of pebbles were dropped through the window. This time, one of them landed on an eyelid. She muttered something in her sleep and rolled onto her side.

There was another moment of waiting silence. Outside, the sound of hushed voices in discussion could just be heard. Then, a rock the size of a fist dropped through the window and directly onto Revka's ear.

"Ow!" Revka sat up, rubbing her ear. "What the hell?" She picked up the rock and studied it in mild confusion.

"Psst!"

Revka peered suspiciously toward the window. "Who's there?"

"Friends," said the voice. "We've come to help you. You're in great danger!"

Revka looked around the jail cell. "Do tell," she deadpanned.

"I mean we're here to help you! It's us, the Tex Arcana!"

"Oh!" Revka scrambled to her feet. She stood on tiptoe, peeking through the window bars. "What's up? Gonna send us a cake with a file in it?"

"What? No! Don't be silly. We're breaking you out. Now, pay attention. Are you both in the same cell?"

"Yes."

"Good. Then go ahead and wake up your friend."

Friend. Revka dutifully went over to where Iyarra was stretched out on a sleeping mat. "Psst!" She nudged the centauress. "Hey, Yarra? Hon? Wake up, the cavalry has arrived."

Iyarra looked around groggily. "Hm? Whassat?"

Revka touched a finger to the horsewoman's lips. "Shh. On your hooves, girl. I think we're about to get sprung."

That woke her up. "What? Really?"

Revka nodded. "Seems like."

"How?"

"Dunno yet. Wait here." She hustled back over to the window. "OK, she's awake. What's the plan?"

"Okay. Here's what we need you to do. First, have her get away from the wall, as far as she can."

"Er, okay." Revka turned to Iyarra. "They say move away from the wall."

"What, like up against the bars?"

"I guess." She turned back to the window. "OK, now what?"

"All right," said the voice. "You should have plenty of time, but we'll need you to put this against your side of the wall. Then you need to get away from it as well. Got it?"

"I guess, only what exactly are we—"

"Wait." The voice dropped into an urgent hiss. "What do you mean it's already lit? Oh, for... Give it here! Yes, now!" The voice returned, somewhat louder and definitely more excited than it had been a moment before. "Okay, here! Drop it by the wall and go! Go now!"

Revka watched as a red cylinder was hastily shoved through the window. Outside, she could hear the sounds of hooves galloping away at speed. The cylinder dropped into her hands. It was a curious thing, paper rolled up and plugged at both ends. A bit of black cord was burning at the end.

Revka had never seen dynamite before, but you didn't grow up in a mining community without knowing a thing or two about explosions. Her mind came to some very swift conclusions, and her hands were already throwing the thing down as fast as they could. *"Holy hell!"* She scrambled backward at top speed and didn't stop until her head banged against the bars of the cell.

Iyarra looked at the fizzing thing doubtfully. "Uhm, is that...?"

"Down!" Revka shouted. Woman and centauress hunkered down, covering their heads, just as the last of the fuse disappeared, followed immediately by most of the wall.

Revka coughed and sputtered, the smoke and the noise putting her momentarily out of sorts. She heard hoofsteps again. As the dust cleared, a small group of robed centaurs emerged amongst the rubble. "Quickly!" one cried. "Before they get here!"

Sure enough, there was a galloping commotion headed their way. As Revka staggered to her feet, the door to the cells flew open and a deputy pushed in. "Good gravy!" he shouted, and fumbled for his crossbow.

Revka grabbed Iyarra's arm and tugged. "Come on!" Iyarra seemed to clear her senses with a good head shake and scrambled to her hooves. She wobbled a bit as she headed for the gaping hole in the wall, still not entirely recovered from the blast. Revka hurried after her, glancing over her shoulder to see the deputy aim his crossbow right at them.

Revka looked around wildly and grabbed a shattered piece of the bench that was lying by her feet. It was old wood, but good and thick. As the deputy pulled the trigger, she quickly raised the broken plank in front of her. There was a dull *thunk* as the bolt lodged itself in the wood. She threw it down and leaped through the hole after the others.

Revka swung herself up onto Iyarra's back. "Okay, not quite what I expected, but under the circumstances, I'll take it."

"Sorry," said one of the hooded figures. "We had to get you out of there quickly, had no time to come up with a proper plan. Fortunately, we have access to some dynamite and a few other...well, useful items." The group galloped along back streets in the shadows of silent buildings, away from the center of town.

"Yeah, about that," said Revka. "You want to tell me why you pitched that thing into our cell? Why couldn't you blow it up on your side?"

"You mean, why didn't we cause a bunch of exploding rocks and debris to go flying into a small, enclosed space with nowhere for you to dodge them?"

"Okay, fair point." Once they'd put some distance between jail and escapees, they moved from shadow to shadow as quietly as they could. Behind them, shouting could be heard. "Er, what happens now?"

"We need to get you out of town," said one of the others. Revka thought it sounded like Babs. "Do you remember the way to the cave?"

"I think so," said Iyarra. "But you know they've been in there. All the way in, I mean. I don't think they're going to be scared away anymore."

"You're right. I'd quite forgotten." Possibly Babs was quiet for a moment. "All right. How about The Gap?"

"Oh, the maze-looking place? Hm, maybe." Revka turned to Iyarra. "Do you remember how to get there?"

The centauress furrowed her brow. "I...yeah, I think so. It's just a bit north of the cave, if I'm remembering it right."

"That's right, yes. Head there. You can hide in the maze till someone comes for you."

"All right. And what are you going to do?"

By now the shouts were getting nearer. There seemed to be more of them. "We," the first figure said grimly, "are going to keep these people occupied for as long as we can. I can't promise you much of a head start, but we'll give it the best we've got." They emerged from the shadow of a building to see the fence that marked the town limits. "We'll join you when we can. Best of luck. Now, get going."

Chapter Twenty

THE TRIP TOOK A bit longer than they expected. Finding their way across the desert at night was no picnic, even when they did have a nice big mountain range to aim for. They got to the foothills easily enough, but it took a bit of poking around, and even some backtracking, before they finally found the entrance to The Gap.

Iyarra was just about dead on her hooves by the time they found the circular labyrinth, so Revka took first watch. She hung out by the entrance and kept her eyes peeled for any sign of pursuers. Iyarra relieved her a little after dawn, and Revka headed back to the spot in the middle of the maze and tried to get some sleep.

She'd been out for a few hours when Iyarra shook her awake. "Psst! Revka! Revka!"

Revka rolled over, squinting her eyes against the sunlight. "Hm? What? What's up?"

"There's people coming! Centaurs, maybe a dozen of them!"

Revka groaned. She sat up, rubbing the sleep from her eyes. "I don't suppose they're our bunch, by any chance?"

Iyarra shook her head. "Doubt it. Looked like a posse to me."

"Figures." Revka rolled up onto her feet and started gathering up their supplies. "Do you remember if there's a back way out of here?"

"I don't remember anything about one, no."

"Crud." She looked around. "I mean, we could hide out here for a little bit, but if they split up and search all over the maze, they'll probably find us sooner or later." She frowned, looking around for ideas.

"Of course," said Iyarra, "There is that secret way out."

"The what-now?"

"You remember. The first time we came here? That one stone in the corner that took us to their hideout?"

"Oh! Right!" Revka frowned. "But we had to follow the exact path, didn't we? I'm sure I remember someone saying that."

Iyarra stepped past Revka to the perimeter of the central area. She moved to one of the openings, tilted her head a moment, and nodded. "This one," she said.

"You sure?"

"The scent trail is still there. Faint, but good enough."

"So, you can follow your own scent?"

"Well, yours actually."

Revka blanched a little and took a quick sniff at her armpit. "Oh. Ish. Well, in my defense, I haven't had a chance to wash since yesterday morning."

Iyarra laughed softly. "I didn't mean it like that. Well, mostly not like that, but I'm pretty sure I can follow the exact path. Just walk behind me and go where I go, okay?"

Revka nodded. "All right, let's—wait." She grabbed a blanket out of one of Iyarra's saddlebags, and shook it over the dusty ground, obscuring their prints. "Okay," she said. "Lead on."

Iyarra began to pace her way along the winding passages, eyes half-closed while she let her nose do the work. From time to time, she would stop at an intersection, sniffing the air some more, before she picked a direction. Revka followed along behind, obscuring their track as best she could.

They'd only been at it for a few minutes, when the sound of voices came from the center of the maze. "Yup, they've been here all right," said someone. "Spread out. Everybody take an exit. I'll stay here in case they double back. Go on!"

Revka cast her eyes heavenward. Could they *never* catch a break? She gestured to Iyarra to keep going, then rolled up the blanket as quickly as she could and dumped it on the centauress' back. No time for subtlety anymore.

Iyarra followed the trail as quickly as she dared. From time to time, they could hear the sounds of their pursuers picking their way through the maze. Any time they came to an intersection, Revka would creep forward, check the crossing passages, and signal when it was okay to proceed. There was a close call when a couple of centaurs trotted past just as they were getting ready to enter a T-junction, but they managed to slip around a back corner in time and wait until the hoofbeats could no longer be heard.

After the longest five minutes of either woman's life, they finally found their goal. Revka let out a quiet "Thank the gods," as they approached the stone disc.

Iyarra nodded. "Tell me about it. I don't want to do that again. Let's just go through the—"

"*Stop right where you are!*"

Three centaurs strode in from another passage, crossbows drawn and pointed directly at the two women. The one in the middle, who was evidently the leader, turned to another. "Elroy," he said, "you still got that rope?"

"Yassir."

"Good. Fetch it out. We'll tie these two up good an' proper so they don't get away this time."

Revka sighed. She raised her hands, very slowly. "You know, this has just been my whole day, you know what I mean? Every time I think things are going my way, *pfft*. Right into the dunny."

The leader snorted. "If you're thinkin' of trying something," he snarled, "you may as well forget it. There's three of us to two of you, and all I gotta do is holler and bring a bunch more running." He turned to the third centaur. "Block the other exit, will ya, in case they get any ideas." The centaur nodded and positioned himself at the passage they had arrived from, planting himself firmly in place and folding his arms.

"Okay, okay, nobody's gonna try anything. You found us, fair and square, but there's just one thing." Keeping her hands up, she glanced back at Iyarra just long enough to catch her eye and flick her gaze back at the stone disc.

The leader tilted his head, leery. "What exactly did you have in mind?"

"Well, I mean, we got broken out of jail, we've been on the run all night, chased by a posse, and now you've got us cornered. All very well and good. *Tres* cowboy. But something's missing, don't you think?"

"And just what would that be?"

"Well, a famous last stand, of course! I mean, what would people think? 'They blew a hole through the jail, ran all night, hid in a maze, and when they were finally found they meekly surrendered and went back?' Come on! I mean, put yourself in our place!"

"Well, I suppose you have a point."

"Point nothing!" Revka shifted her weight, moving one foot back a bit. "Why, it'd be a travesty. It would be" —She took off her hat and held it over her chest, nudging Iyarra to do the same—"against The Code of the West!"

The effect was immediate. The men doffed their hats, closed their eyes, and raised their voices high.

"*The Code of the West!* Right, now…consarn it, where'd they go? Oh, gol dang it…well don't just stand there, boys, spread out! Find 'em!"

* * * * *

The world went black. And then there was torchlight, flickering against the walls of a dark place. Two figures stood silhouetted against the light, holding silent and listening for any noise.

After a long moment, the two untensed. There were no cries, no sounds of pursuit. Wherever they were, they were far enough away that their pursuers were well and truly left behind.

Revka cricked her neck. "Okay," she said, though quietly, because she still wasn't entirely sure where they were. "I think we're safe. For now."

"Are you sure?" Iyarra scraped a hoof along the ground. "I mean, what if they come through the same way we did?"

"Can't. They didn't take the right trail, remember?"

"Oh. Right." Iyarra looked around. "So, er, where the heck are we, exactly?"

"Well, that's a good question." Revka took in their surroundings. They appeared to be in a small, circular chamber. One torchlit passage led away from the chamber. The room was empty, except for a stone circle in the middle, just like the one that had brought them there. Revka wondered if stepping on it would bring them back to the maze. Probably not the best time to find out. "Well, do you remember anything about the last time we were here?"

Iyarra shrugged. "I remember being knocked out and waking up tied, hand and hoof, with a bag on my head."

"Yeah, same here. Not exactly helpful." Revka turned to the passage leading out. "Well, nothing for it. Guess we might as well poke around a bit. Come on."

In fact, there was very little to explore. The passage went along and down, with just a few side rooms, which had been turned over entirely to storage. The rooms had the musty smell of benign neglect, the sort of place used by several people who all thought it was someone else's turn to do the washing up.

The passage led to another chamber, rather larger than the first. This room was square, about ten meters in either direction, with another, larger entrance leading off the opposite end of the room. A design of several shapes nested inside one another dominated the floor, along with a series of incomprehensible glyphs, all rendered in the eerie, luminescent blue of the glowstone. Revka paced around the markings, hands on her hips. "Well, doesn't this look familiar."

Iyarra nodded. "Same markings as in the cave, aren't they?"

"Bet my last copper."

"Well, what are they doing here?"

"I..." Revka paused, tilting her head at the markings. "Yeah, I have no idea." She wandered slowly around the runes, trying to make any sort of sense out of them. They had just enough regularity to them that you could see patterns, certain glyphs showing up more than others. She wished she was clever enough to work them out.

Something caught her eye. What had first seemed to her a bundle of rags cast off in a dark corner of the room seemed suddenly familiar. She poked at the rough canvas suspiciously. Underneath was...*ah*.

Revka fished out the old horse skull and held it aloft. "Well, well." She turned to Iyarra. "I think I just found the beast."

"Unless they just happened to have some horse skulls lying around."

"Cute, but no, I can smell the paint on it." She put it back where she found it and looked around some more. "So, they must have moved everything over here when they got the tip-off we were going to explore the cave. I wonder how they got it here." She thought about that. "Come to think of it, where *is* here? I thought maybe the thing in the maze was like a trap door, but I don't think we did any falling. Also, this place doesn't feel like a cave."

"For once."

"Hm." Revka looked at the large entrance along the far wall. She moved toward it and listened. It seemed there was the distant sound of wind coming from somewhere beyond. She motioned to Iyarra. "Wait here, I'm gonna reconnoiter." She followed the wider passage, which turned to the right after about ten paces. There were remnants of ochre paintings along the walls and a single doorway on the right. At the other end, the corridor turned to the left. She couldn't see what was beyond it, but there was possibly the hint of sunshine?

She checked the lone doorway first. It led to a small chamber, not much more than a closet. Some sacks, a couple of boxes, but nothing of interest. She moved on.

Around the second corner, the corridor opened into a larger space, more of an anteroom. A large doorway stood opposite, with a sturdy iron gate blocking the way. Through the bars, Revka could see the Tandari Mountains stretching out beyond.

The gate was new—relatively new, anyway, compared to the place it was attached to. Someone had taken a lot of effort to bolt it solidly into the stone walls so it couldn't be removed easily. They had also taken the time and trouble to wrap a thick, solid chain around the opening and fasten it with a stout lock. Revka frowned. Unlike the rest of the place, the lock was new and in excellent shape. Still, the bars were more than wide enough for her to slip her hands through, and her tools were...

Revka groaned. Her tools were back at the sheriff's office, locked away with her weapons and Iyarra's saddlebags. "Krep, Krep, Krep, bloody Krep." She hadn't even thought about it till that moment. Here they were, out in the middle of the mountains, with nothing they could do to escape or defend themselves.

She let out a moan and leaned her head against the securely fastened gate, staring glumly at the view.

A moment later, Iyarra came running around the corner in response to Revka's shout. "What's wrong?" she panted, looking around in alarm. "Is there someone here? Are we in danger?"

Revka stood next to the gate, pointing. "Look out there. Look out there and tell me what you see."

Iyarra stepped forward and peered out. "Er, let's see..." She looked out at the view, wondering exactly what she was meant to be looking for. "Well, it's the mountains. I think I see a bit of a path off on that one there, and there's a trail going down from here to..." She stopped. "Wait. Just how high up are we, anyway?"

Revka nodded grimly. "Pretty high up, by the looks of it. And that's kind of a puzzle, because when we were back at the maze, it was pretty much ground level, wasn't it?"

"Just about, yes."

"Wherever that magic-portal thingy took us, we seem to be pretty high up. The breeze is kind of cold and all, you know? Not to mention we seem to be stuck." She rattled the chain disconsolately, glaring at it.

Iyarra leaned over for a closer inspection. "New lock. Good chain, but not the strongest in the world. I could probably kick it open if there's no other way out. I mean, it would take a few tries."

"Well, let's just look around a bit more first. "There may be another way out of here. I'd prefer to keep the property damage to a minimum, if only because this is supposedly the Tex Arcana's headquarters and we've already got enough people after us as it is."

"Okay. Just say the word."

"Right."

Iyarra followed along behind Revka, who wandered back to the main room and began to pace around, thinking out loud. "Okay, we've got this ancient temple kinda place, right? And it has a magical portal to the maze back down in The Gap. Maybe it's a one-way door, maybe it's not, but if the search party is still there, I'd rather not find out just now.

We've got the big opening, which I'm assuming is the front entrance to this place. Fine. So is the magic portal a way to sneak in, or out, or both? And if there's one, maybe there's another? Maybe if we checked the rooms there might be something we can fi—yes?"

Iyarra put her hand down. "Sorry. Didn't mean to interrupt. Only, why is that thing glowing?" She pointed to the glyphs on the floor.

Stylized representations of a star were arranged every few paces and spiraled out from the center. The outermost one, which Revka had just walked over, was glowing a faint blue.

Revka peered at it, then waved her foot over it. Nothing happened. She gently pressed her foot down on the star. The light went away. The girls exchanged glances. Revka tried again. The light returned.

"Okay." She turned and followed the spiral to the next star. Sure enough, a light tap of the foot set it alight. Moving faster now, she worked her way around the spiral, lighting up star after star, coming ever closer to the center. The room took on that eldritch glow, as more and more of the stars were lit. Finally, Revka stepped on the very last one. There was a sound like a bell, and all the stars went out at once.

"Huh." Revka looked back at the room. "Well, that was a bit anticli—"

Iyarra heard the thrum of machinery and sensed movement far below. The circle in the middle of the room began to glow. New symbols appeared on its surface, throbbing intensely in time with the noise. Iyarra sighed theatrically. "It's another magic-portal thing, isn't it?"

"Looks like."

"And we're going to go through it, aren't we?"

Revka grinned. "Certainly."

"Sure we can't just take our chances with the posse?"

"Oh, come on, where's your spirit of adventure?"

"I think the sheriff confiscated it."

Revka walked over and took her hand. "Come on, we'll go in together."

"All right, all right. But if we come out in a bottomless pit or something, don't say I didn't warn you."

Revka chuckled. "Fair enough." The two of them stepped forward until they were at the border of the glowing circle. They exchanged nods, then stepped into the circle together.

There was darkness and a stomach-twisting moment of vertigo. The world began to resolve itself around them, glowing blue runes in a sea of empty blackness. Slowly, details began to resolve themselves. The cylindrical walls, the markings on the floor. They looked up. Sure enough, daylight could be seen high above them where the top of the mountain opened up. "The cave," Revka said. "We're back in that weird cave."

"And it's about time, too," said a voice. "I was starting to wonder if you were going to make it."

Chapter Twenty-One

THE GIRLS TURNED AROUND. Behind them, leaning casually against the entrance to the central chamber, was Mr. Fleet.

Revka let out a breath. "Good grief. Am I ever glad to see you! You would not *believe* the day we've had."

The centaur just chuckled. "Oh, I think I would at that. Been a busy day for all of us, but I do reckon we can pull this one out of the fire yet. You two all right?"

"Yeah. We got to the maze, and we were able to work out how to use the secret entrance again. Unfortunately, the main way out of the temple was locked, so..."

"Yep." Mr. Fleet beamed. "That's about how I figured it. When you two went missing from The Gap, I kinda put two and two together. Did send a couple of the boys up to the temple though, just in case, but I had a feeling you'd find your way here." He buffed his nails up and down his waistcoat. "What can I say? I am, by nature, a pretty good guesser."

"Well, I just hope we didn't keep you waiting too long!" Iyarra gave a friendly smile.

Mr. Fleet laughed. "Naw, no problem at all. As a matter of fact, I was just admiring this fascinating thing." He pointed to the center of the black stone and a pyramid made of some sort of transparent, blue material, capped with an opaque, silvery tip. Revka peered closer. "It looks like a crystal, but the insides are really complicated." Infinite pulses of light flickered through the shape, rainbow hues flashing up and down its length.

"The key," she breathed.

Mr. Fleet tilted his head. "How's that, now?"

"It's the...well, since we know you're one of them, we might as well tell you. It's a key. It, like, takes the sunlight and puts it into the block, and that keeps the big monster asleep. Or something."

"Ya don't say." He stepped forward and took a closer look. "And how did you come by this information?"

Revka grinned weakly. "Would you believe divine revelation?"

Mr. Fleet laughed. "Fine, I won't ask, but I think we'd better bring it with us." He reached toward the key, then hesitated. He turned his hand and brushed the back of it lightly against the pyramid.

"Just a little warm," he said. "That's all right." Carefully, he removed the key and wrapped it up in his coat, which he carefully stowed in one of his saddlebags.

"All right," said Revka, "what happens now?"

"Now, you two come with me. This is not a safe hideout. The temple should be—hardly anybody even knows it exists, anymore—but that was a one-way door. I don't reckon you feel like going all the way back. Fortunately, we've got somewhere we can hide you. Nobody there except trusted folks. I told the others to meet us there."

He wandered into the central chamber, looking up at the long arc of sunlight that stretched most of the way down the sheer wall. "Let's see...yes, we should be able to get there well before dark. Come on, now. Reckon we'd better get a move on."

* * * * *

The three of them wound their way down the tunnel. Revka sat on Iyarra's back, thinking. The past day had been a bit of a blur. What with one thing and another, she hadn't had a chance to puzzle it all out. There seemed to be some breathing room now, once they got to wherever it was they were going. At least they were going to have somewhere decent to hide out. Good thing they had a few allies this time around.

Although...

Revka raised a tentative hand. ""Er...say, Mr. Fleet, sir?"

"Yes?"

"How did you know we were going to show up here? I mean, how did you know there was a...I dunno, a magic doorway from the temple to here? When we were with you before, and we explored this place, I kind of got the impression you'd never been here before."

Mr. Fleet laughed. "Well, I swear you are sharp. As a matter of fact, I hadn't been here before. I knew bits and pieces. Knew about the temple of course, and that there was a way into the heart of this place. It was used for some sort of ceremonials back in the olden days, though nobody comes here anymore."

He turned back at the girls and grinned. "Between you and me, I've been kinda itchin' to have a look at this place, ever since I found out about it. The stuff with the beast was just a good excuse to head up and have a lookie-loo."

"Ah. Right." Revka fell silent and sat back, lost in thought.

Shortly afterward, they emerged from the mouth of the cave. Two of the other centaurs who always seemed to follow Mr. Fleet around were there, standing guard and not looking particularly happy about it.

"All right boys," he said. "Turns out my hunch was correct. Let's shake some legs and we can get there by sunset."

"By the way," said Revka as they started off, "you never did say where we're going."

"Just a safe place," said Mr. Fleet. "Don't worry, it ain't too far. And the sheriff and his folks won't bother you there. We should get going, all right? We'll talk more when we get there."

They began to follow the line of mountains due south, running parallel with them all the way along. The trail was rough until they moved away from the foothills. When the going was sufficiently smooth, they moved along at a brisk trot, not exactly in a hurry, but keeping a decent pace.

The sun was just slipping behind the mountains as the group rounded a scrub-laden hill and found themselves in familiar surroundings. There was the big storage shed they'd spent the last week on, and the much smaller office. Off in a corner was a pile of scrap lumber left over from the building projects. They'd arrived at the job site, the quarry, or mine, or whatever it was supposed to be. *Well, that makes sense. If Mr. Fleet is a secret member of the Tex Arcana, then it only makes sense that Findswater might be too.*

Something about that tickled at the back of her brain. Something that had happened the day before, to do with the office. What had she—

"How-*dee!*" Mr. Fleet called, doffing his hat and fanning himself with it. "We're here, y'all. Told you I'd find them!"

The door to the office opened and out came Findswater himself, flanked by Mr. Tarran and Mrs. Wildberry. They stepped toward the group, their expressions disconcertingly blank. Mr. Findswater came up to Mr. Fleet, nodding curtly.

"Indeed you did," he said. "I must confess I am surprised, but I should probably know by now not to underestimate you, yes?"

"Ha! Well, I was a lucky guesser this time, that's all." He smiled and turned to Iyarra and Revka. "Ladies, I believe you remember our friends from the Citizens Protection Committee. I believe everybody's been introduced. Anyhow, I reckon we can have you folks here nice and safe till we need you later. Don't worry about a thing. Got a couple of mattresses set up for ya, and a fair amount of chow, should be more than enough. After you." With a sweeping bow, he gestured the girls toward the big storage building. Something about it pricked at Revka's memory.

"Doors," she said. "You've added the doors."

"Yup. I believe the crew finished 'er off today while you two were, *aheh*, otherwise engaged." He chuckled and rubbed his hands together. "Just in the nick of time, too. I don't mind telling you, I was getting kinda worried, but things do usually work out in the end, I find. Don't you?"

Revka and Iyarra exchanged glances. "Uhm," said Iyarra, "you want us to go in there?"

"That's right ladies, off you go."

The centauress eyed the dark interior dubiously. "Uhm, I'm not super good with confined spaces," she said.

Revka regarded the opening to the windowless building. The feeling that had been gnawing at the back of her mind since their arrival was really clamoring now. Things were starting to come together, and she did *not* like the picture they were making. Still, maybe she was wrong. Maybe.

Revka turned back to the others and put on a bright smile. "What my colleague here means," she said, "is that she's more suited to wide-open spaces and suchlike. Sitting in a place with no windows or anything isn't what you'd call conducive to rest and recuperation. I'm sure, as fellow centaurs, you can entirely understand. I think, maybe, we might bed down in the office instead, if that's all right? At least it has windows."

"Oh, I don't think that's gonna work out for us." The grin was still there, but there was no friendliness behind it. The others moved closer, fanning out a bit. "Y'see, that really wouldn't work well with our plans at all. And we do have plans, yes indeed we do. As I mentioned before, we've got more work for you two, and it does pretty well necessitate keeping you where we can get to you when we want you."

A memory flashed in Revka's mind. "This isn't any kind of warehouse," she said quietly. "It's a holding pen. Just like we heard them talking about yesterday."

Some of the others muttered darkly at this, but Mr. Fleet only spread his arms wide. "You see?" he said, "I knew y'all was clever! Figured it right out, didn't ya? Yup, we're gonna have a lot of folks coming in through here if all goes according to plan. I mean, it's gonna be pretty crowded once we get 'em in, but that's nothing you'll have to worry about. You'll be long gone by then," he added.

Iyarra leaned down to Revka. "Sorry," she whispered. "What exactly is happening? I think I'm a little lost."

Revka nodded her head toward the others. "We haven't been rescued," she said grimly. "We've been captured."

"Oh, I was kind of hoping that wasn't it. Darn."

"I guess they must have found out we overheard their plans yesterday." She turned back to Mr. Fleet. "Must have thrown you into a panic, sending someone up to town to have us locked up."

"Oh, that." Mr. Fleet chuckled. "Yeah, that was a mistake. I can put my hand up that I had nothing to do with it, though. Young Mr. Findswater here got word as to how Harry had seen you two hangin' outside the office, and he did kind of jump the gun. 'Course, as soon as I found out, I told him right off. Say you're sorry, G."

The younger centaur snorted. "Yes. Fine. Sorry."

"But one thing puzzles me," said Iyarra. "Why would you blow us out of jail, only to drag us back here? I mean, it seems like a real waste of time, not to say dangerous."

"Wait, you think...?" Mr. Fleet suddenly burst out laughing. "Oh, bless your heart! That wasn't us! That was those idiots in the Arcana. A fine mess they made of things, too, I can tell ya. I mean, I was just gonna get the sheriff to remand you into my custody, is all. Can't imagine what they were thinking, blowing up the jail like that."

"Wait. 'Those idiots in the Arcana?' But aren't you...I mean, you knew the sign and everything!"

Mrs. Wildberry spoke up. "You don't have to tell them, Everett. Just toss them in the pen and we can get back to town."

Mr. Fleet held up his hands placatingly. "Now, now. The ladies are confused, and understandably so. I reckon we've got them where we want them now, so no harm in explaining what's what." And now, his smile had morphed into a cruel smirk. "Besides, I want to make sure these two understand the crucial role they are to play.

"So, ladies, it's like this. Yes, I was a member of the Tex Arcana. Or rather, we all were." He swept an arm back toward the others. "Our little citizens committee, you understand. We're what you might call a breakaway sect.

"You see, the Arcana has always been central to the history of the town, and, as such, the society has been made up of the founding families, what you might call the core citizens. Our families have been shepherding this town along since day one. Not just keeping watch over that big creature that's buried down in the mountains, but doing what we can for the benefit of our beloved community, as well.

"Now, along about...I want to say it was around twenty years ago? That sound about right, folks? Yeah. About twenty years ago, there was a bit of a disagreement in the ranks. We were starting to get traffic in from the trading routes, people heading west to The Great Rift. People who needed somewhere to rest, store their wares, maybe do a little buyin' and selling. People were starting to notice our little valley.

"Now, *some* people were a bit worried about this. They favored keeping a low profile. The last thing they wanted was more people running around poking and prodding the way some folks do. They were worried that someone would go and wake the beast up—not that silly costume, you understand, the big one. The *real* one. Some of them even wanted us to close the town off to outsiders, altogether. Now can you imagine that?

"However, some of the more, ah, forward-thinking members of the group began to talk amongst themselves. This was Red Valley's chance to get big. I mean big. A center of trade? Crossroads of the west? Do you know what that can do for a town? And once you get trade coming in, you get people. And when you get people, you get culture. And when you have that, then you get *influence*."

Mr. Fleet was pacing back and forth now, in full monologue mode. "And then we said to ourselves, how do we do it? How do we make that happen? And then we remembered. We have a god. A literal god, stuck underground and snoring the centuries away. Why? Why leave all that power to waste? Why have your very own captive god and not put it to use? I mean, that'd be like having your own gold mine and never picking up a shovel."

"Gold mine!" Revka exclaimed. "Of course! You had Stumpy dump that gold dust into the water so others would think there was gold in the mountains."

Fleet's brow furrowed. "Stumpy? Oh! You mean our friend, Jake. Well, I don't know how you know about that, but yes indeed, you hit the nail on the head. You'd be amazed how many people in town have sunk a little money into what they're sure is a gold mine, but of course, all of us here know we've got something better than gold down there, yes indeed."

He stopped and looked over the girls appraisingly. "You know, I am beginning to have second thoughts about the two of you. I mean, you are pretty goldang clever, and quick on the uptake to boot. Decent fighters, good at improvising. I'm starting to think I should give you two ladies the opportunity to join in our little endeavor. We can always use more capable hands around here. I reckon you two are more than accustomed to getting your hands dirty. I tell you what, maybe we can talk it over and see where things lead. There's a future in it for you. We got dental."

"Yeah," said Revka, "I don't think—wait, you got dental? Really?—I mean, no. No. I'm sure it's a great deal and all, but I don't think we'd be a good fit for the job."

"Yeah," said Iyarra. "We kind of have a thing about any job that involves waking up ancient gods. It's nothing personal."

"Oh, I think you should hold off before you give a definitive answer. I mean, given the alternative and all. You see, you already know too much about our little operation. We can't let you wander around. Heaven only knows who you might talk to. So if you can't be of use to us, well, then at least we can make sure you aren't in the way."

"You're crazy," said Revka. "There's no way you can get away with this. When people find out—"

"Find out? What's there to find out? A couple of drifters came into town, got in trouble with the law, and split. End of story as far as most people are concerned. Nobody's gonna look for you. In a couple of days, they'll probably forget you were ever here and assume you ran off into the desert. Now, I'm not saying I can definitely square things with the law if you decide to take me up on my generous offer, but I guaran-damn-tee that if you don't, nobody is ever going to see either one of you again."

Revka sighed. She tried again. "All right. But look, even supposing you do wake this thing up with whatever ceremony you have in mind, how do you know it's not going to just turn around and squish you? Gods are not exactly known for being easy to work with."

"Your concern for our well-being is touching," said Mrs. Wildberry. "I assure you that we have been researching the binding and channeling of gods for a very long time. Quite a lot of it was from our training as part of the Arcana, though they hardly understood the value of what they taught us."

"Sister Wildberry is correct," said Mr. Fleet. "We didn't just jump into this thing yesterday. We've been putting the pieces together ever since the split. You just happened to come in when we were about to make it happen. I guess you're just lucky that way."

"Yeah," Revka grumped. "Lucky old us."

"Well, I think that ought to do it for now. I'm sure you'll have other questions later, but they can wait. I don't know about you two, but I have had a heck of a long day." He turned to the two henchmen by his side. "Go on, get them in there."

Revka and Iyarra were marched at crossbow-point into the holding pen. "We'll be along tomorrow, sometime," Mr. Fleet called after them. "Probably in the evening. I hope it ain't too hot for you in there. We'd have put in some ventilation but, well, you can't have people getting in and out all the time. Just try and stay cool till we get back. There's plenty of water so you don't dehydrate, and a bucket in the corner. I'm sure y'all know the drill by now. Boys?"

The doors swung shut in unison, coming together with a metallic clang that echoed through the empty building. There was the sound of chains, then hoofsteps, then only silence and the barest slivers of light pushing through the cracks in the darkness.

Chapter Twenty-Two

SEVERAL HOURS PASSED. THE gold of the daylight coming through the seams of the building moved to crimson, then darkness. All around them was the chilly silence of the desert night.

Revka sat in a corner near the doors, gnawing on some jerky. "Well, this is pretty ironic."

Iyarra looked up from one of the sleeping mats. "What is?"

"Oh, all of this." Revka swept an arm around the room. "I mean, we spent the last week or so building this place, only to find out it's a holding pen for slaves. And lucky us, we're the first ones to try it out."

"Yeah, that's pretty terrible," agreed the centauress. "Only..."

"What?"

"Is it actually ironic? I mean, I'm pretty sure it's just a coincidence."

Revka's brow furrowed. "Same thing, isn't it?"

"I don't think so." Iyarra rubbed the back of her head. "I think it's like, you have to expect one thing and get the exact opposite."

"So, if we had been like, boy, I'm sure glad we're not going to be locked away in this thing, then that would have been ironic? Do I have that right?"

"I think it's more like if we had built the place to lock someone else up in it. Or maybe if we—"

"Iyarra?"

"Hm?"

"This is maybe not the time."

"Oh. Right. Sorry."

Revka gnawed at the jerky some more. There was that and flatbread for them to eat. Nutrient-dense foods, she noticed, and ones that kept well. Shame about the flavor. She dusted her hands off and looked back at the centauress. "How's the leg?"

Iyarra swung her right rear leg back and forth a couple of times. "Better," she said. "Still kind of sore, though."

"Figures they'd make the doors centaur-proof," Revka muttered. "I could have sworn a few kicks would have had that chain open."

"Well, yeah," said Iyarra. "But it sounds like they barricaded it from the other side too. I guess they figured we might be able to break out otherwise."

Revka lay back on the other sleeping mat. "I swear, we never seem to be able to catch a break. Now, any decent guard, they'd have a flimsy door that could be knocked down or removed or whatever. Right?"

"Would they?"

"Sure." Revka continued, warming to her subject. "Or at the very least they'd use ordinary cell doors with the bars nice and far apart, and the keys hanging a few feet away, just close enough that you could toss your belt at them until they fell down, then fish them over and get out. You know?"

"I can't say I've ever seen a cell like that."

"Yeah, me neither. People just don't know how to behave anymore."

Revka got up and wandered back over to the walls. The metal plates they had so carefully attached to the wall were still firmly in place, fit together so close that she couldn't so much as slide a fingernail between them. Not that it made too much of a difference. The fact was that no amount of leverage was going to pry them off, even if they had tools.

She leaned back against the wall, sulking. Another fine mess they'd gotten themselves into. Doors barricaded shut, walls impenetrable, concrete beneath their feet, and a roof above. Pretty much boxed in, any way you looked at it. She let her eyes wander, staring blankly around the room. If only she...

"Iyarra?"

"Hm?"

"I think I might have an idea."

"Really?"

"Yeah. I think we're going to have to do something stupid."

"Oh? How stupid do you mean? Like, kinda stupid or real stupid?"

Revka eyed the roof. "Oh, I'm thinking pretty thoroughly stupid."

"Oh, *well*, why didn't you say so?"

* * * * *

"You got it?"

"Right. I'm good. Just hold nice and still...there."

"All right. Just let me know when you're ready."

Revka shifted her feet so she was balanced on Iyarra's shoulders. She steadied herself, leaning forward and bracing herself against the wall. She gazed up at the roof beam less than a pace away. This was going to work.

Probably.

"Okay," she called down to Iyarra. "Ready for phase two."

"All right. Hang on." The centauress planted her hands against the wall and slowly pushed back. She began to walk her hind legs forward, one cautious shuffling step at a time. She splayed her forelegs out, bracing them against the wall.

Revka walked her hands up the wall, as Iyarra boosted her up. Getting closer…if she just managed to close this gap, she could grab the beam. "Okay," she said. "Looking good, here. I think—" She felt her legs buckle and dared to look down. "Yarra!" she hissed. "Lean closer, will you? I'm losing my purchase!"

"Sorry!"

Revka suddenly found herself nearly flat against the wall, her center of balance threatening to yank her backward and down if she so much as breathed wrong. "Notthatclose! *Notthatclose!*" She kept her hands flat against the smooth metal wall, trying to stick to it through sheer mental will.

Iyarra shifted back a little, and Revka felt her body weight stabilize again. "Good grief!" She panted, waiting for her heart to stop its thumping.

"Sorry about that," said Iyarra. "This better?"

"Much, yes." Revka looked back down again. "You know, I just realized, maybe we should have dragged the sleeping mats over here, just in case."

"That would have been a good idea, yeah."

"Can you go up any more?"

"A little, I think." The centauress shifted and eased herself closer to the wall. "Okay. That's about it. Can you reach it?"

Revka batted her arm, her fingertips just grazing the roof beam. "Almost, I think we can do this. Time for phase three."

"Aw, really?"

"I'm afraid so."

"Darn it. I hate phase three."

"It's all right; just take it nice and easy." Revka leaned forward a little bit more, keeping herself stable against the wall. "I'm ready when you are."

Sighing, Iyarra moved her forelegs up, bracing them against the wall so her hands were free. Licking her lips, she brought her hands just above her shoulders, palms facing upward, and took a couple of quick breaths. "Ready."

Revka stepped onto the waiting hands and held as still as she could. "Okay, nice and easy, now."

Iyarra grunted and began to push upward. Revka slowly rose, until she was able to get her hands around the roof beam. "Got it! Great!" she called down. "Just a little more, and I can scramble up!"

"Don't wanna rush you," Iyarra hissed, "but you're not getting any lighter."

"OK, brace yourself. One, two," Revka crouched as much as she dared and gave a little leap, just enough to wrap her arms securely around the beam. "Three! All right." She moved back from the wall, shuffling one arm at a time, until she had room to swing her legs up and over. In a moment, she was lying on her back along the beam and staring up at the tin roof. "Okay. We got this."

"You good?"

"Yup."

"Okay, I'm going back down."

"Great. Maybe drag the mats over here just in case."

"On it."

Revka examined the roof. There were thinner timbers up here, just enough to support the sheets of tin that had been nailed into place. She reached up and braced her arms against the rafter directly above her. Having secured herself, she walked her feet up until each one was braced against a metal sheet, straddling the rafter between them. She tested each one in turn, feeling to see if either gave under pressure. Both metal sheets were nailed in pretty firmly, but it did seem to her that the one on the right had a little more give to it.

Might as well start with that one, then.

Bracing her left leg, she brought her right one back and kicked the metal sheet as hard as she dared. The resounding clang was impressive, but the sheet flexed only a little. That seemed to be about it. She shifted her weight and repositioned her foot, to aim closer to the point where the metal was secured to the wood. She began to kick at it again, pounding it as hard as she could. The metal roof shook and echoed with every kick, but she held on tight and kept going.

She clenched her hands around the rafter. It was a bit of a reach, and her arms were starting to ache. She steadied herself and redoubled her efforts. Again and again, she brought her foot against the sheet, pounding it in heel-first right at the join. It may have been a trick of the dark, but it seemed like it was starting to come loose, a little, where her blows were concentrated. She gritted her teeth and redoubled her efforts. "Come! On! You! Stupid! Thing! Come! Loose! Stupid! Dumb! Nails! *Ugh!*"

"Uhm, Revka?"

"Not now, not now! Get! Loose! Dammit! Get! Loose!"

"Revka!"

"Oh, for...what?"

"The door!"

"What about it?"

Down below, the door swung open. Silhouetted against the moonlight stood two of Mr. Fleet's men. They were both carrying crossbows.

Revka sagged. She smiled weakly at the two men. "Uhm, hi. Just...trying to get some fresh air. Haha." *Oh, Krep.*

* * * * *

"In retrospect," said Iyarra, "I suppose we should have realized they might have left guards behind. Really, we should have seen that coming."

Revka didn't answer. She just lay sprawled on one of the sleeping mats, bound hand and foot. The trip down off the roof beam had not been pleasant, and the reception she got upon landing only made things worse. Even if they hadn't bound her hand and foot, the roughing up she received at the hands of the two goons pretty much put an end to any clever plans, for the time being.

Iyarra hobbled over to Revka's side and knelt beside her. At least she could move about a bit, though thanks to her ropes, only at a slow and wobbly shuffle. She looked down at her partner with concern. "Revka?"

"Hm? Oh. Sorry. Just thinking." The woman rolled around to face the centauress. "This has been a heck of a trip, hasn't it?"

Iyarra grinned. "Well, we've had better, that's for sure." She leaned in closer. "Are you too badly hurt?"

Revka managed to shrug. "Not too bad. Bruises, mostly. Nothing that won't heal in a week or so."

Iyarra winced. The guards had seemed to feel that picking a fight with a large, muscular centauress was not a recipe for success, but they had no problem with giving Revka "a lesson," once the two were safely tied up. The centauress shuddered at the memory. If the other one hadn't had his crossbow aimed right at her head...

"You know what the worst part is?" said Revka quietly.

"Is it getting beat up before you could escape?"

"Well no, that was pretty bad too."

"The fact that we built this place ourselves?"

"OK, that sucks too, but no."

"Oo! Is it the fact that we might be about to get fed to some ancient monster by a bunch of cult loonies as some sort of twisted urban renewal program?"

"Okay, fine. That's definitely worse, but what I mean is that I thought we could trust Mr. Fleet. You know what I mean? He was always so nice, and gave us work, and even spoke up for us. All the time he was just...fattening us up. Just burns me, you know?"

"Oh, that. Yeah." Iyarra nodded. "That's bad too."

"I mean, I didn't even see it coming, you know? I like to think I can read people pretty well, but... Well, this guy, he just blindsided me. Did you pick up on anything?"

Iyarra shook her head. "Search me. He always smelled fine to me."

"Oh." Revka fell silent, staring into the darkness.

"So, what happens now?"

"Well, first of all, I'm going to need your help with something."

"Of course. What is it?"

Revka nodded her head to the far corner. "I gotta use the bucket. Tied up like this, it's going to be a real logistical nightmare. Then, I think we need to talk about our future."

* * * * *

"Well, top of the morning!" The morning sunlight burst in through the opening doors and ushered in Mr. Fleet. "How's everybody doing?"

Revka glared up at him and didn't deign to reply. Iyarra, who had been lightly snoozing, stirred awake and blinked uncomfortably at the sudden incursion.

"That good, eh?" Mr. Fleet chuckled. "Well, now. Sounds like we—" He stopped, a puzzled look coming over his face. He pointed. "Uhm, what happened over there?"

"There was an accident with the bucket," said Revka. "Kind of hard to use it while all tied up."

"Oh. Right. Well, never mind. We'll get that taken care of, but first, I understand we had a little bit of an incident last night, didn't we?"

"Oh, hell." Revka sighed. "Look, it's not as if we even got anywhere. We—"

"Oh now, don't you worry about it." Mr. Fleet waved a careless hand. "Listen, I'd be disappointed if you hadn't tried something. That's the whole reason I had Jed & Clem here stay overnight. I told them if anyone could find a weakness in this place, it would be you two. Well, we'll just have to reinforce the roof a little bit, maybe put some spikes on the joists, but we can talk about that later."

Mr. Fleet knelt down on the concrete floor and leaned his arms on one foreleg so he was level with the two prisoners. "Now then, you've had a night to think about it, and you tried your hand. And bless you, I don't blame you a bit for trying, but now, it's what you might call the moment of truth.

"See, I like you girls. I do. You work hard, you're resourceful and smart—just not *too* smart." He grinned. "So my offer stands. Come work with me. Any of my boys'll tell you, I take good care of my people. And who wouldn't love to be on the winning team? But let me tell you, this is a limited-time offer. So, you'd better speak now, hear me?"

Revka and Iyarra exchanged glances. There was a nod from the centauress, and Revka returned it. "All right." She turned back to Mr. Fleet. "Yeah, we talked it over last night, and well, I guess we don't have a choice, do we?"

Mr. Fleet beamed. "See?" he called over his shoulder to the others. "I told you they were smart." He stood up, dusting off his forelegs. "Right. Get these two untied, and we'll head to the other camp. Get you cleaned up and fed, the world will look a lot different."

A few minutes later, the group set out. The girls were unbound but still flanked by Mr. Fleet's men. Fleet himself moseyed along at the back, along with Harry, the foreman.

"I don't know about this sir," said Harry. "I mean, for myself, I'd just cut 'em and forget 'em."

"Oh, ye of little faith," said Mr. Fleet. "They're smart, I told you. Whether they mean it or not, they know the only way forward is to play ball with us. And that's just what we need."

"Yeah, but can we trust them?"

Mr. Fleet lit a cigar. "Just long enough, Harry," he said. "Just long enough."

Chapter Twenty-Three

"CAMP" TURNED OUT TO be a small group of tents and a few sacks of supplies just outside the entrance to The Gap. Mr. Fleet pointed the girls over to one of the tents. "Y'all can get cleaned up in there. Cookie should have vittles ready by the time you're done. We all eat over there." He pointed to a larger canopy spread out next to a chuck wagon.

In the tent were a bucket of water, some soap, a couple of flannels, and even a brush. Much to the girls' surprise, the items they'd surrendered at the sheriff's office were neatly stacked in a corner.

"Wow," said Iyarra. "I guess he really *is* connected."

"Tell me about it." Revka grabbed a rag and began to scrub. "You get past the whole summoning-an-evil-monster-to-do-your-bidding part, and he's a pretty decent boss. I mean, we've worked for worse."

"Dear lord, have we?"

As they emerged from the tent, several minutes later, the smell of cooking wafted over and hit them right in the appetite. Two stomachs rumbled in unison.

"There they are!" Mr. Fleet waved to the girls from beneath the canopy. "Come on an' join us!" He gestured as they joined the group. "We got beans, griddle cakes, and coffee. Grab a plate and dig in."

"Thanks."

"Yeah, thanks." The two loaded up their plates, and the next few minutes were filled with the silence of people who had better things to do with their mouths than talk.

"So," said Revka, once the initial nosh was out of the way, "what are we doing out here?"

"Well," said Mr. Fleet, "we're going to be doing some of the incantations and things here. When they put that thing away, they wanted to make sure he didn't just, y'know, slip out. So they locked him up real good." He pointed to the entrance to The Gap. "This place is the key. Now, from what I hear, you found the passage to the old temple, right? Following one of the four trails?"

"Right, yeah. The one that goes...what would that be...northwest? From the center?"

Mr. Fleet grinned. "Actually," he said, "as I understand it, any one of the four trails would have taken you there. I mean if you followed the routes exactly of course."

"Yeah," said Iyarra, "Come to think of it, why does that make a difference? I mean, if you go to the place shouldn't it work no matter how you got there?"

Mr. Fleet shook his head. "No, no, there was...oh, let me think. My pappy told me about it once, a long time ago. It's like, the way you traverse the path, it's like weaving a spell, from how he described it. There's certain points you have to hit in the right order, as I recall. I guess it's like saying the magic words the right way for a spell. Anyhow, that's just a small part of what we're going to be doing.

"See, that's not the true purpose of the maze. I mean, it will do it, if you get the paths right, but that's what you might call secondary. The real trick is to invoke the opening."

"Now, tomorrow night the moon is gonna be..." He stopped, snapping his fingers. "Dangit. Clem, what's that called when the moon is halfway between full and new? Like right down the middle?"

Clem furrowed his brow. "Uhm. Is that gibbous?"

"No, no. That's when it's all fat, I think. Pretty sure. Well, never mind. Doesn't matter. Point is, it's going to be that way tomorrow night. Now, people go on about full-moon this and full-moon that, for doing magic, but I'll let you in on a little secret. The half-moon—is that what it's called? I'm gonna call it that—the half-moon is where the real magic's at. That's the moon of doorways, of thresholds between one world and the next. Holler out to the dead on a half-moon, they just might hear ya. And when you holler out to a god...*well.*

"Anyway, we're gonna do a little magic then, see what we can work up, but first, we've got some preparation to do. That's gonna be today and tomorrow, for the most part. Y'all are gonna need to help us clear out the maze. A lot of it's been neglected over the centuries and all. So, everybody eat up, and we'll get on to work."

The rest of the day was spent hauling brambles and tumbleweeds out of the maze. They cut down some shrubs which had grown up in some of the long-abandoned corridors. The long, hot work kept them occupied till nearly sundown. Mr. Fleet had put one of his men with them to, as he put it, "help with the cutting and hauling." No doubt, he was also keeping an eye on them. Understandable, but it did rather curb any attempts at conversation between her and Iyarra.

Lunch was much the same as breakfast. Dinner came with sourdough biscuits and a gravy that looked and tasted like library paste. Revka couldn't help but remember what the others had said about never asking a centaur what went into glue. Still, no one seemed to complain too much. It was amazing what a day of work in the hot sun did for one's appetite.

That night, the group lit a campfire and sat under the stars. Mr. Fleet was full of tales, talking about the history of the valley and his plans for the future. "We're gonna be the queen of cities, you mark my words," he said. "With the help of our divine friend, the barren ground shall become lush with food, and water will spring forth from the desert. Why, I foresee a day when our modest little town will take up the entirety of the valley. We'll have to move the thungas out into the prairie.

"Oh, I wish you could see what I see." Mr. Fleet's voice took on a wistful note. "Vast tracts of homes, all alike, with perfectly manicured lawns. Gated communities with easy access to schools and grazing land. And shops! Grand stretches of shops all under one roof where you can buy anything you want: clothes, household goods, books, you name it. And happy centaurs and people walking around munching on soft pretzels and chocolate-chip cookies big as your head. Restaurants will have every kind of food you can imagine, and they'll even sing to you and bring you a free piece of cake if it's your birthday. There will be organic hay and small-batch, artisanal braw, locally made of course. It'll be a never-ending place of wonders, a veritable paradise on earth." In the firelight, his eyes gleamed. "It'll be *glorious*."

"And run on slaves and blood sacrifice."

Mr. Fleet smiled at Revka. "Well, you can't make an omelet without cracking a few eggs, as they say, but yeah, we'll need some...unofficial help in the early stages. Once things are fully established, we can probably go easy on them. I mean, once the secret's out and all. That's the important thing, keeping everything secret at first. We gotta keep everything hush-hush until the deal is sealed, you know what I mean? Don't want any goody-goodies throwing a wrench into the proceedings. Not when we're so close."

"But you're really going to go ahead with sacrifices?" Iyarra asked.

Mr. Fleet shrugged. "Well, that kinda depends. We'll see what the god wants. If we can get away with thungas, that's all the better. If not...well, there's always crimes, and there's always punishment."

That remark had what could charitably be called a sobering effect on the evening's conversation. The group broke up shortly afterward, and everyone not on watch duty went off to bed.

* * * * *

The next morning dawned clear and cold. Revka and Iyarra emerged from their tent to the familiar smell of the chuckwagon.

"Morning, people." Mr. Fleet emerged from his tent just as the girls were sitting down with their plates. Revka raised an eyebrow. Pretty much every time she'd seen Mr. Fleet, he'd been dressed up sharp in a white button-up, black waistcoat, and bolo tie. The rolled-up sleeves of his simple denim shirt drew mild surprise. He caught her expression and grinned. "Got a lot of work today," he said. "Don't wanna dirty up my good clothes before tonight, you know what I mean?"

"So, what are we doing today, boss?" asked Harry.

"Well, we have a few more preparations for tonight. A lot of that's gonna be on me and the others, when they show up. That should be sometime in the afternoon. Mostly, your jobs will be to assist us in the ceremony and keep a watch out, in case anybody figures on interfering. I'm gonna want you all pin-sharp tonight, you hear me?"

There was a chorus of yesses around the campfire.

"Fine, that's fine. Now, everyone eat up, then meet in the center of the maze. All right?"

"Yessir."

"Understood."

"Mm-mmph."

"Dangit Clem, don't talk with your mouth full."

* * * * *

When the group filed into the center of the maze, Mr. Fleet was already there. The cleanup crew had removed a lot of dirt and brush, and now the map of the maze was clearly visible all the way around.

"All right, ladies," Mr. Fleet said. "Got a little job for you. Each of these four pathways will go to a different corner of the maze. Of course, you have to follow the exact path, but there's a couple of these that haven't been used in Krep-knows how long." He pointed with his hoof at the line that marked the northwest path. "This one we've been using pretty much all the time, but we gotta make sure we have all of these correct. Now, if you look here." He pointed to the southwest path. "You can see there's gaps in the maze. It goes all the way along to here, then the trail kinda fades out for a bit, then it picks up over here."

Mr. Fleet knelt by the maze, tracing along the paths with his finger as he talked. "Now, it seems to me that there are about three different ways to get from one point to the other. If you look at the map here, you can see there's this straight shot here, and this other little path with a dogleg, or possibly even this bit where it winds around some. So, what we're gonna do is this.

"I've worked up a map of this section. I want y'all to work out which is the right route. Just go to this spot here." He took out a crumpled piece of paper and showed it to Revka and Iyarra. "Then try one of the paths. If it's the right one, it should zap you straight to the temple. You should be able to come right back using the disc they got in there. If it's not the right one, you'll need to come back here and start again from the beginning. Got that?"

"Yessir."

Revka kept her face carefully blank. *The temple, eh? That just might work to our advantage...*

"Curly?"

"Sir?"

"You go along with 'em so they don't get lost." There was that smile again.

If we live through this, I swear I'm going to knock that grin off his face at least once.

Curly hesitated a moment, then nodded and stepped up between the girls. "Yessir. As you say, sir."

"All right. Off you go, then. Don't forget to mark the map when you find the right passageway."

* * * * *

The three of them filed their way through the maze, following the map made by Mr. Fleet. The route was easy enough to follow, but like the other trails, wound around and around in what seemed to be a needlessly convoluted manner. It was several minutes before they came to the point where the trail stopped.

"All right," said Revka. "We lose the path here." She scraped her boot on the ground, making an X. This spot was a four-way junction, with two passages crossing each other. "Now, it looks like the path picks back up along about"—She traced a finger along the map, then pointed forward and a bit to the left—"Over there. So, we've got a passage to the left, one to the right, and one going straight." She looked back at Curly. "Any preferences?"

Curly wasn't listening. He was too busy looking into every corner and side passage. Revka watched him. Now that she looked, he clearly had something on his mind. He kept pawing at the ground. His ears were standing straight up, and his tail twitched behind him like a metronome.

"Listen," said Revka, "are you okay?"

"I—what? Yeah. Yeah, I'm fine. Whichever's fine." He licked his dry lips, eyes flicking from one passage to another.

"Uh-huh." Revka looked up at Iyarra. "How about you? Any feelings one way or another?"

"Not particularly."

"OK, you good with going left first?"

"Suits me."

"Curly?"

"What? Uhm, yeah. Fine. Fine."

"All right." Revka handed over the map and pointed. "Here's the route. I'll let you lead."

Curly took the map and, with extreme reluctance, took the lead down the left-hand path. The group picked their way along, double-checking the instructions at every junction.

"Let's see," Curly muttered, glancing downward. "Right here, then...wait, did we already make a right?"

"There are two rights in a row," Revka pointed. "This is the second one. You're fine."

"Oh. Right." He moved to the right-hand passage, muttering to himself. Iyarra looked over at Revka. "Is it just me," she whispered, "or—"

Revka clapped a hand over Iyarra's mouth. She leaned forward and mimed cupping a hand to her ear.

"Oh. Right. Sorry." They followed the rest of the path in silence.

When they arrived at the point where the trail picked up, Revka drew another X in the ground. "OK," she said. "Looks like it's just a short way to the end. Shall we?"

The end, when they got to it, was exactly like the other one: a large circular area with a giant stone disc in the center. Revka thought that the glyphs on this one looked a bit different from the other one they'd seen, but she wasn't sure. "Well," she said to Curly, "shall we give it a shot?"

The centaur hesitated, scratching at the ground. "Uhm," he said, "I think Mr. Fleet wanted one of you to test it. I'm probably not qualified." He hovered near the open passageway. "Go on, now," he said, gesturing to the stone disc. "Give it a try."

"Okay," said Revka. "I just hope the trip back is working all right. Don't wanna leave you here all alone."

This had the desired effect. Curly had the dark complexion of someone who spent their life in the outdoors. Even so, he managed to turn pale. "I—I mean, maybe just one of you go? Just in case?"

"Oh for Krep's sake," Iyarra said. "*I'll* go." She stepped forward onto the stone disc and waited. Nothing.

Revka tutted. She fished out the map and drew a tiny X on the left-hand path. "Well, that's one down, anyway."

Iyarra grumped. "Oh, well. So now we try another route?"

Curly sagged. "Dangit," he muttered.

Revka traced her finger along the maze. "Well, first I figure out the fastest way back to the center, but then, yeah, we try another route."

They started back toward the center of the maze, Revka strolling alongside Curly as he turned the map this way and that. "So," she said conversationally, "Hope you don't mind my saying so, but you seem to have something on your mind."

"What? No! Shut up!" He waved an impatient hand at her, then glanced nervously at the surrounding stones.

"Only, I can't help but notice you seem to be a bit on the jumpy side, that's all."

"Dangit! I ain't jumpy! Who said I was jumpy? I...oh, what's the use?"

Iyarra stepped up and gave him a sympathetic look. "Do you want to talk about it?" she offered.

"You won't...you won't laugh? Or tell no one?"

"On our honor," said Revka. "Right, Yarra?"

"Cross our hearts."

"Okay." Curly took his hat off and mopped some sweat from his brow. "It's just that...well, my grandmama, she had all these stories, you know?"

"Like the one about the cave?"

"Yeah." He took a deep breath. "I mean, I know it's all stories an' that, but—"

There was an eerie, unearthly howl. It seemed to come from no one spot, but somehow all around them in every direction at once. Curly froze in place, eyes bulging with fear. He looked around wildly, his legs nearly buckling underneath him. "Oh my lord," he cried out, "what was *that?*"

Revka, who had almost cried out herself, managed to stop herself just in time. Just over Curly's shoulder, Coyote sat perched on a rock. He winked at the girls and touched a finger to his muzzle. *Oh.*

Revka organized her face into a mask of perfect innocence. "What was what?"

"You didn't...you didn't hear anything?"

"Don't believe I did," said Revka. "How about you, Yarra?"

Iyarra tore her attention away from Coyote, who was pulling faces at the other centaur. "What? Oh, nope. Don't hear a thing. Don't see anything either."

"Okay," Curly breathed out. "Maybe it was just, I dunno, hearing things. Yeah." He made an effort to pull himself together. "Just a story," he said to himself. "Just a story."

Revka moved closer. Time to turn the screws a little. "A story, huh? Well, Iyarra and me, we love stories. Don't we?"

"Oh yes. We'd love to hear it."

"It's just...it's just my grandmama, she said...'you ain't supposed to go in The Gap,' she said. Cos of the critter what lives there. She said, anyone what goes in there, they—"

"*Currrrrrr leeeeeeee!*" Coyote was closer now, slinking along the top of the stone wall. Curly whimpered. "Ohhhh, gods tell me you heard that!"

"Heard what?" said Revka. "There's nobody here but us three...in the middle of the maze. All alone."

By now Curly was a mess. He trotted in place, his head on a constant swivel, ears on the alert. "This ain't right," he muttered, "this ain't right!"

"I remember a story I heard as a kid," Revka said. "There were these creatures, nobody could hear or see 'em unless they were coming after you. They'd pick out one victim at a time, so they said, and they'd hunt 'em until they caught 'em. Of course, the real danger was if they caught your name. They have that, they'll follow you to the end of the world."

Curly stood rooted to the spot, eyes closed, trembling. "Stop it," he whispered, "I don't wanna hear it!"

"I heard one time one of 'em set its sights on a guy, he took off out of his town, went all the way to the coast. Got on board a ship for the Green Lands. When they docked, he didn't come out of his cabin. So they went to get him..."

"Oh, gods..."

"And there wasn't any trace of him at all. Nothing left but a single horseshoe."

Curly yelped. "Look, I gotta...I gotta do something, okay?" He looked around wildly. "Looks like we're about to the middle of the maze again. You reckon you can try the other paths yourselves?"

Revka gave him a big, helpful smile. "Why sure," she said. "We'd be happy to. Wouldn't we, Iyarra?"

"Oh, no trouble at all."

"Great! Great." He hurriedly forced the map into Revka's hands. "If Mr. Fleet asks, I was with you all the time, all right?"

"Well, if you're sure." Unseen by Curly, Coyote had crept up till he was hanging over the centaur. He grinned toothily, catching Revka's eye. He licked Curly's ear.

The centaur let out a scream and galloped down the path, moving as fast as he could. Coyote fell back onto his stone perch, rocking with silent laughter. He winked at the girls, then hopped down.

"Pretty good story, just now," he said. "Nice work."

Revka grinned. "Hey, glad you liked it."

"I thought it was a fine example of the oral tradition," he chuckled. "Anyhow, got a message from the boss. Let me see that map."

Revka handed it over. Coyote perused it a minute, then pulled a quill from behind his ear. "All right," he said, "you're gonna wanna take this route here." He quickly drew in a convoluted path connecting the two halves on the map. "Go ahead and try it out real quick, just to make sure though, eh?" He tapped the side of his head. "You never know."

"We'll do that, thanks."

"Don't mention it." Coyote tipped his hat to them and bowed, disappearing behind a segment of the wall.

Revka smiled up at Iyarra. "Well, shall we?"

Twenty minutes later, they found themselves at the crossroads again. Revka glanced down at the map. "OK, according to Mr. Coyote, we want to take a right here."

"All right."

Several minutes later, they found themselves back at the stone disc. Revka patted Iyarra on the shoulder. "Well, shall we?"

Iyarra nodded. She took a deep breath and let it out slowly. Centauress and rider stepped onto the stone disc and promptly disappeared.

A few minutes later, they popped into view again, right at the same spot they had left. Revka squinted at the sudden glare of sunlight. "Dang," she muttered. "Forgot how dark it was in there."

"Well, at least we know the path works."

"Yup." Revka double-checked the path marked out on the map. "That oughta do it."

"Suppose we'd better get back then," said Iyarra. "I'm sure Mr. Fleet will be wanting to hear the good news."

"Yup. I bet he's got some other work for us too, so maybe we don't need to be in any particular hurry."

"Well, it's probably best that we keep on acting busy. I mean, what with, ah..."

"*Shh!*" Revka clapped her hand over Iyarra's mouth and leaned forward. "Careful," she whispered, "anybody could be listening in."

"Right. Sorry. Sorry."

"All right." Revka sat back up. "Anyhow, let's head on back to the others. I dunno how much more prep work they've got for us, but I'm pretty sure that tonight is going to be a busy one."

Iyarra nodded and headed back into the maze. "That is the understatement of a lifetime."

Chapter Twenty-Four

THE SUN WAS CLOSE to setting as the rest of the group arrived. Revka couldn't help but notice that it was pretty much the entire Citizens Protection Committee the girls had been introduced to around the table...how long ago? A few days? Felt like ages. They were all in extremely jovial spirits and chatted amiably with Mr. Fleet as they made the final preparations. There was more an air of a social occasion than a dark-god-awakening ritual. Some of the cultists, to Revka's considerable surprise, even brought dishes to pass.

The core group of the cultists was huddled around the central spot in the maze, where the key stood in a place of honor on a rough stone plinth. They were doing something Revka couldn't see but which involved handfuls of multicolored sand. While they were thus occupied, she sidled over to Iyarra.

"Can you believe this?" she whispered. "What is with these people?"

Iyarra shrugged. "Search me, I've been to exactly as many evil cult ceremonies as you have. Well, unless you did some before we met."

"Not me."

"Me neither. Maybe this is how they always are, and we've just had them wrong all along."'

"I mean, I guess that's possible, but they're acting like this is some kind of picnic or something. I mean, they're awful and all that, but I do feel that if you're going to dress up in red robes and wake a gigantic sleeping god from before the dawn of time, having a potluck table and lemonade is kind of ruining the effect."

"I see what you mean." Iyarra nodded. "You'd expect, like, roast spiders on little crackers. Or bat's blood, maybe. Stuff like that."

"Exactly. Not potato salad."

"I mean, they do have deviled eggs," Iyarra added. "That's kind of evil."

"Eh, a bit of a stretch."

"Now that I think of it, the most evil thing here is the lime gelatin salad."

"Oh? Looked all right to me, though I don't know how long it'll stay good in this heat. What's wrong with it?"

"Well, you know the rule about never asking a centaur what goes into glue?"

"Uh-huh?"

"Goes double for gelatin."

In the inner circle, Mr. Fleet clapped his hands for attention.

"All right, you people. Looks like the sun will be setting here pretty soon. We're gonna want to get started right at twilight, so let's go ahead and get ourselves organized. Clem, Phil, go to the entrance and stand guard. We don't want anybody crashing our little do without an invite. Those who have been designated couriers to the four points, prepare and cleanse yourself now, please. And somebody cover up that potato salad so it doesn't go bad, will you?"

The cultists donned matching crimson robes, the same ones that Revka had seen that night by the warehouse. Iyarra and the other workers were given plain black robes. There was a bit of fuss when they realized they didn't have any human-sized ones for Revka. Fortunately, Iyarra still had Revka's cloak stowed away, and it was judged more than sufficient for the job.

As the sun touched down upon the tip of a nearby peak, the cultists took their places around the inner circle. There was a fire going there, mostly made up of the scrub and brush of the desert, but oddly scented with hints of camphor and mint. Also, and it may have been Revka's imagination, but it did seem to her that there were strange colors mixed in with the usual yellow-orange flames. She watched the heat ripples rise above the flames. For a moment, it almost seemed that the world she saw through them was not quite the one she knew.

Mr. Fleet stood at the head of the circle and stretched his arms out wide. "Friends!" he proclaimed, his voice echoing off the ancient stones. "We have gathered here this evening for a great work, one for which we may be justifiably proud. This night represents the culmination of many years of work, but it also represents a new beginning. Tonight, my friends, we cast off the shackles of fear! Tonight, we cease to cower from greatness, but reach out and grasp it with both hands! Tonight...oh, tonight, we will rend the veil between man and god, and we shall harness no less than immortal power for the glory of ourselves and our beloved town! This is our moment of opportunity, friends! Shall we take it?"

The robed figures cheered, waving their fists and stomping their hooves. "Hot dang!" called a voice that Revka recognized as that of Deacon Mushrat. "Let's do this thang!"

Mr. Fleet chuckled. "Calm down, brother," he said. "We must have dignity. Now, if you will be so good as to lead us in the invocation?"

The deacon stepped forward, the firelight playing weird patterns on his hooded cloak. He held his arms aloft, paused for dramatic effect, and began to intone.

"Oh, ye who sleepeth beneath this place, hear our plea. O father of the mountains, great and powerful art thou. See, we have come to this place to pay adoration to you, to worship at thy feet, to free you from your eternal prison of stone.

"This we do gladly and with joyous hearts. On this night, we shall rend open the prison that holds thee. We shall crown thee lord of this land and shall stand as thy servants. We shall spread your glory across this world, and all will know your might and tremble.

"Oh, great and powerful one, all this we shall do and more. We ask only one boon of thee. That you will accept our humble valley as thy home, and that you use thy power to make it a place worthy of your magnificence. Let there be great towers that brush against the ceiling of the sky! Let there be great works of statuary to thee of such grand size and magnificence that the world must turn away in shame for their own feeble efforts. Let the barren wastes be made rich and fertile, let the water flow in abundance. Let every tongue speak of thy glory and the glory of this, thy capital. We ask not in our own sake, but only that thou shalt have a throne worthy of thy greatness.

"This we ask as your humble servants, with all adoration and glory to your magnificence, and so we say...amen!"

"Amen!" the others chorused.

By now the sun had disappeared behind the mountains, and the stars were just beginning to come out. Now that the world had darkened somewhat, Revka saw that there were, indeed, unfamiliar colors in the fire. Traces of green danced at the very tips of the flames. Deeper in the heart of the fire there seemed to be something odd, some mass that changed from blue to red even as she watched.

Mr. Fleet stepped forward again. "Let the gate be made ready. Those who shall walk the paths of the four winds, take your stations now. The rest of you, don't wander off. I'll need help preparing the sacrifice."

Four of the cultists stationed themselves at the entrances to the four paths, each joined by two attendants. Iyarra had been assigned to go with Mrs. Wildberry, who would be taking the southwest path through the maze. Mr. Fleet had asked Revka to stay behind and help him, "...as I need someone who can follow directions properly." There was some more chanting, and Mr. Fleet threw a bag of something-or-other into the fire. At once, four glowing, blue lines spread out from the central flame to the entrances to the four paths. The four groups set off, each down its own trail. The blue lines followed them, glowing eerily in the deepening twilight.

Mr. Fleet rubbed his hands together. "Well, it'll take them a few minutes to get to their proper places, so we can take a quick breather till then."

"Pardon me asking," said Revka, "how will we know when they've made it?"

The centaur just grinned. "Oh, don't you worry about that. We'll know, all right. Won't be no doubt about it."

* * * * *

Iyarra and another centaur she didn't recognize followed after Mrs. Wildberry, torches in hand, marching along as they followed the path carefully laid out earlier. Mrs. Wildberry held her map at eye level, peering through her half-moon glasses. On more than one occasion, she had to call the other two over to help.

"No see, we already passed that part." The other centaur, whose name was Zeke, pointed at the map. "Remember? We did that left and the left again and then that kinda curlicue thing. That's the only place on the map that does that."

"Hmmmm." Mrs. Wildberry peered at it again. "So, we're at this crossing, are we?" Her finger stabbed a four-way intersection.

"No, we went through that one," Zeke replied. "Couple minutes ago? You were telling us about your grandkids, remember?"

"Oh. Right, yes. Er...so...?"

"I believe we're right here." Iyarra pointed at another intersection down the path a bit.

"Yup, that's us," said Zeke.

"OK, so we go...?"

"Left."

"Left?"

"Right. I mean, yes. Yes, left."

"Okay." The group filed into the left-hand path and continued on their way. Iyarra looked back at the blue line snaking behind them. Apparently, (according to Mrs. Wildberry) it would stay blue as long as they were on the right track. They seemed to be doing all right so far, knock on wood.

Iyarra wondered how much of this they knew was going to happen. It seemed like they had done their homework, but on the other hand, they seemed more than a little coy about the actual details. Maybe they just didn't trust the others? That seemed plausible. Still, she didn't much like being kept in the dark. Hopefully, they could just get this over with and get away.

Iyarra stopped her reverie as she saw the others disappearing around the corner. She shook her head. It wouldn't do to fall behind. She hurried after them, the blue line following in her wake.

* * * * *

They emerged at the end of the line. Once again, it was a small open space with one of the stone discs right in the middle. Mrs. Wildberry held up her hand. "Nobody step on the stone," she said. "Just find a place around it."

The three of them shuffled into position. Behind them, the blue trail closed the gap to the stone disc. It may have been Iyarra's imagination, but the trail almost seemed to throb in the dim, evening light.

"Now then," said Mrs. Wildberry, "I need you two to hold these and be ready." She fished out a rolled bandage and a small pot of balm and handed them to Zeke and Iyarra, respectively. "We've got the line here, and now we need to seal it. That will open our portion of the lock."

"An' how do we do that, ma'am?" asked Zeke.

Mrs. Wildberry didn't answer. She just fished in her saddlebag and drew out a dagger. For a moment she turned it this way and that, the torchlight catching the blade. Then, in one swift movement, she brought it fast along the tip of her index finger, opening up a thin slit from which bloomed a rivulet of dark blood.

The centaur woman held her hand over the stone disc, face down. Blood began to drip into the lines carved into the stone unknown ages before. As the three of them watched, the blood seemed to multiply, spreading itself and following the carven passages until it reached the spot where the glowing blue line touched the disc.

Instantly, the blue light washed over the disc, tracing over the crimson path to the center. A deep thrumming noise announced a change, and wisps of green-blue magic curled up from the disc like smoke.

The three centaurs watched in awe, mesmerized by the eldritch sight. It was only when Mrs. Wildberry gave a yelp and clutched her hand to herself that everyone was brought back to reality.

"Mercy sakes!" she muttered. "That really does smart! Miss Iyarra, put some of that balm over the cut, will you? And Zeke, be ready with that bandage."

A couple of minutes later, they had her finger all wrapped up and as good as it was going to get. She flexed it a couple of times, only wincing a little. "Well, that hand ain't gonna be good for much for a couple of days, that's for sure." She smiled a little. "Still, I reckon it's a small price to pay."

Zeke spoke up. "Now what do we do, ma'am?"

Mrs. Wildberry put the knife and other items away. "Now we head back. Just follow the line back to the center, should be no problem. One of you go ahead of me with a torch, though, will you? It's starting to get on to dark and my eyes ain't what they used to be."

"Yes'm." Zeke nodded and headed toward the exit. Mrs. Wildberry and Iyarra followed along behind. As she left, Iyarra cast one last glance at the stone disc. The magic was still streaming upward from the stone, disappearing into the night.

Iyarra shuddered and hurried after the others.

* * * * *

Back at the center of the maze, Revka watched a third stream of magic light up the sky. "One more to go," she muttered to herself.

Mr. Fleet nodded. He rubbed his hands together, grinning like a child on Christmas. "I tell you what, if this ain't the damnedest thing you ever saw! And we're only just getting started."

"Oh, I believe you, all right." Revka eyed the scene warily. The closer they came, the less okay she was with the whole idea. It was slowly dawning on her that, holy Krep, they were actually going to *do* this thing. She could feel her stomach begin to knot up. She would definitely feel better when Iyarra got back. Maybe they could, well, excuse themselves, call of nature or something like that, and make a run for it. They could maybe talk their way past the guards at the entrance, find their way back to town, and sneak through before anyone called the cops. Lord knew it wouldn't be the first time.

A little nagging thought tickled at the back of her brain. There was something she hadn't thought about, something amiss. Well, they were getting to resurrect a giant primordial god, that was pretty darned amiss right there, but no, this was something different. A single note, just a slight bit off and so easy to miss in the symphony of terror playing its way nonstop through her mind, but...

A memory clicked. Revka looked around. There were a couple of other cultists milling around and a few more of the hired hands. It was what she did *not* see that really stuck out. Now that she knew what she was looking for, its absence was more than a little bit obvious.

She cleared her throat. "Er, Mr. Fleet?"

Mr. Fleet looked up from the fire. "Mm? What's on your mind, Miss Revka?"

"Pardon me for asking, but I seem to recall that you mentioned there was going to be a sacrifice? As a way of getting the god's attention?"

"That's right, yes."

"Only," she waved an arm around vaguely. "I don't see that we've brought anything. I thought you mentioned a thunga or similar? Is there, like, one outside or something?"

Mr. Fleet just smiled. "Tell me, you ever heard of the great prophet Djal?"

"Djal? Doesn't ring a bell, no."

"Well, I'll tell you." Mr. Fleet's voice seamlessly slipped into oratory mode. "One time, the great prophet, Djal, went forth into the mountains, taking with him only his beloved son. 'Where are we going?' asked the son, 'and why?' And Djal said to him, 'Behold: we are going to a spot that has been shown to me by our god. There we shall make sacrifice unto him.' And they came to a place, far from the cities of man and centaur, and climbed atop a great bluff. There, Djal did direct his son to gather wood and get a fire going.

"By the time the sun was about to set, the fire was burning bright. Father and son knelt to make their prayers. When they finished, the son turned to his father and said, 'The place for sacrifice is ready, yet there is no sacrifice, as we have brought no beast.' And Djal said unto him, 'Fear not, my son. For our god shall provide.'"

"Uh-*huh*," said Revka. "Well, that's, uhm, certainly a nice story there, but what happened? Did the god provide a sacrifice?"

"Oh, he did indeed."

"So...what happened?"

Mr. Fleet smiled. "Tell you what, how about I just show you?"

* * * * *

Mrs. Wildberry returned to the central area, along with her two escorts. Mr. Fleet bowed. "All well, sister?"

"Smooth as a baby's hinder," she said. "Everything going all right, so far, Everett?"

"Going just fine, thank ya. We've had three beacons lit so far, and I'm expec—" He stopped as a fourth wisp of smoke emerged from the maze. "Ayup, there it is. Four for four, can't get better than that." He rubbed his hands together in anticipation. "Just about ready for the next stage. Oh, gentlemen?"

A couple of the hired hands looked up.

"Go ahead and attend to that thing I mentioned earlier."

The men nodded and wandered around the fire over to where the new arrivals were standing. One leaned over to Zeke and whispered something in his ear. Iyarra tilted her head, trying to catch it, but was unable to make anything out. *What were they—?*

Suddenly, there was a knife at her throat. A voice in her ear hissed, "Hands behind your back. Now." Too surprised to put up a fight, she put her hands back. In a moment, her wrists were tied together and her legs hobbled. The men worked quickly, too quickly for them not to have done this many times before. Before she knew it, she was rendered helpless.

Mr. Fleet walked over to her, still smiling. "Sorry about this, but as I was saying to your colleague, y'all are clever. Too clever, if I'm honest. If I brought you on, I'd be watching my back the whole time. And, as Miss Revka so conscientiously pointed out, we *do* need a sacrifice." He nodded to a cultist, who moved aside. Behind them, Revka lay bound and gagged.

"We do, indeed, have some special work for you." Mr. Fleet smiled at Revka. "It's not the most pleasant task, but look at it this way: y'all are about to be the stars of the show.

"Now, you may be trying to come up with one of your clever little plans, but bear in mind there's sacrifices and there's *sacrifices*. We can make this happen quick an' painless, or we can draw it out a good long time. In the olden days, they'd rip the beating heart right out of a body. Now, I don't think we need to go to that extreme, but it is always an option." He turned to the others. "Keep them separate, just in case."

As Iyarra was dragged away and out of sight, Mr. Fleet moved back to the fire. He pulled the hood of his cloak over his head, and the rest of the cultists did likewise. A horrible silence spread out from the heart of the maze. Even the crackling of the fire seemed muted. Mr. Fleet spread his arms outward.

"Dearly beloved," he intoned, "let us begin."

Chapter Twenty-Five

THE LAST RAINBOW HUES of sunset slipped below the horizon as the ceremony began. Torches had been lit around the central area of the maze. In the middle, a struggling Revka was dragged to the fire between two of the hooded centaurs.

Mr. Fleet reached over with one hand and whipped the gag away. Revka glared at him and spat.

"Temper, temper," he said, his voice as infuriatingly calm as always. He reached down to her chin, turning it so she was facing him. "I suggest you adjust your attitude," he said quietly, "or you would not believe how bad a time you're gonna have." He raised his voice again, looking out at the others. "Sorry about that, brothers and sisters." He grinned. "Some folks just don't know how to behave in church!"

There was a scattered chuckle, the kind of laugh that comes when people are nervous and on edge and desperate to break the tension. As Revka looked around the group, it occurred to her that some of them were not entirely on board. Up until this point, it had probably been all dreams of glory and power, but now they were about to watch another sentient being get slaughtered. It was not sitting well with some of them.

Revka could just see Iyarra. She had turned her face away, but even from across the fire, Revka could see tears reflected in the firelight. Her hands, still bound tightly behind her back, clenched into fists. If they got out of this, Fleet and all of his bunch were going to pay for every tear.

Beside her, Mr. Fleet was droning out an invocation to the god that slept below, asking it to bless their work and smile upon this, their first sacrifice. Revka found it hard to concentrate. She found herself scanning the area, peering into the dark passages of the maze beyond. For Krep's sake, where...

Mr. Fleet was going full tilt now, swooping and bellowing his words like an old-time country preacher. They stood on the *threshold* and were going to bring forth a *great* and *glorious* new era, and the *world* would tremble beneath their feet. This was no time for fear, this was no time for doubt, this was the *moment* that they, the very *elect*, would reach out and grab the future with both hands. The energy in the circle reached a fever pitch.

"And now," he crowed, pulling out a long thin dagger, "Oh ye what sleeps below, awake! Awake! And look well upon our sacrifice!"

Revka took a deep breath. She braced herself. Any second now...

"Er...hold up. Sorry, can we hold up just a second?"

Mr. Fleet turned and looked at the interruption. "Hm? Oh, now what? Who said that? You done wrecked my momentum."

A hooded figure raised a tentative hand. "See here now, Everett. Just what exactly you plannin' on doing?"

Mr. Fleet rolled his eyes. "I'm bakin' a cake, Brother Tarran. What the hell does it look like?"

"Only, I just...well, I didn't think you were *actually* gonna... I mean, that's a human. It ain't like an animal or something. I mean, you're not...you're not, are you?"

"What Brother Tarran is trying to say," said Mrs. Wildberry, "is that I think we were under the impression that if there was going to be a sacrifice, it would be more of a, well, symbolic act."

"Symbolic."

"Yes, exactly!" Brother Tarran's hood nodded vigorously. "I mean, Everett, we've all studied the same texts. Surely, it's the intent behind the sacrifice, not the actual sacrifice itself...that..." he trailed off, withering under Fleet's glare.

"Intent? Really?" Mr. Fleet shook his head. "I do not believe what I am hearing here. We are here, we've done the invocations, we've got everything in place, and you pick now to get cold hooves."

"Well for pity's sake," said Mrs. Wildberry. "We didn't sign on for no cold-blooded murder. I know I certainly didn't."

Fleet looked around the circle. "Well, now. I'm sorry if invoking the powers of an almighty god may involve some slightly unsavory deeds. I suppose some of you thought this was all gonna be just fun an' games and nobody getting hurt. Well, this is serious business. Every one of y'all is in this up to your necks. Don't even kid yourself about backing out now.

"But, you know, fair's fair. Maybe you can't bear to be a party to this. Well, it's real simple. Anybody wanna take these girls' places as our sacrifice, just raise your hands now. Anyone? Anyone at all? That's what I thought. Now, if I may be allowed to continue..."

Mr. Fleet raised the dagger, pointing it right down at Revka's throat. She felt herself tense up, bracing for the plunge of the blade.

A chance movement caught her eye. Nothing definite, a suggestion of darkness moving against the blackness of the maze. It looked like...

It looked like a lanky upright coyote wearing an old top hat. In the darkness, only his eyes were visible. They flickered momentarily, reflecting the flames, and in her head, she heard a whisper, *Get ready...*

A large rock came sailing out of the darkness and hit Mr. Fleet's hand, causing him to drop the dagger and lose his grip on Revka. The woman dropped to the ground and rolled away as fast as she could. Members of the Tex Arcana charged out of the maze and began to attack.

There was a rapid series of thumps as a half dozen crossbow bolts crisscrossed through the air and into the enemy. Most hit shoulders or chests, though one went straight into the darkened crimson hood of one unlucky cultist, who screamed and collapsed where they stood. The Arcana, clad in their black robes, closed with the other cultists and started swinging.

Mr. Fleet was livid. He whirled around, his face going purple with rage. "Stop them!" he cried. "Use your daggers, you idiots! Cut their throats!"

"But sir," said one, "the Code of the—"

"Screw the gods' damned code!"

There was a moment of shocked silence on both sides. Fortunately, the Arcana were the first to recover, and several took the initiative to land an extra punch or kick. They had the advantage in numbers, but as the fight progressed, it became clear that most involved didn't have a lot of experience in hand-to-hand combat. Only Mr. Fleet's hired hands showed any real prowess. While they were only a few, there were enough that they could turn the tables, all things being equal.

One of the hired goons pulled a knife from a sheath on his belt and crept toward one of the Arcana members, who was busy exchanging blows with a rival cultist. The goon maneuvered his way closer until he was right behind them. He raised his knife, taking aim at the upper back. The goon cried out as a ton of centaur crashed into him. He dropped the knife and hit the dirt hard, howling with pain.

Iyarra jumped (as much as her ropes would let her), landing hard on the other centaur's leg. He howled with pain, cursing and threatening her, but he wouldn't be putting up any more of a fight if she was any judge.

The red cultist stopped to stare just long enough for the Arcana member to lay him out good and hard. Once he was down, they turned to see Iyarra, smiling sheepishly.

"Hi," she said. "Look, I know you're busy, but would you mind undoing these ropes?"

* * * * *

On the ground, Revka had rolled onto her stomach and managed to squirm out of the way of the flailing hooves. Just a couple of paces away, Mr. Fleet's dagger glinted in the firelight. Moving carefully, she inchwormed her way forward, closing the distance as fast as she dared.

The clearing was full of fighting centaurs. She tried to find a path clear of the forest of dancing and stomping hooves, constantly on the move. She darted forward any time a space presented itself. At last, she got to the dagger. After a couple of tries, she managed to get the handle between her teeth.

Great. Now what.

She looked around, trying to find a place where she could cut herself loose. The main central area was...well, there was no chance, that was all. Too many centaurs, too much fighting. She'd have to sneak to one of the side passages. She looked around and soon located the nearest one. Right past Mr. Fleet and one—no, two other centaurs who were fighting with him. Damn.

She grunted and started shuffling toward the darkened passage.

* * * * *

Up above, Babs and another one of the Tex Arcana were confronting Mr. Fleet.

"I truly wish it hadn't come to this, Everett." The older centauress held a crossbow, aiming it at Mr. Fleet's head. "Your father was a good and noble man. I can't imagine what he would think to see you now."

"Now, that's just a low blow, ma'am," said Mr. Fleet. He eyed the crossbow warily, being careful not to make any sudden moves. "Bringing my daddy into it. Since you bring it up, he was indeed as good and noble as anybody I ever did meet, but he was somewhat lacking in vision, at least in certain subjects." His eyes flickered around, trying to spot the fallen dagger or any weapon. "All y'all who have guarded this thing for centuries, afraid of its power...I mean, think of what we could have accomplished by now!"

"Only chaos and destruction, Everett." Babs shifted a bit, keeping Fleet in the firelight. "A thing like that cannot be bid. It cannot be bound to servitude or appeased with sacrifices and prayers. It is not some giant wishing pot to fill with your ridiculous fantasies. It is a *monster*. It is some terrifying thing from a universe other than ours, and it works in ways we cannot begin to understand! My gods, man! You read the sacred texts! When this thing came through it couldn't even fit into our world, for goodness' sake! And you want to treat it like some sort of penny-slot machine? Insert sacrifice, get wish? It's madness!"

Mr. Fleet began to edge away from the fire, trying to ease his way into the cover of darkness. Around him, the fight was not going well. Several of his supporters were still active, but the key ones—the ones he knew could fight—were starting to go down. It was time for a change of strategy.

"You think we don't know what we're doing? We've all read the same texts as you. Hell, my papa practically taught me to read using the *Secret History,* but that's not all we read. See, I've been getting other books sent in, special books like you don't generally find on the shelf. There's been other things like this before, if you know where to look. Those fantastic creatures were brought to heel by the greatest and most powerful magicians of their times. Frankly, ma'am, I see no reason not to join their exalted ranks."

Babs shook her head. "Is that it? Really? All of this? Just glory seeking? Everett, I thought better of you."

Mr. Fleet took another step back. "Not for me, ma'am. Not for me. For the town. We're gonna make it the greatest and grandest city in the world. It will be a city of never-ending light, wealth coming in by the cartload every day. The world will come to our doorstep, and we will stretch our influence out over the land. Even Lemuria won't have had nothin' on us! Don't you see? This town has a glorious future ahead of it. All it needs is the right people in charge."

"People like you and your friends, eh?"

He shrugged. "People who aren't afraid to take charge." He stepped back again, his rump brushing against cool stone. Babs still had a decent shot at him, even in the low light. He raised his hands slowly, keeping them where she could see them. "But look, I ain't got no weapons. I'm no threat to you. Just cool down and we can talk this out." For a fleeting moment, his gaze shifted, glancing over her shoulder. "Let's just not do anything one of us might regret, huh? Everyone just stay nice and calm and—"

There was a yelp behind Babs. The centaur who had been sneaking up on her screamed and dropped his knife, hobbling off into the darkness. Before she could react, Mr. Fleet dropped down and grabbed the knife. He stood back up, a dangerous glint in his eyes.

"Now," he said, "as I was saying..."

* * * * *

Down on the ground, Revka shifted the knife around again, getting a better grip. Trying to stab someone when you're holding the knife in your teeth isn't very easy at the best of times, and these were about as far from the best of times as you could get. Still, she'd managed to send him off limping. There had been a bad moment when he'd almost stepped on her in his panic to get away, but she'd managed to frantically shuffle out of the way in time to avoid being pancaked.

There was a clear path up ahead and darkness beyond. She glanced around quickly to make sure there wasn't any oncoming traffic and hurriedly crawled her way forward. As she approached, a shape began to emerge from the darkness. She saw a red-hooded figure—one of Mr. Fleet's people, then—lying on its side, motionless. The face was hidden, but there was something odd about the way the hood hung about it...

She squirmed closer. The shapes began to resolve themselves better. She realized there was a crossbow bolt sticking out of the hood, which had tented itself around the shaft. Revka shuddered, horrified but, she had to admit, also a bit curious. She really, really shouldn't look. Maybe if she used the knife to prop up the hood a little more...

A glint of light caught her eye. On the ground, in front of the hood, were a broken pair of pince-nez. Ah.

She shook her head and steered herself back toward the darkness.

* * * * *

On the other side of the clearing, Iyarra was on the ground, frantically working at the rope that bound her forelegs together. The Arcana member that she had helped (Phil?) had undone the bindings on her wrists before plunging back into the fray. She grunted with effort, trying to reach down to her lower legs. She pushed all the breath out of her lungs and just managed to scrabble at the rope until she found the knot. All she had to do was figure out how to undo the knot, without being able to see it, while maintaining an extremely uncomfortable position and hoping nobody came along and stabbed her. Great.

Her fingers fumbled around the knot, looking for a loose end. She got hold of one and carefully traced it back into the knot. *Let's see...the rope went under this bit and came out here, then if I tug just so...*

One of the red-robed cultists backed into her. He had been shuffling away from one of the Arcana and hadn't noticed her on the ground. He staggered and glanced downward, just in time to see an angry centauress rising up, fist first.

The uppercut sent him reeling, staggering off in the other direction. The Arcana member pressed their advantage, raining several blows on him, one after another, until the cultist hit the ground with a thump.

Iyarra grunted. She shook her hand out, bent down, and tried to remember where she had left off.

* * * * *

Babs and Mr. Fleet circled each other warily, each holding their weapon ready, but neither quite ready to be the first to attack.

"You're only putting off the inevitable," said Mr. Fleet. "If it's not us, then someone else will eventually come along. Wouldn't you rather it was someone you could trust to do what's right for our people? What are you afraid of?"

The high priestess shook her head. "We have guarded the secret of this mountain for centuries. Until your group came along, we'd never had the slightest bit of trouble. The future is not as inevitable as you would have it be."

"Oh, but it is." The gleam was back in his eye. "This is going to happen, ma'am, by the gods it is. And do you know why? Because this is our destiny, that's why! Everything that has happened has steered me to this moment. When your group falls, we shall bring a god himself to heel, and then...well, there ain't gonna be no stopping us!"

"No stopping you? Look around, man! You're losing! Even if you did somehow defeat us, there aren't enough of you left to finish the ceremony! You've lost, that's all! Show some sense, man!"

"Sense? *Sense!?*" Mr. Fleet bellowed. "Damn it, woman! Kill 'em all, see if I care! This is my destiny, and you can't do a dang thing against it! I am the Elected One, the great god's hands on this earth! He has chosen me—*me*—to free him and bring him forth to rule upon this land!"

His voice dropped now. "He comes to me in dreams, you know. Ever since I was a little'un...tellin' me all about my destiny, and how he would raise me up to be foremost among men..." He sighed wistfully. "He's a-gonna take me by the hand, and raise me to the exalted place, he is. And I shall rule the world by his side, and I shall live forever. And all shall look upon us and tremble. The kings of the world will pay homage to us. The lesser gods will kneel before us. And that stuck-up bitch Julia Baker will wish she never threw me over for that Cornwell boy."

Babs shook her head sadly. "Really? This is what you've become? I used to think so highly of you, boy, but now it seems you're just another damned lunatic."

"Lunatic?" His eyes flared. "*Lunatic!?* How dare you! I am god's chosen one! I am going to be king of this world! Do you hear me?"

The priestess rolled her eyes. "Oh yes, that definitely sounds like something that a sane person would say." She held out a placating hand. "Look, put down the knife. Everett. Listen to me. It's over. It's all over. Let's get you home. We'll get you help. Please."

The centaur stared at her. For a moment, he seemed to waver, but the mad fire returned to his eyes. "No," he whispered. "No, you will not take this from me." He shifted his grip on the knife, licking his dry lips. "The ceremony's gonna go on. There's gotta be a sacrifice, and by god, there's going to be." He was smiling again. "Yes, a very worthy sacrifice indeed. Why not?" He advanced on the older woman, raising his knife above his head. "Quite a prize indeed, a high priestess. Worthy, indeed, for our god. Yes, yes...of course! That's why you're here! He has chosen you for this glorious moment!"

Babs aimed her crossbow right at Mr. Fleet's head. "Back down!" she shouted. "Everett, so help me, I'm not afraid to use this." But Mr. Fleet just kept coming. The high priestess was backed right up to the central fire now, and still he came. In his eyes, the fire danced.

"Just hold still," he said. "This won't hardly hurt a bit."

* * * * *

In a darkened place only a few paces away, Revka had finally managed to find somewhere she could work on the ropes in peace. She spit the knife onto the ground and squirmed her way around so that she was able to grab it and begin to saw it back and forth across her wrist bonds. She thought back to the stories she'd read in her youth, tales of heroes using a sharp rock, or hidden knife, or, in one instance, a passing alligator to snip themselves free in the knick of time. Funny how they never mentioned just how awkward a move it was. She could only do short sawing motions back and forth. The knife kept slipping in her fingers, and she'd come close to cutting herself a couple-three times already.

Still, it seemed to be working. The rope felt like it was beginning to give a little. She clenched her jaw and kept sawing just as fast as she dared.

* * * * *

Iyarra flung away the last bits of the rope from her forelegs and heaved a sigh of relief. She arched her back, and stomped a little life into her hooves, feeling the blood flow freely again. Now. All she had to do was free her hindlegs, and she was back in business.

Her hind legs...right...

She looked back at them, frowning. Maybe if she...? No, that wouldn't work. She tried backing up until she was resting on her haunches, but her legs—and the rope binding them—stayed resolutely out of reach.

Sighing, she made to stand. Her body wobbled disconcertingly as she tried to haul her rear half upright. This turned out to be a lot harder than she had anticipated. She grunted, pushing her hind legs up while scrabbling her forelegs forward. Her rump managed to get off the ground, and it felt like she was going to make it, but the momentum gave out and she dropped back down with a resounding thump.

"Oh, Krep," muttered the horsewoman.

* * * * *

Babs held the crossbow aimed straight at Mr. Fleet. "For gods' sakes, Everett, put down that damn knife before someone gets hurt." Her hands only trembled a little, as she fumbled for the trigger.

"I'm not afraid to use this," she lied.

Mr. Fleet was too far gone for mere threats to have any effect. He just laughed and swatted the crossbow out of her hand. With a triumphant cry, he grabbed her arm, putting the knife right up against her throat. "Everybody stop where you are!" he shouted.

Around the fire, the fighting came to a halt. Cultists on both sides stopped what they were doing and turned to see what was happening. Mr. Fleet held his knife at the priestess's throat. "It's over," he bellowed. "You hear me? It's all over!"

The crossbow rattled to the ground, the safety catch jostling loose in the process. The bow wobbled a bit before coming to a stop. There was a movement in the darkness. A distinctly canine toe reached out and nudged the stock—not much, not much at all, just enough to change the way it was pointing.

The foot withdrew. Anyone paying attention may have heard a throaty chuckle.

* * * * *

"Now," said Mr. Fleet, once he had everyone's attention, "all you just stay where you are, and I will make this quick." He gave them a cruel smile. "Interfere, and you'll only prolong her suffering. I can promise you that." He raised the dagger again. "In the name of He Who Sleeps Below…"

"*Hi-yaaaa!*" Revka, newly freed, sprang out of the darkness. She brandished her knife, charging toward the two centaurs. "You're in for it now, you two-tim—*whoa!*" Revka wobbled and slipped when she stepped on something in her path. She fell backward, hitting the ground ass-first with a thump.

The crossbow, which had been through a lot in the past few minutes, gave up the ghost with a *twang*. A bolt rose out of the darkness and struck Mr. Fleet in the spot most likely to get his attention.

Mr. Fleet howled with pain. He threw his knife up in the air, and involuntarily jumped away. Too late, he realized that he was jumping straight for the fire. He tried to change direction in midair and fell onto his side, straight onto the heart of the blaze.

His knife flipped through the air, the blade catching the firelight as it tumbled in a lazy arc. There was a moment when the world seemed to go into slow motion, the blade tumbling round and round on its downward journey, until it dropped blade-first onto Mr. Fleet's lower breast.

A single bead of blood rose out of the wound and dripped into the fire. The flames leaped up, the whole becoming suddenly enveloped in the same blue-green magic that still rose from the four corners of the maze. An intense burst of light. A scream of terror and rage. Darkness.

Revka sat on the ground, waiting for the afterimage to go away so she could see again. After several seconds, the scene resolved itself. The fire was back to normal. No more magic, and no more Mr. Fleet. She stared in mild bemusement at the place where he had been.

"Uhm, sorry," she said. "Was that supposed to happen?"

Chapter Twenty-Six

THE HIGH PRIESTESS WAS the first to recover. "Well, it would appear our Mr. Fleet has been hoisted by his own petard." She looked around the circle. "You all know me, and I daresay I know all of you as well. Those of you who cast in your lot with Mr. Fleet, well, he's gone now. You backed the wrong horseman. I suggest you pack it in and surrender and not give us any further trouble. I think we can see to it that this whole affair is dealt with quietly and with a minimum of fuss. That is, as long as you are willing to cooperate."

There was a susurration of disgruntled muttering, but none of the other cultists seemed inclined to put up too much of a fight. Revka suspected that seeing their leader get swept up in a storm of magic had flattened their enthusiasm rather more than anything else could have. There was a general shedding of cloaks and surrendering of weapons.

A few minutes later, Revka emerged from behind Iyarra and patted her on the flank. "All free. This is some good rope, though. We should keep it."

Iyarra cocked an eyebrow at her. "Seriously? This is the stuff they tied me up with and you want to keep it?"

"Well, you know. Waste not want not. I'd go get mine, but I had to cut through it." She coiled up the rope and tucked it away in one of Iyarra's saddlebags. "Anyway, we're fine now. All's well that ends well, and all that stuff. Let's pack it in and head for town. Did anybody see what happened to that potato salad?"

"I think I stepped in it," said a robed figure.

"Bummer. Well, never mind. We'll grab a bite at one of the saloons." She turned to Iyarra, who was staring distractedly at the fire. "Ready to go?"

No answer. The centauress stood facing the fire, staring into it with a puzzled expression.

Revka cleared her throat. "Uhm, Yarra? Hello?"

Iyarra shook herself out of whatever reverie she had been in. "What? Oh. Sorry. Just thinking."

"About what?"

"Well, actually I was wondering if it's really over."

Revka shrugged. "Of course it is. We stopped the sacrifice, killed the head bad guy, and now we've got the rest surrendered. Job done, right?"

"Well, yes, but…did we stop the sacrifice, actually?"

"What do you mean?"

"I mean, Mr. Fleet just kind of disappeared and—"

"Well, yeah, but he wasn't the sacrifice, remember?"

"Well, *I* know that and *you* know that, but, well, does the monster know that? See, the way I figure it is Mr. Fleet didn't just burn up. He went somewhere. Probably wherever the sacrifice was meant to go, you know? So, this monster, or god, or whatever it is gets a bunch of prayers saying, hi there, here comes our sacrifice, please wake up for us. And then a few minutes later along comes Mr. Fleet through the magic door."

A robed figure raised a hand. "But he wasn't meant to be the sacrifice," they said.

Babs frowned. "True, but now that I think of it, that probably doesn't make much of a difference."

"Yeah," said Revka. "Like, if someone gets killed and sent to a god and they're like, I'm sorry, there was a mistake, I wasn't meant to be the sacrifice, the god ain't likely to say Okay, you can go back then."

"Well, hell." Phil looked up at the mountains surrounding them. At the four corners of the maze, the wisps of magic were, if anything, even stronger.

"So," said Revka, "if he just became the sacrifice, then does that mean it worked, or…?"

A distant rumbling rose from far below the surface of the earth, shaking the ground beneath them. The air took on the sticky, staticky feel magic practitioners come to associate with a high magical field.

The group huddled together near the fire. As they watched, the four columns of magical light, one by one, went from blue to red.

Babs took command. "Everybody! Out of here, right now!" She grabbed a torch and started down the path to the outside, the others galloping after her.

Revka groaned. "I suppose it's too late to withdraw the question." she said to no one in particular.

Iyarra rolled her eyes. She grabbed Revka and hauled her toward her saddle. "For Krep's sake, get on!"

"Wait!" Revka tugged herself free and darted over to the plinth where the key still sat, undisturbed. She grabbed it, then hurried back to

Iyarra. Revka hauled herself onto Iyarra's back, tucking the key into a bag and hanging on tight to the centauress. "Okay! Go!"

The horsewoman took off, racing after the others. Fortunately, it was a straight shot to the entrance. The group exploded out of the entrance to The Gap, sweeping up a small group of other taurs in their wake. They kept running until they were well clear of the mountains. Revka clung to Iyarra's back, not even daring to risk a glance backward, until they were far into the desert night.

The group clustered together in a patch of clear ground, quite a distance from the mountains. The quake had gotten more intense so that even at this distance they could still feel the movement beneath their feet. The group watched in silent horror as the mountains shook. Revka dismounted from Iyarra's back and slipped a hand through her saddle strap to keep herself upright on the trembling ground.

"Good gravy," said a familiar voice. "What in tarnation happened in there?"

Revka turned around in surprise. "Maisie? What the heck are you doing here?"

The cowtaur tipped her hat. Beside her stood Gabby and Tom, who nodded in greeting. "Oh, Miss Babs knew we was friends of y'all's, so she got word over to us about the shindig tonight. We were what you might call in reserve, in case things went really bad."

"Really?" Said Iyarra, "Weren't there some guards outside?"

"Oh there *were*," said Tom, "til we showed up and, uh, had a little word with 'em."

"Eyup," said Gabby.

"Oh," said Revka. "Well, I can't say it's not good to see you guys. Even if it could be better circumstances."

The mountains, silhouetted against the sky, were changing shape. They buckled and heaved. Pieces crashed against each other with echoes that boomed across the desert night. In the cracks and fissures that now ran along the length of the mountain range, an ethereal green light pierced the starlit sky. One by one, the four columns of light changed to pure white. No longer drifting upward like smoke, they became turbulent pillars of magic, flaring upward with terrible purpose.

The ground surged. The valley rippled and buckled as the mountains began to shift and tumble away. A boulder the size of a small castle tumbled down and hit the ground with an impact that knocked everyone off their feet and kicked up a cloud of dust which caught the eldritch light and bathed the scene in an ethereal haze.

As the group got back on its hooves (or in Revka's case, feet), a new sound joined the infernal cacophony. The undulating howl, deep and unearthly, went past the ears and straight for the spine. Everyone who heard it shuddered, their senses reeling from horrors undefinable.

Revka looked up. Beyond the green haze, there seemed to be something moving. Something big.

"Sweet mother of mercy," Babs whispered. "What have we done?"

* * * * *

Back in town, Jack Hadok stepped outside. It was a nice night, warm but not too bad. Not a cloud littered the sky. Just the night to get a pleasant buzz on. He pushed his old hat back on his head and strolled up the street, whistling tunelessly to himself.

On the edge of his hearing, there was a rumbling like distant thunder. Must be some storms along the mountains. Funny, that. Well, as long as it wasn't raining on him, he was satisfied. He glanced again at the sky, but there still wasn't a cloud to be seen.

Jack stumbled a bit as he passed the old livery stable. He felt his feet moving out from under him, almost as if the ground was weaving. Now, the old man was no stranger to the ground shifting around under his feet, but usually, it had the decency to wait for the trip home, after he'd had a few. Funny it getting such an early start tonight. He stood still for a few seconds, waiting to see if it happened again, then shrugged and carried on.

There was another sudden jolt. This time there was no mistaking it. The ground slid to the side, sending the old man reeling. He thumped against the wall of the stable, clinging there for a few moments, while he caught his breath. "What in—"

The third jolt hit. Buildings creaked and groaned. Around him were the sounds of falling items and shouts of alarm. Just above him, the block-and-tackle lift into the stable's loft came away and dropped a large crate right in his path.

Jack Hadok stared at the crate, his old heart racing. He looked up at the building, then back to the crate, and finally up at the sky. Then, he pulled off his hat and threw it to the ground. *Dag nab it!* he shouted to the world at large. "All I wanted was a lousy drink!"

Grumbling, he snatched his hat up, dusted it off, and stomped off back home.

* * * * *

Back in the desert, the group watched in horror as the dust began to settle. The weird, indistinct shapes that had been masked by the debris cloud slowly came into focus. Revka quickly wished they hadn't.

The creature. Just like Discordia had shown them, though of course that had been a vision, something that couldn't hurt them. Here it was, up close and personal, and extremely terrifying. She felt her legs go to jelly. She was barely able to hold herself up. She wanted to leap onto Iyarra's back and run away, far into the desert night, and keep running until all this was left behind, but how could you run away from something like this? Where could you possibly hide?

Deacon Mushrat, who had divested himself of his red robe, stared up at the thing in disbelief. "Sweet mercy!" he whispered. "What is it?"

"That," said Revka quietly, "is the 'god' you wanted to wake up. The one you thought would make all your dreams come true."

"But, it's—it's—"

"Yeah."

"And we woke that up?"

Revka smiled mirthlessly. "Yeah, congrats on that, by the way."

Mrs. Wildberry shook her head. "No," she whispered. "No. It wasn't supposed to be like this at all. It was..."

Babs reached over and slapped her on the face. "Who are you to say what it was supposed to be? This is a god—no, not even a god! It's a thing beyond our comprehension. A creature so alien to us we could not begin to understand it, let alone bargain with it! It is a thing that cannot exist here, that cannot be destroyed, and *you idiots let it out.*"

Somehow, despite all the chaos and destruction, the area of The Gap with its maze was still intact. At least, the four shafts of magic were still rising up to the heavens. It seemed to Revka that they might be even taller now. You could almost think...

One of the streams touched a distant star. The star flared brightly, then a thin trace of white began to move away, plotting a course toward a nearby star. When it made contact, this star also flared, and the path took off in a new direction toward another one. All four of the magical streams had reached the dome of the sky. All four were tracing paths of light across the darkness.

The group watched in horrified fascination. "What's it doing?" asked one of the Arcana. "What's going on?"

Babs tilted her head. "It looks like they're each tracing a path. It looks like it might be random, but I really can't be sure."

"Random, yeah, but...does it seem to anyone else they're getting closer to each other?"

There was a gasp. Iyarra covered her mouth as she stared up at the stars, wide-eyed. "Oh my gods," she whispered. "I know what it is."

Revka turned. "You do? How? I mean, what is it? Sorry. Answer the second question first."

The centauress pointed. "Look at that one, the one on the far right. Don't you see?"

"I...see what?"

"It's the maze. It's the same path we took to open the door to the temple, remember? There's that little dogleg curve. And I'm pretty sure that path over there is the one we had to map out this afternoon."

Revka goggled. "Holy thunga, she's right! That's exactly the path we took! So, that means...actually, what does that mean?"

"Search me." Iyarra shrugged. "But there's no way it's a coincidence."

"I think," said Babs quietly, "that the maze was a map of the stars all along. It was a guide to...well, whatever we're seeing now. Of course, we always started from the center and worked our way to the four stations. I can't imagine what's going to happen when those four paths meet in the middle, but I'm not at all sure I want to find out."

A bone-shaking, earth-rattling roar pulled everyone's attention back to earth as the giant creature waded through the rubble of the mountains. The residual magic coming up from the ancient stones cast eldritch shadows on the creature, which rippled and shifted in ways no natural thing should. It shuffled forward, unsteady on what would have to be called its legs. It seemed utterly disinterested in the small group, its attention focused entirely on the conflagration in the sky.

"Oh, gods," whispered Revka, "what is it doing?"

Babs just shrugged. Around them, several of the others were groaning or screaming and covering their eyes. Some had begun to weep, and one—it appeared to be Mr. Tarran, the banker—had curled up on the ground in the fetal position and was industriously sucking his thumb. Revka recalled that, aside from her and Iyarra, the group was seeing this thing for the first time.

Honestly, she couldn't blame them.

The four traces of light wound their way from star to star, drawing ever closer. It was now clear they were converging upon the star known as Nautus, the navigator. Revka thought back to her childhood, when her father would take her out in the cold night air and teach her the stars. He had always pointed out the navigator star. *No matter where you were in the world, or what time of year it is, Nautus always points exactly due west.* He called it the sailor's friend and said that, as long as you knew where it was, you could find your way home.

Revka wondered what else it might point to.

The creature waded forward, eyes fixed on the stars. If anything, it seemed as drawn to them as the small group who stood helplessly watching the four traces of magic converge.

As the fourth trail touched Nautus, the world seemed to change. Revka had braced herself for a burst of white light, or an earth-shaking boom. There was only a disconcerting ripple across reality, as if the world had suddenly been glimpsed through the heat haze of a roaring fire, and then returned to its normal self. The star briefly flared, and all was still again. The world held its breath.

And the sky...*split*.

A light opened at the spot where Nautus still shone, rapidly growing up and down from the star. As the group watched in horrified fascination, the rip began to widen, pulling away to the sides. It was as if the sky they had lived beneath all their lives was nothing more than a cheap curtain being pulled aside. For the first time, they could see what lay behind it.

Black. Not the black of the night sky, not the black of the caves they had been in. Those were living blacks, places that, while they may have had little or no actual light, still had something of the living world in them. They were part of nature. This was different. This was a black forged of solid void, a black born of eternity and absolute nothingness. It was the ultimate black. As Revka gazed at the void, she could almost feel it drawing her in.

She grabbed hold of Iyarra's arm. The centauress was trembling, unable to turn her gaze away from the sight. Revka gave her a reassuring squeeze, though it was anybody's guess who she was trying to reassure. The gap in the sky widened, the curtain of stars being pushed aside as if they had never been more than an illusion all along.

"My god," whispered one of the cultists. "It's, it's...I can't."

"And you thought you could tame it," said Babs quietly.

The figure behind her shook its head in sorrow. "We didn't know," it said. "I'm sorry. We didn't know."

"Well," said Babs. "There's no doing anything about it now. What could stand against such a thing as that?"

"The key!" Revka snapped her fingers. She dug out the pyramid from the saddlebags. "Of course!"

Babs regarded the object. "It was nice of you to retrieve it, but I'm afraid it's a bit late for that, now."

"No, no! You don't understand. Wait. Uhm, anyone got a pole or something? A stick? Maybe a broom handle?"

"Now who's going to have a broom handle in the middle of the desert?"

"Never mind." Phil stepped forward. "You can use my quarterstaff."

"Perfect." Revka rammed the pyramid onto the end of the staff, then took a quick breath. "Okay." She reached up and turned the tip clockwise, just as Eris had shown her. There was a soft whirring noise, and the corners folded themselves up until they were pointing to the tip. Inside the pyramid, a strange pulsing light appeared.

"Good lord," whispered the high priestess. "How in the world did you know to do that?"

"Eh, long story." Revka grinned sheepishly. "But basically, once it gets enough energy we can blast the thing." She looked at the tip. It was mostly dark, but little cracks of blue light were crawling their way up from inside the pyramid itself. She shook it impatiently. "Come on," she muttered. "Hurry up."

On the ground, the giant creature made its way to The Gap. It raised what Revka had to assume were its arms and let out a long, unearthly wail. It was no mere noise, but a sound carved of pure emotion. Waves of raw feeling washed over all who heard it. Anger there was, and loss, and...fear? Revka shook her head. *What could a thing like this have to fear?*

From beyond the tear in the sky, there came an answer, a deep, thrumming sound that washed over the valley. Revka had once heard that singers in the capital had special training to project their voices out as far as possible without having to sing loudly. This was like that: the noise had an unpleasant quality, a feeling like it was going through her somehow. She didn't like it one bit.

There was movement in the darkness behind the sky. Nothing definite, a shifting of shades. Something was moving back there, something huge. If the creature before them was the size of a mountain, then whatever this was it was big as...as...

Revka shook her head. There was nothing to compare it to. Possibly an entire mountain range, and even then, only maybe. It made her head hurt trying to take it in all at once.

The creature was calling louder, now. There was a new note. One of…joy. Revka blinked in surprise, as the wave of elation washed over her. What in the world could it mean?

Babs shook her head. "We have to stop it," she whispered. "Whatever it's doing, it's happening now."

In Revka's hands, the tip of the pyramid was almost entirely saturated with magic. She hefted it, licked her lips, and took careful aim. Around her, the world seemed to ripple in unreality. If she concentrated, it seemed that she could just see the faintest outlines of other creatures, new ones filing into the valley. The gods of this world were coming back, ready to do battle again. Eons ago they had barely been able to subdue the smaller monster. What chance could they possibly have against this new titanic horror?

"Wait." Iyarra held up a hand. "I don't think—"

"There's no time!" The high priestess turned to Revka. "For gods' sake! It's trying to let the other one through!" She grabbed the staff from Revka and aimed it at the creature. All around her, Revka could feel the magic building up. At the end of the staff, the tip of the pyramid shone out like a star.

"No, really," Iyarra raised her voice, something she almost never did. "Please, just listen to me…" But the others were paying no attention, only watching the creature approach the opening. Revka's mind raced. *What is Iyarra talking abou—*

Something clicked. Revka looked up at the scene again, but this time through different eyes. And suddenly the pieces fit together. *Of course.*

"Stop." She reached up and grabbed the staff away, snatching it out of the priestess's hands before she could react. She tossed it to Iyarra, who trotted a few paces back, holding it tightly to her.

The pyramid went pure white from base to tip. An incandescent lance of pure magic shot out from the tip and into the night sky.

Babs wheeled on Revka. "What are you doing?" she screamed. "It's going to kill us!"

"No! Wait! I think we've got this wrong. Just hear us out." She turned to Iyarra. "Go ahead."

"I don't think it's going to let the other in," the centauress said. "In fact…"

Just then a network of tentacles slid through the hole in the sky. They spread themselves out, then swept back down to where the creature was standing. The tendrils interlaced themselves behind the creature, forming a kind of cradle that carefully gathered it up.

The tendrils began to lift, tugging the creature toward the darkness. It had ceased its cries and was now burbling contentedly. As the group watched, the titanic beast was gathered up into the darkness beyond.

There was a sudden rush of warm air, and another wave of emotion washed over the watchers. This time, there was no fear. No anger. There was only a feeling of relief, of being safe and loved. A feeling of home.

The rift began to close. The sky healed itself, drawing back over the stygian blackness and leaving only the star-filled infinity of the night. Below, the magic glow emanating from what was left of the mountains faded away to nothingness. For a long while, nobody said anything, just stared up at the stars that twinkled innocently above.

Finally, Brother Phil spoke up. "Is that it?"

Babs nodded. "I believe it is, yes. That's really it."

"But..." He shook his head in bewilderment. "What the hell happened out there? What does it all mean?"

"It means we were wrong," said Iyarra. "We thought it was a god, or a monster, but it wasn't any of those things."

Revka nodded. "We saw how big and scary it was, but we didn't have a clue about the truth. It probably got lost, is all. They do that, you know. Trust me. I had brothers."

"What the hell do you mean?" said Babs.

"It's simple," said Iyarra. "It was no monster. It was a lost child, and its momma just came for it."

Chapter Twenty-Seven

IT WAS DAWN, AND the sun came up over a very different world. The small group stood at the foot of the rubble where the mountains had been, surveying the new scenery.

"All right," said Babs. "Now, do we have our story straight? Everyone?"

Iyarra nodded. "We were hiding out, and you were looking along the mountains to try and find us."

"Right," said another figure. "And we got out there to The Gap, figuring they were hiding in the maze—"

"—when all of a sudden a giant earthquake hit," continued someone else.

"Which we barely managed to escape."

"Except for Mr. Fleet and G Findswater," added Revka.

"Yes, of course. And the terrible ne'er-do-wells who facilitated your escape from the jail."

"Yup. Dead and gone. Not a trace of 'em."

The high priestess nodded her approval. "Good job, everyone. Now, for heaven's sake let's stick to the story. We may get through this without any embarrassing questions."

"Actually," interjected Mrs. Wildberry, "How did you know to find us there? I thought we kept things secret."

Babs smiled. "The two ladies here," she gestured to Revka and Iyarra. "They got word to us yesterday afternoon."

"Yester—but, they were here the whole time, surely?"

Revka grinned. "Mr. Fleet had us trace out one of the paths from the maze. When we did, we stepped onto the disk to make sure we got it right. Naturally, it took us straight to the temple, and guess what, we weren't the only ones there."

Babs nodded. "I had sent a couple of our people to the temple to guard it in case the cultists tried anything. Happily, the ladies were able to fill them in on what was happening, and we were able to arrange an intervention. We came in through the temple portal, of course, so we were able to get ourselves in position while you were occupied."

Mr. Tarran nodded. "I see," he said. "Well, I guess that explains that."

Deacon Mushrat snorted. "I still don't see why we're going along with this," he growled.

"Well," said Mr. Tarran patiently, "would you rather the whole town knew what we were *actually* doing out here?"

The deacon blanched. "Well, er..."

"Exactly," said Mrs. Wildberry. "We'll protect each other."

"That does bring up a problem, though," said Revka. "I mean, Iyarra and I are still fugitives and all."

The banker coughed. "I, er, believe I might be able to assist on that front. I can take the sheriff aside and have a little talk with him. I rather feel I can get him to see reason, especially if you two will agree to leave town peaceably?"

"Oh, no worries about that," said Revka. "We weren't figuring on hanging around, but what makes you think you can talk him into letting us go?"

Mr. Tarran, who was no stranger to making sure he was on the winning team, gave the women a helpful smile. "Well, my family has always been financiers. As such we have multiple investments in different businesses in the town, including several along Merrybone Lane. I happen to know a lot about who goes where, and does what, and with whom. I, er, trust I make myself clear?"

Babs smiled. "Ah, indeed? And the sheriff always struck me as such an upstanding and moral man." She leaned over to the banker. "I don't suppose you could give me a hint?"

"Certainly not, madam. I would never stoop to low gossip." He paused. "However, if he refuses to play ball, who knows what might leak out."

Revka smirked. "Okay, now I'm curious."

"Speak for yourself," said Iyarra. "I'm guessing I don't want to know."

Revka chuckled and gave Iyarra a pat. "Fair enough. Well, shall we head that way?"

The sun was just burning away the last of the early dawn chill as the group trotted up the main street.

"All right," muttered Babs, "everyone remember what we agreed. Don't go off script. Don't volunteer anything. And for heaven's sake don't mention the—"

"Hey!" A centaur waved from where he was lounging in front of the bank. "Y'all see the monster?"

The group exchanged glances. "Er, what?"

"You know, the monster! The big one what was stompin' all around the mountains last night! Fair woke the whole town up, you know? I mean, you did see it, din'ja?"

Babs looked at Revka, who just shrugged. So much for secrecy. "Oh, that one," Babs said. "Yes, yes we did see that, now you mention it."

"We weren't sure which monster you meant," said Revka.

"They say it was the legendary beast—you know, the one that was here when folks first settled here and all that? Well, the sheriff an' them rode down this morning. He said the mountains is crumbled down all along the back of the valley! Mayor reckons that we could flatten it out and get a straight shot to The Great Rift, so people don't have to go round the mountains anymore!"

Mr. Tarran rubbed his chin. "You don't say? A pass through the mountains would be extremely popular. Of course, they'll have to come through our town to get there." He brightened considerably. Things were looking up.

"Indeed," said Babs. "And just think, your bank can provide some nice, interest-free loans to the city for development."

Mr. Tarran's face lost a little of its brightness. "It...it can?"

"Oh, yes." Babs's smile stayed on her face, but her hand clutched at Tarran's arm. "After all, it's for the good of the town, right?"

Mr. Tarran sagged. "I...for the good of the town. Yeah. Fine."

"Speaking of the sheriff," said Babs, "is he back in his office? There are things we'd like to discuss with him."

* * * * *

A few hours later, Iyarra and Revka were cooling their heels in the sheriff's office. They were not, apparently, under arrest. It was just that the delicate negotiations with the law were taking longer than expected. Until things could be properly hammered out, the deputies preferred to keep the two where they could see them. As Revka understood it, they were free to go where they liked, provided they didn't actually go anywhere.

Iyarra leaned down to Revka. "How's it going in there?" she whispered.

Revka glanced up. She was holding a glass against the wall of the sheriff's office while the deputies were out for a smoke break. She held up a finger to Iyarra, motioning her to wait a moment.

A few seconds later, she removed the glass and put it down on a nearby desk. She sat back slowly, a curious look on her face. Iyarra nudged her. "Well?"

Revka shook herself out of whatever reverie she had been in. "Wha? Oh. Yeah. Well, the good news is, I'm pretty sure we're going to get out of this. Seems Mr. Sheriff is quite well known on Merrybone Lane. Guy has some interesting hobbies, from the sound of it."

Iyarra arched an eyebrow. "Ohhhh? Do tell?"

Revka looked around. "Ask me later, maybe when there's no one around."

"Aw, fine." The centauress grinned and gave her girlfriend a nudge. "That good, eh?"

"Well, not so much good as...odd. I mean, I've heard some things in my day, but this...I mean, I must have heard wrong, probably. Possibly."

Iyarra covered her mouth in time to stifle a grin. Revka sat back in her chair, staring off into the distance. "Tell you one thing," she said, apparently to herself. "I'll never look at a watermelon the same way again."

A few minutes later, the door opened and a delegation of the Tex Arcana members trooped out, along with a curiously subdued Sheriff Lestrange.

"Well, it's fixed," said Babs. "There's a convoy heading back east tomorrow morning. If you can stay out of trouble until then, you can leave with them and that will be the end of it. Sound good?"

Revka smiled and nodded. "Sounds great," she said. "I think we've pretty much had our fill of the wide-open spaces anyway. What do you say, Iyarra?"

"Oh, definitely."

"Splendid." Babs clapped her hands together and rubbed them with satisfaction. "Well then, I think that's all for now. Do come by the meeting place tonight, though. I think we're going to have a small celebration. Nothing too fancy, just an informal get-together. There's this bottle of Ephesian lightwine I've been saving for a special occasion. Thought we might break that out. Maybe get a few nibbles to go with it. What do you say?"

Iyarra nodded her head politely. "That sounds lovely. Thank you."

"Wonderful. I'll let the others know. Will a cheese tray be all right?"

In the corner of the room, the sheriff, who hadn't said a word since coming out, quietly poured himself a cup of coffee.

Revka headed toward the door with Iyarra. "Sure. Maybe with some fruit, if you can get it?" She waited until the coffee cup hit the old centaur's lips. "I know I, myself, am partial to a nice, juicy watermelon."

There was a very satisfying moment as the sheriff spat coffee flying halfway across the room. Revka just smiled and stepped out into the street.

* * * * *

The next morning, the two were wandering down the main street on their way to join the wagon train back east. They'd had a nice send-off the night before. The sun was shining, and each could feel the tension of the last few days dissipate in the face of a new adventure. Around them, centaurs strolled up and down the street on various errands.

"I mean, it's not a bad little town," Revka was saying. "Pretty decent, actually. Nice folks. They figure, with the mountains out of the way, they're going to be getting busy once they lay out a path to the coast."

"That will be nice," said Iyarra as she strolled beside her. "Have you ever been to The Great Rift? It sounds like it's really something."

"Not me. Not yet, anyway. Why, do you want to check it out?"

The centauress gave her a weak grin. "I think I'd rather just head back east, for now. I miss having grass beneath my hooves."

"Fair enough," Revka grinned. "Well, maybe one day we can come back, and—"

"*YOU!*"

Revka spun around. There, standing in the middle of the street, was Big Jake. He was facing away from them, glaring down the street. Revka peered. Dusty Steele, trail boss extraordinaire, exited a nearby shop. He practically gleamed in the early afternoon sun as he turned and regarded the bulltaur.

"Well now," he said. "Look who's here. Haven't seen you since McBee's Canyon." The centaur paused. "How you doin' there, Mr. Big Horn?"

Big Jake snarled, scraping a hoof along the ground. "I'm gonna beat the livin' daylights out of you," he growled. "Bout time someone knocked that smug little grin offa your face. And I reckon I'm just the one to do it."

Dusty rolled his eyes theatrically but made a show of rolling up his sleeves. "Well, I did have plans for today, but I suppose I can spare you a few minutes. No," he said to a couple of centaurs who had stepped up beside him. "This here is my fight, though I'm much obliged for the offer." The two nodded and stepped back to join the crowd that had materialized the moment it had become apparent there was about to be some violence.

Jake and Dusty began to close on each other, moving forward warily, each watching the other like a hawk. When there was less than a centaur's length between them, they began to circle, looking for an opening, a weakness they could exploit. There was a hush, the crowd going quiet except for one child in the back complaining to his mom he couldn't see. Steele made a quick feint, then another, trying to spur the giant bulltaur into making the first move. They continued to circle each other, arms out, eyes locked. Finally, Big Jake snapped "Oh, to hell with this!" and went in swinging.

Clouds of dust kicked up as the two battled. Dusty was no slouch. He had speed and good technique, but to any experienced observer, it was clear there was only one way this was going to go. Big Jake didn't bother with dodging or weaving. He just kept swinging his fists in Dusty's general direction. It wasn't the most sophisticated technique, but a few lucky shots were all he would need.

They battled their way down the street until they wound up near one of the blacksmith shops. The forge was empty, the workers having stepped out to watch the show. The two fighters tussled back and forth, grappling with each other, trying to trip each other up. Dusty got in a lucky shot, right in Jake's solar plexus. This knocked a little wind out of the bulltaur, and the trail boss pressed his advantage, bringing blow after blow in rapid follow-up.

Suddenly, the bulltaur lashed out. Entirely unprepared, Dusty went sailing backward and bounced lightly against the doorway to the forge. His rear legs buckled beneath him as he tried to get back on his hooves. It was too late. Big Jake pressed forward, bringing blow after blow, until Dusty was on the ground, his upper half weaving unsteadily as he clung to consciousness.

Big Jake grinned. He loomed over the trail boss, cracking his knuckles. "Now, you got any last words? Better make 'em quick, Mr. Smart Mouth. Because I'm about to—"

"Wait!"

Big Jake's head snapped around, glaring. "Whut? Whozat? Who said wait?"

From somewhere in the back of the crowd, a voice called out. "You can't just hit a guy when he's down!" The female voice was a bit low and husky, and somehow familiar. He peered in the direction of the voice but couldn't see much more than the top of their ebony mane.

Big Jake snorted. "Can't I? Well, why the hell not?"

"Yeah," said another voice in the crowd, "best time if you ask me."

"You can't because it isn't honorable!" the voice replied.

"Well?" he said. "So what? Neither am I! Hell, not being honorable is kind of my whole thing! Now, do you mind?"

"It's more than that!" the voice cried out. "It's against *The Code of the West!*"

And every single person, every taur and tauress, down to the tiniest foal, doffed their hats, closed their eyes, and solemnly intoned in unison, "*The Code of the West!*"

There was a muffled clang. When everyone opened their eyes again, Big Jake seemed...different. His fists had dropped to his sides, and his eyes had a somewhat glazed quality about them. Dusty Steele braced himself for the killing blow, but it never came. He scrambled back up to his hooves. The bulltaur merely stared at him, slack-jawed. The trail boss pulled back his fist and let fly with a haymaker.

The effect was immediate. Big Jake staggered, went cross-eyed, mooed, and keeled over onto the ground, out like a light.

The crowd cheered. Centaurs rushed to slap Dusty on the back and congratulate him. A group of well-wishers dragged him to the nearest saloon for a congratulatory drink before he hit the road. Big Jake lay prone on the ground, not even putting up any resistance when the sheriff's men came to drag him off to jail.

Back in the darkness of the forge, Revka carefully put the large iron hammer back where she had found it and crept out the back way.

Codes are all very well and good, but the thing about iron is, it gets things done.

* * * * *

They say that the sun never sets on those who ride into it. As the wagon train passed out of Red Valley and into the desert, the rising sun hung bright in the eastern sky like a beacon guiding them home.

Perched on a mesa at the edge of the valley, Coyote watched them go. A long line of wagons snaked its way out of town and into the wilderness. Soon they would arrive back east with their goods and— more importantly—news of what had occurred. He turned his head to the back of the valley, to where the mountains had once stood, and looked closely. If he concentrated, with the right kind of eyes, he could just see the future. A sprawling city, lit by a galaxy of lights, teemed with centaurs and humans and elves and every type of person, all intermingling and forging a new future together. It was, he decided, definitely something worth sticking around for.

* * * * *

In the convoy, Revka sat perched on Iyarra's back, gazing out at the scenery, silently ruminating. It had been quite an adventure, but she felt very glad to be heading back east. She'd heard somebody say once that the best part of traveling was coming back home. She wasn't sure she agreed, but just then and there, she could kind of see what they meant.

Iyarra looked over her shoulder at her girlfriend. "Hey, penny for your thoughts?"

"Hm? Oh, just thinking. I haven't been back home since I first left. Was kind of wondering how things are going there, you know?"

"We can go up and visit if you like."

"Well, if you're sure. It's pretty cold up that way. Even in the summer, it's a bit nippy."

"I don't mind. Besides, I'd like to see where you came from."

"Yeah, well. It's been so long, heaven knows what it's like now. Probably my siblings are all settled down and got kids and whatnot. Not sure I'd fit in anymore, you know?" Revka sighed. "You can't go home again. You know who said that? Perdu the Sage."

"Yeah, but wasn't he the one who once got lost in his own house?"

"Well okay, that's a point."

"It wasn't even that big a house."

"All right, geez. Anyway. It has been a while since I saw everyone. Haven't thought about them in ages, you know? And now I can't stop wondering."

Iyarra smiled. "Well, think it over. We've got a little time."

Revka patted her girlfriend's back. "Yeah, yeah, we do."

* * * * *

On his distant mesa, Coyote leaned back, took a long look at the world, and laughed and laughed and laughed.

The End
(y'all)

About K.L Mitchell

K.L. Mitchell was raised all over the south in a series of increasingly tiny towns until she finally joined the Air Force out of a desire for some Culture. She's spent most of her professional life working on computers in one capacity or another, and occasionally manages to get them to actually work.

She's been writing for fun most of her life, and for publication since about 2011. She's written for multiple websites and local publications, and in 2013 was a recurring columnist for the Kansas City Star. She lives with a gray cat named Molly and would like to be an astronaut when she grows up.

Connect with Kelly

Email: k_l_mitchell@mail.com

Facebook: https://www.facebook.com/KLMitchellHere/

Cover Design By : Rachel George
www.rachelgeorgeillustration.com

Note to Readers:

Thank you for reading a book from Desert Palm Press. We appreciate you as a reader and want to ensure you enjoy the reading process. We would like you to consider posting a review on your preferred media sites and/or your blog or website.

For more information on upcoming releases, author interviews, contests, giveaways and more, please sign up for our newsletter and visit us at Desert Palm Press: www.desertpalmpress.com and "Like" us on Facebook: Desert Palm Press.

Bright Blessings